Being Emerald

New Atlanta Series

Sylvia Ryan

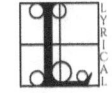

LYRICAL PRESS
Kensington Publishing Corp.
www.kensingtonbooks.com

Lyrical Press books are published by
Kensington Publishing Corp. 119 West 40th Street New York, NY 10018

All Kensington titles, imprints, and distributed lines are available at special quantity discounts for bulk purchases for sales promotion, premiums, fundraising, and educational or institutional use.

Special book excerpts or customized printings can also be created to fit specific needs. For details, write or phone the office of the Kensington Special Sales Manager:
Kensington Publishing Corp.
119 West 40th Street
New York, NY 10018
Attn. Special Sales Department. Phone: 1-800-221-2647.

Kensington and the K logo Reg. U.S. Pat. & TM Off.
Lyrical Press and the L logo are trademarks of Kensington Publishing Corp.

First Electronic Edition: March 2015
eISBN-13: 978-1-61650-621-6
eISBN-10: 1-61650-621-0

First Print Edition: March 2015
ISBN-13: 978-1-61650-622-3
ISBN-10: 1-61650-622-9

Printed in the United States of America

To the only person who really knows me.

Acknowledgements

Thank you, Penny for taking the time to teach.
Thank you, Jessica for wanting to learn.
Thank you, Donna Johnson for being my biggest fan and
for catching what everyone else missed.

Chapter 1

The distant explosion vibrated the worn wood floor beneath Rock's feet. *Oh yeah. That one's going to hurt.* Exclamations echoed in the cavernous space of the beautiful Sapphire Zone Historical library. Bright light filtered through the massive doors as a handful of patrons filed out to investigate. Rock turned his attention away from the diversion and wove through the stacks. He cut sharply down a roped-off nonfiction aisle where three books lay exactly where Xander's letter had said they'd be. He scooped them off the shelf and dropped them into his bag. With the task complete, Rock joined the others on the front steps, blending into the crowd of faces pointed toward rising smoke in the Emerald Zone.

Since the Gov realized they'd been stumped by codes taken from old paper books, nonfiction was off limits without an official escort. Patrick O'Connor, the first guardsman to jump ship and fight for what was right, had known their value to the newly formed Resistance.

His bag weighed down with more knowledge, Rock whistled as he descended the stairs and turned toward the Emerald Zone.

General Morgan was shrewd enough to know he couldn't ban books and cunning enough to present his library restrictions as "safety precautions" for the good of the people. Like all good politicians, he knew the delivery of the words were as important as the words themselves. If it still appeared they lived in a democratic society, the masses wouldn't notice or care that their reading materials were controlled.

Rock couldn't contain his smile as he walked toward the smoke billowing from the Peacekeeper's armory. *Two birds, one stone.* Nothing brought him more joy than another opportunity to piss Morgan off or bring him down. Xander, his best friend and leader of the Amber Resistance, was a brilliant strategist. To help Rock occupy the few days between Onyx Zone recovery missions, Xander always had a spectacular plan waiting. It was Rock's big old *fuck you*, signifying he'd made it back alive from another mission. Morgan had to know it was him doing the destroying, but Rock hadn't been caught yet. He glanced up at the rolling black cloud melding with the white puffy ones of the beautiful New Atlanta day. The sight filled him with absolute glee as he pressed on, his long strides devouring his four-mile hike home to the Emerald Zone.

The Resistance was winning this conflict because, after a quarter century, Ambers, the dregs of society, had a unique way of thinking outside the box to solve problems. It was also how they waged war. Since the first pandemic survivors arrived in New Atlanta, continued existence hinged on finding alternative ways to meet their needs. With no medicine, they used roots and herbs. With no families, they forged surrogate ones. With a wall built to keep them in, they made nirvana and kept everybody else out. His father had always told him a man could go crazy focusing on what he couldn't do or didn't have. Instead, in a culture of love and unconditional acceptance, Ambers had flourished, focusing on everything else. They'd been forced to since the Repopulation Laws had been enacted.

A squealing streak of pink ambushed him with an "Oomph!" He staggered back and then hoisted the young girl into his arms.

"Please can you look for crayons? The store is out." A smile marked with dimples graced the blue-eyed girl's cheeks.

The girl's mother stepped closer. "Dallas, leave the nice man alone."

Ignoring her mother, Dallas hugged his neck tighter. "Pleeease," she whined.

"Hmm, crayons. That's a tall order, sweetie."

"I know. My mom told me they were all melted."

"Not all. They're just much harder to find now." Smiling at her sweet innocence, he said, "I'll see what I can do."

"Thank you." She tightened her arms around his neck and smacked a loud kiss on his cheek.

He set her down with a pat. She ran back to her mother, excitedly relaying their conversation.

While the public filled the walkways and gawked at the latest act of war, he ducked down a side street to avoid being noticed again. When he was on the streets in uniform, as he was now, and sometimes even when he wasn't, people approached him. Often, it was just to thank him for his service, and occasionally with requests for specific items paired with promises it would be worth his while if he brought them back. He was a minor celebrity, a Santa Claus of the post-pandemic era.

By midafternoon, he sat in a bar, eating a hamburger. In front of him sat the first of many beers he planned to consume before he passed out.

He perpetually worked for the Resistance. The few days he spent inside New Atlanta's walls was no exception. Few friends to the Resistance had access to the bar the National Guardsmen frequented after shift. Those who did wouldn't be caught dead there. Too dangerous. He didn't care. He liked to take advantage of the power-drunk National Guardsmen, who always got a little sloppy when pumped with free shots.

Raising his arms and feigning more intoxication than he actually felt, he shouted "Another round for the house!" His role in this crowded bar filled with Guard was easy. Keep them lubricated and keep them talking. Getting information from them was like taking candy from a baby. "Hey, where's that guy?" Rock snapped his fingers a few times. "Uh, Irish, red hair, about four feet tall?"

Jason, a lanky kid who'd been a gold mine on previous nights of drunken intel gathering, laughed. "Shaugnessey?"

"Yes, that's him."

Jason leaned in. "He's one of the missing."

"Yeah, missing the ability to hold his liquor."

Jason didn't laugh. "No." He looked over his shoulder, darting a glance at the men nearest them. "Guard are going missing,"."

"Since when?"

"Nobody's really sure when it started. So many people disappear in New Atlanta, but Guard command noticed about six weeks ago. Put us through training on how to increase the chances of surviving an abduction. Since then, five or six more have dropped off the face of the earth."

"The Resistance?" Rock asked, though he knew it wasn't.

"Don't think so. We think someone is fixing to take over and is getting rid of the obvious wild cards." Jason raised his arm. "Be right there," he called to a group entering. "Hey. I'll talk to you later, man."

"Yeah." Rock slapped him on the shoulder. "Later."

Rock stayed, buying drinks and talking up the enemy for hours but heard little else he could pass along, so he headed home.

After a short drive, he entered the enormous house and dropped his bag on the kitchen island. After opening some windows and praying for a breeze, he pulled out one of the books he'd stolen. *The Modern Clinicians Guide to Hypnotherapy* was a training manual. He dropped it back into his bag and grabbed *Privileged Information: Top Secret Mind Manipulation During the Second Cold War* and *Keeping Secrets*. He kept *Privileged Information*.

Slightly buzzed and utterly exhausted, he settled on the couch and read until he could no longer keep his eyes open.

* * * *

"No!" Rock jerked awake. His raw bellow had provided escape from the nightmare but released only a tiny part of the desperation bottlenecked at the base of his throat. He struggled to catch his breath as air heaved fast and raggedly in and out of his lungs. Touching his hand to his chest, he found he was soaked with perspiration, not the thick pool of blood in the dream. Twenty-four hours in New Atlanta was all it took for flashbacks to invade his head. They were always a problem in the dead quiet of this house. So much easier to avoid the demons when they were drowning in the noise of the Amber Zone. He swung his feet to the floor and attempted to leash the rampage every muscle of his body was primed to let loose.

His heart raced and hands shook, spurred by the unspent adrenaline saturating his system. It was no small task, but his body eventually settled.

He stood, drawn to the solitary kitchen light illuminating the center island and casting long shadows on the cream-colored walls of his great room. He filled his lungs, pulled his shoulders back and rolled his neck before letting the breath go. He never slept well inside the city. This place was toxic, with the stress of imminent danger never leaving until he was outside the walls again.

He walked to the rich dark wood cabinets lining the back wall of his kitchen and grabbed a glass. With trembling hands, he filled it with water, leaned against the counter and downed it.

The nightmares made him pissed all over again. Then they made him hurt to the depths of his soul. Sometimes he thought the torment of Emily's absence would never leave him, remaining as his hell on earth eternally.

Surrounded by the prison of slick granite counters and monstrous stainless steel appliances, his temper rose. He hated this fucking house. He detested his life and loathed the man he'd become since he'd been forced out of the Amber Zone.

"God dammit!" He flung the glass at the far wall. A satisfying crack, then exploding shards sprayed the kitchen, tinkling as they hit the floor. Rock clutched the edge of the counter, trying to rein in his fury. His bare feet against the tumbled marble tile filled his vision as he forced himself to regain his composure. During his year in the Emerald Zone, he'd only been inside the city walls for a handful of weeks, but even that was too much. Every second since he'd been condemned to this home had been miserable. He'd never even bothered to walk upstairs, preferring to sleep on the couch in the living room whenever forced to be inside his lavish prison.

Rock sat on a high stool at the island and stuck his earbud in his ear. "Call Dad." He thanked God his dad didn't give a flying fuck their conversations broke the law banning communication with Amber citizens. "Let them listen. Let them try to do something," his father had shouted through his earbud when the new injunction had been put in place. "They all can kiss my ass."

"The dream again?" his father asked in a rough, sleepy voice.

"Yeah."

"It's been a while since the last one. I thought maybe you were done with them."

"Me too. I got my next assignment today. Go date is July fourth."

"Jesus," his father hissed. "That fucker is messing with you."

"He's good at the game. My job is different too. I'll bodyguard the woman who runs the Fine Arts and Artifacts Program. I've got a couple of months to train her before we go to DC."

"The new assignment explains the dream coming back after so many months."

"You think?"

"Being responsible for a woman. The anniversary of Emily's death as the go date. Hell yeah, he's stirring things up, fucking with your head."

"So, same shit different day."

"Yeah, son, same fucking shit. Have you met the woman yet?"

"Yeah, briefly."

"I saw a video highlighting the mission the other day. It's been on steady rotation in the feeds. She was in it."

"Laila?"

"Yes."

Rock could practically hear his father rolling his eyes. It bothered his dad that he left women relatively unnoticed since Emily's death.

"In the interview," his dad said, "she seemed certain she knows where the Declaration of Independence and Constitution are being stored."

"I guess we'll find out."

"She's pretty."

The words grated. "Subtlety still escapes you, Dad. Always has, for both of us."

"Huh."

Rock knew that sound. Knew it wasn't good. "What?"

"He's putting you in a position to have to protect another woman. He has to know it would crush you if you failed."

"You think Morgan's going to try to kill her?"

"Maybe. I wouldn't put it past him. He'd be completely absolved of any wrongdoing if the mission just never returned. Plus, I think having the people's focus on the freedoms this country was built on is the exact opposite of what he wants. You have to wonder why he'd bring so much attention to the retrieval of documents that will so blatantly undermine his rule in New Atlanta."

Rock hadn't considered that. "You think he's counting on us not to come back?"

"Well, in your case, isn't he always?"

He weighed his father's words. "Maybe this time he'll plant someone to make sure of it."

Normally, being killed outside of New Atlanta wasn't a worry because he trusted his team, but his usual team wouldn't be with him this time. "Shit."

"Some people think this Washington trip is a suicide mission."

"Every mission is a suicide mission, but I get what you're saying. I have to find out more about the program and the woman running it before I get a good sense of what fucked up scenario he's throwing me into. Whatever it is, I'll handle it."

"I don't doubt it, son."

"I'm getting tired of this bullshit. I'm done, Dad. I can't anymore." Months ago, his plan to leave New Atlanta permanently had come to him like a lightning bolt of divine inspiration. The Onyx Zone recovery missions had given him a sense of freedom that, over time, had grown to an almost uncontainable need. He was more alive in the dilapidated and overgrown places he'd traveled than he ever was in New Atlanta. Often, he walked off by himself and enjoyed the absence of restrictions, and the relative safety of being away from the Gov's eyes and long-armed reach. Ironic. When he'd first started working in Onyx, Rock had hoped to die in there. His general aversion to being alive had diminished over the last year, but not his aversion to life inside Emerald Zone walls.

"All right, son. I suppose I knew it was coming."

Rock ran his fingers through his hair again and stopped the motion, gripping a fistful of it on top of his head. "You need to visit with Xander." His mention of the Amber Resistance leader's name caused several seconds of dead air. His father didn't know it yet, but Xander held a letter for him. It outlined the plan. They would meet at the drop house and disappear together.

"All right."

"I'll talk to you soon." He disconnected the call. The man was his lifeline. He'd been waiting for the right way to break the news he was leaving. Now that the tunnel from Amber to outside the walls was completed, his father could leave with him. They would be together under one roof again soon. Most days, that knowledge was the only thing that kept him going and kept him sane.

It had been almost a year since he lost the woman he loved and the companionship of his father, friends—every important relationship in his life. A year since the devastating removal of the physical touch he needed. For twenty-seven years he'd been wrapped in the soft comfort of another's bare skin brushing his countless times a day.

Then it was gone. He'd never get used to the deprivation of it, the hollow feeling in his belly that seemed like a permanent part of him now.

He was dead inside. He still drew breath. He still had thoughts, though he tried as hard as he could to eradicate those causing him to feel anything, but he wasn't the same man who'd lived and loved in the Amber Zone. He'd constructed layers of protection around himself. That shell, like the bark of a tree, shielded the ever-hemorrhaging wound with a rough, dark barrier. He rarely allowed himself to acknowledge his raging anger and desperate need for human contact. If he allowed himself to feel all the emotions that crowded him every day, he'd have probably killed himself, or somebody else, by now. Every waking minute held potential for Rock to totally lose it, to explode in a dangerous fit of pent-up fury. He was like a diamond created under immense pressure, becoming something hard and cold.

This next mission would be his last. He was going to walk away. He couldn't wait.

Chapter 2

Laila Lewis stood in the hallway, just outside the door of the conference room. This initial briefing marked the beginning of the final two months of training and preparation before the mission. The Fine Arts and Artifacts Recovery Program was her baby. The trip to DC was the culmination of thousands of hours of specialized education, apprenticeships and the ultimate goal of her life's work.

For years, the anticipation had been practically overwhelming. But today, facing the sea of Black Guard uniforms, her excitement was muted by fear. She had no interest in engaging in polite conversation with any of the people here. Rock was the exception. No uniform, but still in black. He was a goliath, standing head and shoulders above the rest. Two hundred pounds of badass, standing there with bulging arms crossed over his chest. Armed men in camouflage stood at attention against the white walls, no expression, no movement, like pieces of furniture. Nobody sat at the massive conference table yet.

A high-level crowd attended, and her heartbeat jumped when she spotted General Morgan. His scar bit into his upper lip, making him appear as if he sneered whenever he spoke. "Fucking hell," she said under her breath. She had a difficult time staying in the same room with the man for too long. His evil overwhelmed her.

Laila took a deep breath and locked her defenses into place. She strode into the room and sat in one of the rolling, black leather chairs surrounding the dark-wood conference table.

Someone called for everyone to take their seats.

She was not the only woman present. Sydney Parr, an Amazon—tall, leggy and muscular—would be riding in the other truck with Garret during the mission. She was a legend in her own right because of her rank and reputation in one of the Onyx Zone Recovery Teams. Recently, she'd received the distinction of being the first woman accepted into Morgan's National Guard.

She sat across the table from Laila, next to Rock. She was close to him. Laila scrutinized them, the distance between them, the general air of formality. They didn't seem to have any kind of relationship. She was relieved. The first time she'd met Sydney, the woman had spared her a disinterested glance before returning to converse with someone else. She seemed like a bitch, and Laila had steered clear of her since.

General Conrad Morgan rounded the table and sat on Laila's right.

She tensed, and her anxiety spiked.

He nodded. "Miss Lewis."

She returned his nod with a well-practiced smile. "General."

They focused on Garret, National Guardsman, mission head, and navigator in charge of getting the four of them to Washington DC. He was tall, like Rock, but his coloring was Sapphire all the way, with sandy hair and green eyes. He had a clean-cut boy-next-door kind of look. He appeared to be the polar opposite of tall, dark and hostile directly across from her.

While Garret ran down the list of significant dangers they would face during the trip, General Morgan slid his finger over Laila's thigh. Her stomach twisted. She steeled her expression, hiding the cringe she so much wanted to be there, and shored up her barriers.

Morgan's energy, slimy and demented, slithered like a snake over her skin.

Adrenaline raced through her veins. She moved only her eyes and looked at his profile. His good side. During meetings, he'd always seated her to his left so his disfigurement was hidden.

Morgan glanced across the table.

Rock's singular gaze zeroed in on the spot Morgan touched her.

Putting on a show, the general made sure Rock saw what seemed like casual affection.

Rock scowled fiercely at General Morgan. Her new bodyguard took his life into his hands with open hostility pointed at the general. Rock's gaze rested on her face before leisurely sliding down her body.

When he turned his attention back to Garret's description of the route they'd take north, Laila could not do the same. Seemingly of its own accord, her interest lingered on the hulking, intimidating man across the table. This mountain's job was to keep her alive. He was an Emerald, like her.

She rubbed the newly tattooed emerald green band around her wrist. Garret had revealed Rock grew up in Amber, like she had. Rock didn't look like the type of person raised in the accepting Amber environment. But, what a person presented to the world was not necessarily what lay beneath the surface.

When Laila tuned into a person's energy, she was able to get a sense of the person and their feelings. She closed her eyes and blocked out the drone of Garret's voice. Relaxing, she exhaled, reached out with her senses and collided with an impervious barrier. He was totally closed off.

Opening herself a little more, she tried to sense the man behind the leave-me-alone-façade. At first, she got nothing. With some concentrated effort, her energy brushed past his defenses and mingled with his.

Her empathic gift was sensitive, and with so many people in the small room, the likelihood she'd feel only him if she opened herself up more was iffy at best. In a room full of people, there was never a guarantee she sensed the person she thought she was. She pretended to read the compad on the table in front of her, took in another deep breath, and opened herself a bit more.

An initial sensation of being under immense pressure morphed into a storm of torment and anger. His hell felt deep and tragic. It overwhelmed her.

She opened her eyes, and their gazes clashed. His eyes blazed as if he'd sensed her attempt to feel him. But that was impossible.

She tried to break the connection, but couldn't fend off the unbearable tsunami of his pent-up emotions. They pelted her, embedded in her soul like buckshot in soft flesh.

Despite repeatedly trying to push the emotions away, they only disappeared when he returned his attention to Garret's presentation.

By the time she'd rid herself of his feelings completely, she was shaken and nauseated. The connection had been less than a minute, but the vast, nuclear bomb-like intensity of what lay inside him had her heartbeat racing and adrenaline pumping. It was the first time her empathic connection had been so intense she'd had trouble breaking it.

Her chair scraped loudly against the floor as she excused herself. She hurried down the main corridor, into the mercifully unoccupied ladies room.

Breathing hard and assessing whether she was going to vomit, she steadied herself with a hand on the wall next to the sink. Her hands shook as she cupped them under the faucet. She gulped in several mouthfuls of water before cutting it off.

"Are you okay?"

Laila jumped and swung around.

Rock stood behind her in the doorway.

Not wanting anyone to see her like this, especially him, she turned away quickly. She took a couple more hitching breaths and lifted her gaze to his reflection in the mirror, nodded. "Yeah. I'm...good."

Gazes locked, they stood in silence, forming a personal connection. For the next few months, they were a duo in a team of four. She was sure those seconds were an allowance of time and attention Rock didn't give just anyone.

"Don't worry. I'll keep you safe. You'll be prepared to defend yourself if you need to." The tone of his deep voice was gentler than she'd heard him use with other people, making it easier to school her expression into some semblance of composure.

"Okay." Her voice quavered. She was completely unraveled. Too many strong energies in such an enclosed space.

"Come on. They're waiting for us."

She gave her stomach a few more seconds to settle, and then preceded him out the door. They walked side by side down the hall, the quick snap of her heels on the tile in sync with his combat boots.

Impulsively, she slipped her hand into his, and he didn't blink at the touch. Almost to the door of the meeting room, his steps faltered. He slowed, looked down at their joined hands, and up until their gazes connected for an endless second. His expression revealed he'd not known she'd grown up Amber.

Laila crooked a finger, a request for him to come closer. He brought his head near hers.

"Thank you," she whispered.

Simply because of his nearness, she sensed his mood again, and the change was absolute. The siege of anger, hatred and pain had lessened.

"Come on." He freed his hand, and stepped aside so she could enter the room.

Everyone looked at her when she re-entered. "I'm sorry, gentlemen. I'm feeling a bit under the weather today."

General Morgan's expression conveyed concern. "Well let's wrap this up, then."

Laila nodded her thanks to the General, sat, and avoided eye contact with everyone in the room.

When the meeting adjourned, she remained at the table to avoid getting pulled into a conversation. The problem was Sydney Parr remained, too.

She didn't need to look up to know Sydney's striking, light green eyes bore down on her. She could no longer pretend she hadn't noticed Sydney wasn't leaving. With her caramel skin and dark hair, the exotic-looking woman's bitchy glare made Laila feel like shrinking away. Sydney scanned her face, then the new emerald tattoo circling her wrist, and malevolence marred the woman's beautiful features.

The prejudice and slurs would come next. She might have an emerald band around her wrist, but to most, it didn't matter. She would always be an Amber—stupid, diseased, inferior.

"You're Emerald now?"

"Yes." Laila smiled and looked pointedly at Sydney's Sapphire tattoo. "And you're not."

"Don't let that green around your wrist make you think you're better than everyone else. You're still spawned from inferior stock."

"I earned my designation. I wasn't born into it like you were. Looks like you were a mere eye color away from growing up in Amber with me." Laila knew better than to bait the woman like that, but she couldn't help herself.

"He's not into you."

"Who?"

"Morgan. It was pretty obvious he was touching you to irritate Rock."

"I agree."

Sydney nodded. "As long as you know your place."

Rock walked back into the conference room. His gaze ping-ponged between them, finally landing on Laila. He stared at her, as if he inspected her insides. Peered directly into her soul.

She fought the urge to squirm. He did an excellent job of making her feel as if he knew her better than she knew herself.

He frowned and gestured toward the door. "Sydney, may I speak with you?"

"Of course. Excuse me." As she rose from the table, she gave Laila a sugary-sweet smile. "It was nice chatting with you."

Rock followed Sydney out.

Laila berated herself for standing up to Sydney and pissing her off. She'd handled those kinds of comments better. Ultimately, she didn't regret what she'd said.

Taking a jab at Sydney was not the only situation she could have handled better that morning. She couldn't lose it as she had in the meeting. Letting emotions, hers or another's, draw unwanted attention to her could be a fatal mistake. One she couldn't afford if she was going to complete the mission—both missions.

Chapter 3

Laila lay wide-awake in her dark bedroom. It was becoming a pattern. The night before, she hadn't been able to sleep for more than an hour or two. The whole move to the Emerald Zone had her out of sorts.

Five years ago, when her IQ testing promptly landed her a Sapphire designation and a one way ticket out of the Amber Zone. It had been a brutal adjustment. She'd thought she was going to a new, better place. She'd been a child who dreamed of happily ever after with the Sapphire Zone being a land of unicorns and rainbows. It had taken no time at all to realize she was expected to pick up the unicorn shit.

Her naiveté at the tender age of twenty-one was laughable. No one had told her when she'd been hustled off into Sapphire that the majority of people living in her new zone would treat her as if the tattoo around her wrist was still amber instead of the rich blue she'd worked so hard for. Her physical characteristics marked her as Amber. It didn't matter what color was around her wrist.

The Emerald Zone didn't seem much different. Bigger house, different color around her wrist, but still, the day in and day out of her life remained the same. People stared at her as if they might be able to spot her defects. She rarely left her apartment, except to go to her office. In the past five years, as Morgan Jr. came into power, the National Guard's constant, intimidating presence and the growing undertones of fear she sensed in practically everybody she met made her increasingly uneasy. Mostly she hid, submerging herself in her program.

Tonight, she was more tired than she could ever remember being, yet her mind refused to rest. She didn't consider herself a worrier, but the complete upheaval of her life, combined with the growing apprehension about her Resistance mission had led her to this—another stint of tossing and turning, racing thoughts, and now, something new to think about—Rock.

She swung her feet off the edge of the bed. The late spring breeze moved the curtains of the window overlooking her street. She'd seen him arrive at his home, which was across the street from her own new monstrosity.

To know someone like him was so close was maddening. Her heartbeat gave a little flutter. She'd met him once before, on the first day she'd been granted access to The Onyx Zone Recovery Compound. They called it OZ. It had been an introduction in passing, shared hellos and then they'd gone their separate ways. She'd been to the compound several times since, transferring items necessary for the trip from her office in the Peacekeeper's Compound to the tiny, makeshift space they'd allotted her in OZ. Many times she'd sat there alone, gazing out the window, watching Rock jog the perimeter of the compound before the heat of the day became oppressive.

Maybe he suffered like her.

She stood and pulled the curtain back.

A faint light radiated out his front windows. She checked the time. Ten fifteen. Laila slipped on her flip-flops, treaded down the steps and out her front door. His house was modern and looked larger than hers. Its jutting roofline accommodated vertical transom windows at the peak before another plane sliced down the front of the house.

She felt him even now as she crossed the street and entered his yard. He was calm and lonely. The rage from earlier in the day had diffused. The connection between them dumbfounded her. It was as if a part of her had slipped into its rightful place the first time she'd reached out to see if she could feel him.

He'd been raised Amber. If he didn't want company, the door would be locked. She turned the knob, and the door swung inward into a silent great room bathed in dark shadows. He sat toward the back of the space underneath a light. Goose bumps rose on her arms as she approached him. His back was to her as he fiddled with something at the kitchen island.

She cleared her throat. "I saw your lights on."

There was no element of surprise in his expression as he glanced up at the single light shining over his head. "Barely."

She smiled. "How do you stand it? It's a ghost town here." She laughed nervously. "I thought I saw tumbleweeds rolling down the street."

He shrugged. "I'm not here often."

"I can see that." She scanned the clothes spilling out of the duffel bag on the floor of the great room.

"You were Amber?"

She faced him and met his gaze. "Yes. I was designated Sapphire due to my IQ scores." The intensity of his stare made her uncomfortably self-conscious, causing her to turn away. She crossed to his refrigerator, opened it and stuck her head into the cool air. "Milk? That's all you have?" She glanced over her shoulder and caught him shoving whatever he'd been doing into a drawer. "What's that?"

"A project."

"Really? You're going to make me ask?"

"I don't want you to ask. It's none of your business." He walked to the fridge, opened the freezer and pulled out a bottle of clear liquid. He poured some into two short glasses and handed her one. He downed his and refilled it.

Laila took hers and wandered into the great room. It was difficult trying to slip back into her old self—Amber Laila. That girl didn't fit as comfortably as she used to. That fact saddened her more than she wanted to acknowledge at the moment.

Flipping on the video feed, she plopped down on the couch. Rock followed and lowered himself next to her. They sat shoulder to shoulder. "Where'd they put you?" he asked.

"Across the street."

He nodded. "They're filling the street house by house. You're the third person to get designated Emerald since I got here last summer." He clinked his glass with hers. "Welcome to the neighborhood," he practically growled, then threw back his drink. "What happened this afternoon when you left the meeting?"

She couldn't tell him the truth, and refused to lie. She raced to find the right words, and the longer his stare bore into her, the angrier his expression became. Finally, she shrugged and gave the same lame excuse she'd used earlier. "I felt a little overwhelmed."

"By Garret's presentation?"

She broke their eye contact and feigned interest in the video playing. "No." She felt him staring at her. Waiting.

"Morgan was touching you. Has he done that before?"

"No. I think his advances were for your benefit."

"Probably were. Sorry about that."

"I'm not the only person who thought so."

"Sydney?"

Laila nodded.

"Let me know if she bothers you again. I told her to communicate through me from now on."

"Why?"

"It didn't take a mind reader to tell she was being nasty. It was written all over your face."

"Oh." He smiled down at her. He was gorgeous when he smiled. "Thank you again."

"You're welcome."

"I got the distinct impression there was some hostility there between you and Morgan."

"That is an understatement."

"I'm not a fan either."

His gaze was hard. His jaw clenched. "Don't worry. Now that I know you don't want him touching you, he won't get the opportunity again."

"Nice sentiment." She shifted and laid her head against his arm. "But Morgan can pretty much do whatever he pleases."

"No, he can't. Not this time," he mumbled.

Laila let the comment go. Even with all her barriers up, she felt his anger flare, but it was nowhere near the level he'd escalated to that afternoon.

Tucking her hand between his bicep and torso, she snuggled close. It had been so long since she'd felt the trademark unconditional acceptance from another Amber. She'd never gotten an opportunity to experience the protection and care an Amber man instinctively exhibited. Maybe now. She sighed, contented. After all the years living alone in the Sapphire Zone, she finally had the touch, the sense of belonging she needed again.

God, she'd agonized at the loss all those years ago. Eventually, she found the only way to cope with total isolation was by locking her emotions down and ignoring her need. Her refusal to let the solitude affect her helped her survive the complete disconnect from everyone and everything she'd ever known. Now, sitting there, the locks broke and relief flooded her.

"It feels so good." She didn't need to elaborate. She'd felt his loneliness.

Rock wrapped an arm around her shoulder and pulled her in so her cheek rested on his chest.

"I missed it so much," she whispered. She wasn't alone anymore. Laila tried to swallow around her tight throat. But with her next breath, her composure fractured. Hot tears streaked down her face. When he squeezed her tightly and shushed her, his massive arms weighing heavily and giving comfort, she cried harder. He rested his cheek on the top of her head and rocked her tenderly.

Mortified, she started to pull away. "I'm sorry."

He pulled her into his side. "Nothing to be sorry for."

She gave up trying to hold it all in.

Chapter 4

By the flickering light of the video screen, Laila cried in Rock's arms. He held her, stroking her hair and shushing her. His chest was tight and his stomach swam with a queasy feeling of foreboding. His earlier conversation with his father replayed in his head and his commitment to this woman who had so little and needed so much solidified.

He absorbed her weight as she burrowed into him, desperately clutching the material of his tear-dampened shirt. She was starved for the unconditional acceptance and physical touch they'd grown up with.

"Lie down. Put your head in my lap." His voice was gruff with emotion, even to his own ears. She tilted her head back and gauged his expression with hope-filled eyes. His heart broke for her, and not able to face her pain, he had to look away. She stretched across the soft leather of the couch, her head pillowed by his thigh. He sought to ease her misery through the continual movement of his hands, trailing his fingers along the exposed skin of her arm and smoothing her hair away from her face. Her sobs subsided into an occasional hiccup.

Soon, his hand at her waist moved with the rhythmic rise and fall of her breathing. She seemed smaller than she had when she sat across the table from him at the briefing. Her coconut-scented hair drew him closer and made his mouth water. Tonight, instead of her professional attire, she wore a tank top and lightweight shorts. This was a side of her he hadn't seen.

He'd barely survived a year outside the Amber Zone. The pervasive hush here seemed amplified, especially when he'd first arrived. It was the complete opposite of the life they'd been used to. Amber was full of noise, of people, of sex. And, it was safe. Even with all those people crammed into tiny little spaces, he'd never felt safer.

Until a person lived in an environment where pitfalls and perils were everywhere, truly understanding the monumental effect safety, or lack of it, had on a person's life wasn't possible. Laila had been living without that particular state of being for five years. A year of it had fundamentally changed him. The citizens of Sapphire and Emerald didn't hide their true feelings regarding Ambers. How many times had their prejudice left her alone and ostracized? No wonder she'd lost it. He was one friendly face in a sea of nefarious humanity.

A fleeting whisper caressed his consciousness. *What had she been like before?*

This changed everything. He would keep her safe, try to calm her fears and soothe her suffering. And she was suffering, even though she tried exceptionally hard not to show it.

In sleep, the ugliness of her pain vanished. She looked peaceful now. Her thick chestnut hair, gathered at the back of her head with a band, curled over her shoulder. For hours, he ran his fingertips through the heavy strands. Closing his eyes, he absorbed as much as he could of the year's worth of touch he'd missed. He memorized the feel of her smooth skin under his work-roughened hand. Appreciated it. Having Laila Lewis sleeping in his arms was a comfort to him, too. With the exception of the time he'd examined Jordan's amputated limb, this was the first time in an entire year he'd deliberately touched a woman. He absorbed as much as he could of the touch he'd missed.

Was he enough of a bastard to inflict his twisted brand of care on this innocent? Laila reminded him of Journey, and she'd done well in the tightly controlled world he lived in. He didn't really have a choice. He knew no other way and didn't really have the inclination to change.

He spent the night watching her sleep and mentally lambasting himself for the direction he would take her life because it wouldn't be an easy path. As the sun rose, chasing away the shadows from the room, Laila finally stirred. Without opening her eyes, she murmured, "I'm sorry about last night. It's been years since I cried because I missed Amber. I guess I had a lot more bottled up inside than I thought."

Rock brushed the pad of his thumb over her cheekbone then down, across her bottom lip.

She peeked up at him. "Forgive me?"

He mustered a smiled. "Forgiven."

"Oh." She pushed up from his lap, suddenly looking wide-awake. "Today's a training day." She stood and stretched. "I need to take a shower and change."

"Take your time. I planned on starting with the basics today. Tomorrow our strict nine to five training schedule begins. You'll have to wear clothes you can move in and shoes you can run in." He perused her body for what had to be the thousandth time in the last few hours. "No skirts."

"What time are we leaving?"

He unfolded his stiff body and glanced at the oversized clock hanging over the wide, arched entry to the kitchen. "About an hour?"

"Okay." She stopped near the front door. "But today you can only have me until two. I have an errand to run after that." Instead of leaving through the front door as he'd expected, she turned and trudged up the stairs to the second floor.

The second floor he'd never been to.

He walked to the bottom of the steps, intent on saying something, but heard a door shut and water running. He stood frozen, mouth hanging open.

When he'd gotten to Emerald, he hadn't even wanted to look at a bedroom. He hadn't wanted the acres of mattress spread out on either side of him as he slept. At least when he crashed on the couch, he could fool himself into thinking the cushions at his back were a soft, warm body.

He grabbed the handrail, hesitated then walked to his downstairs bathroom and snagged two clean towels.

As he climbed those stairs for the first time, he left a piece of his past behind. It was time to take his first steps in a new direction.

He knocked then opened the only closed door on the landing. The big, fern-colored bathroom had a slanted ceiling with a skylight that bathed the room with morning sunlight. "I brought you some clean towels."

"Thank you. Do you have any shampoo? There isn't any in the bottle." Her vague form moved in the steam behind the pebbled shower glass.

"Yeah. I'll get some." Downstairs, he rummaged around in the cabinet underneath his bathroom sink and found the items he thought she'd need.

Back upstairs, he put the toilet paper on the tank and set the soap, shampoo and conditioner just inside the shower door.

"Thank you," she called.

He straightened and looked over his shoulder. "Get used to it. I'll be taking care of you from here on out." He didn't wait for her to answer or offer an opinion to that statement, just closed the door behind him.

Rock stood on the landing at the top of the stairs. There were two doors on the right and one to the left. He went left and found the master bedroom with an attached bath. Leaning his shoulder against the doorjamb, he scanned the suite, taking in the details of a room left alone for a quarter century.

Like the bathroom, it had skylights and high windows along the top of the vaulted ceilings. Rectangles of cheerful sunlight painted the cream-colored carpeting. A riot of white, twisted sheets lay on the foot of a chunky four-poster bed. He picked up a frame sitting on the nightstand. His stomach twisted as he studied the faded family picture of a smiling couple and two small boys in front of a Christmas tree in the downstairs great room. He tossed the photo onto the bed, stripped the sheets and brought the bundle down to the laundry room. He chucked the picture into the garbage can and threw the linens in the washer.

Breakfast was prepared when she joined him, fresh-faced and smiling, in the same shorts and tank from the night before.

"Eggs and potatoes okay?"

"Yeah." She held up a toothbrush he'd never seen before. "I used your toothbrush. I figured you could put it in the dishwasher." He must have blanched because she tilted her head and said, "What?"

He tried to squash his smile as he dropped the toothbrush in the dishwasher's silverware basket.

"What?" she asked again.

"Not my toothbrush."

Her eyes widened. "Oh…girlfriend's?"

"No. You can have it after it's run through the washer. It's yours now." She shrugged. "Okay."

Sitting next to each other at the island, Rock barely tasted his breakfast, too fascinated in the slow withdrawal of Laila's fork from between her lips and the momentary flutter of her eyelids when she groaned her pleasure. When Laila pushed her half-eaten food away, he slid it back. "Get used to having a big breakfast. You're going to need your energy on training days."

"I can't eat all this every day. My clothes wouldn't fit me in a week."

"You're not going to have to worry about that."

"I still can't eat another bite, Rock." She jumped off the stool. "I gotta get dressed. I'll be back."

"No skirts." He got up from his stool and slotted the dishes into the dishwasher. The ambient temperature of the suddenly silent great room lowered five degrees when she walked out the door, and the pervasive feeling of solitude returned. The woman was a storm, churning up long repressed feelings he'd buried deep. She brought some life back into what had only been an existence two days before.

In his downstairs bathroom, he stripped himself of his jeans and turned on the shower. While he waited for the water to warm, he looked at himself in the mirror as if through Laila's eyes, assessing things he hadn't paid much attention to for a year. He was haggard with a week's worth of whiskers shading the lower half of his face. His once super-short cut, worn when he was in the Amber police department, was now shaggy to the collar of his T-shirt. The combination made him look wild. He shaved in the accumulating steam and then stepped into the shower.

The original plan of glossing over the training so he could focus on more terrorism while in the city was out. He'd assumed Laila was just another snooty academic raised in privilege and viewing him as the help. One who, he'd thought, would have a stick prominently stuck up her ass and be a pain in his. What one night did to his perspective was mind-boggling. This was *not* that.

He cared. She roused his protective feelings and it left him feeling like an itch in just the right part of his brain had finally been scratched. Her voice strummed the horrible silence away. His soul purred with anticipation of what was to come. He hadn't been looking for a companion, yet here she was. She had his name written all over her in blinking neon lights.

Now, he was more suspicious than ever that Morgan was fucking with him and setting them both up to die. He ran down training exercises he might be able to use to help her master some of the skills he'd neglected during his initial planning. He needed to train her to follow a command without question and defend herself whether he was with her or not. To some degree, he'd done it twice before. Not overly well, since Emily was dead. He'd been easy on his girls back then, indulging their playful acts of defiance. He wouldn't make the same mistakes this time.

Over the din of the shower spray, Rock heard Laila enter the house and call his name.

"In here. I'll be out in a second." He finished quickly, stepped out of the shower and dried off. He'd forgotten to bring clothes into the bathroom with him, so he wrapped the damp towel around his waist and strode to his clothes piled haphazardly next to his duffel bag.

Laila sat, waiting on the couch, following him with her gaze. He grabbed his pants from the floor and released the towel from his waist.

Chapter 5

Ho-ly Crap. Laila had thought no man could look sexier than Rock, when she'd finally gotten a good look at him yesterday before the meeting. But the twenty-four-hours-ago Rock was just crushed by the right-this-second Rock, hands down.

He was broad and tanned, with water dripping from the ends of his tousled hair and landing on his shoulders. Droplets rolled seductively down his chest past so sexy nipple rings and badass tattoos. She wanted to catch the drops with her tongue. No need for that pesky towel. He was perfect. Muscled, but not too much, obviously powerful, and with an air of danger that wrapped the irresistible package up in a bow. The day she'd noticed those little gold rings in his nipples, winking in the sun as he jogged around the compound, she couldn't drag her eyes away. She'd stolen quick glimpses of his tattoos, and wondered what words meant so much to him he had them permanently written into his skin. Good God, no man had a right to be that gorgeous. He probably had women drooling all over him. Beautiful women, like Sydney with the striking green eyes. Laila wondered how much he availed himself to them.

She was nothing special, painfully average compared to the women outside the Amber Zone. Her self-esteem had always come from her intellect. She was intelligent, but rarely does one hear a man brag about how smart his woman is. She used to be spontaneous and fun, happy. Those great qualities had disappeared since she'd left Amber.

He said, "I'll be ready in a minute. Then, we can go."

"Okay." The word came out guttural. She cleared her throat quietly and continued her appreciation.

He turned just enough to give her an eyeful. *Oh my God.* He was circumcised. She'd never seen one like that before. Growing up in Amber, she'd seen many naked men up close and personal. None of them looked like that.

It answered one question about Rock. He was definitely older than she, old enough to be born in a world where medical care was available for everybody.

She was not. Laila had been one of the first babies born in New Atlanta, her mom having traveled pregnant to the relative safety of the city.

She glanced from his cock to his face and found him looking at her, the side of his mouth curling up.

"Everything okay?" He pulled pants over his muscular ass. No underwear.

"Yes."

He buttoned, zipped, and then walked to where she sat. "Your mouth says yeah, but your face says no."

"Nope. I'm good."

"Don't worry. I'll go easy on you today."

She nodded, happy to be distracted from the direction her thoughts had been going. Visions of military type boot camp had made her wary of mission prep for months.

His boots were set in a wide stance, anchoring girders wrapped in blue jeans. He appeared invincible. He turned and a lock of his shiny black hair fell on his forehead like a comma. Like Superman. He reached toward her and his biceps bulged under his black T-shirt. "Come on. Time to start your training."

Laila spent the morning trying to wrangle some focus from her brain. Side by side, they leaned over a map of the eastern US while he traced the route they'd be taking. She found the size of his hands and the smell of his soap infinitely more fascinating. He taught her the mix ratio of gas and the additive that would make fuel out in the Onyx Zone useable, but she found it hard to turn her attention away from the veins hugging his forearms as he poured. The morning had been a little boring and gave her mind too much time to wander.

After lunch, they knelt side by side while he patiently taught her CPR and first aid. His words fanned over her skin when he knelt with her over the CPR dummy. His gentle brown eyes met hers every few seconds, assessing whether she understood. First aid was a hands-on activity. They spent the early afternoon in each other's personal space. His gentle example of tourniquet tying on her upper thigh prompted goosebumps and tummy twirls with every brush of his fingers against her sensitive skin. She could be in real trouble with this man. He'd be so easy to fall in love with.

Before she knew it, it was two o'clock, and Rock let her go for the day. She scrambled down the corridor of the main building, purposely losing him. Afraid he would offer her a ride, she slipped out of OZ without saying goodbye.

The streets were relatively empty during the trek from one end of the Emerald Zone to the other. The heavy military presence kept the streets absent of terrified civilians. It wasn't far. The zone was small, a residential neighborhood, a strip mall and various military and governmental compounds.

Bizarre. She was calm. Maybe because she'd had a lot of time to mentally prepare. Next month would mark a year since the organizers of the Sapphire Resistance, Jordan Ford and Kate O'Connor, visited her apartment. Thanks to the video piece about the mission, it was common knowledge Laila was going to be given Emerald status before she left for DC. Her Emerald designation gave her entry to places inaccessible to most. They recruited her for the Emerald Zone cell.

Fast moving clouds threatened rain, so Laila wasn't melting in the midday sun. The trip took less than an hour, but by the time she arrived at the Peacekeeper Compound, a faint headache rooted at the back of her neck and radiated outward in all directions.

In her office upstairs, she changed into a full, flowing skirt and a camisole, checked her hair, and then spent some time just sitting, cooling off.

She'd never been called to do anything for the Resistance, like so many other women had. No, they'd saved her, squirreled her away for the time she'd be transferred to Emerald.

Her time had come. And she was terrified. Right now, her focus wasn't on the mission to retrieve artifacts, but on mustering the courage she'd need to complete her assigned Resistance tasks.

Finally, Laila took a deep breath and opened the door.

Morgan's office was in the same building as hers, but on a different floor. She headed toward the elevator. Since the failed attempt on his life, he was paranoid of everybody and kept himself well guarded, making him increasingly hard to get to. The building was a dead zone, and few people had access to the compound or the man. Even Morgan's own Guard were restricted unless assigned to work there. The Gov must have deemed her non-threatening to have placed her office in the same building. If she didn't accomplish this task, it most likely wouldn't get done.

The high-pitched ringing in her ears was more distinct in the utter silence of the elevator. A bell chimed, and the doors opened.

She traveled down the corridor to General Morgan's office, her heart beating double time against the steady rhythm of her footfalls. The stark fluorescent lighting clashed with the bright white floor, exacerbating her headache to tremendous proportions. She felt as if she was advancing on her own execution, instead of a life threatening game of cat and mouse.

Maybe she was.

When she'd pledged her support to Jordan all those months ago, she'd been aware she'd be chosen to complete dangerous assignments when the time was right. This was important, and meant more than mere loyalty to the cause. Laila dreamed about seeing her mom again. For that to happen, the Gov had to fall.

Stopping in front of the two guards standing outside of his offices, she ran her sweaty hands down the front of her skirt. "I need a moment of the General's time, if he's available."

The soldier nodded and touched his earbud. "Sir, Laila Lewis is here to see you." He listened. "Yes, sir," he said, then to her, "I'm sorry, Miss Lewis, but I have to search you for weapons before you go in. Spread your arms, please." He didn't wait for her consent before resting his hands on her shoulders, and didn't look sorry while he slowly ran his hand over every part of her body, including her breasts and crotch. When he was done, he winked at her.

"Liked that, did you?" she asked in monotone.

He ogled her then opened the outer door to Morgan's prison-like office space, glanced back at her and nodded. "Go on in."

When the outer door closed behind her, she moved forward to the steel door in front. Placing her hand on the knob, she waited for the buzz to indicate the lock was disengaged. Instead, the door swung open.

"Laila, this is quite a pleasant surprise," the General said with a disfigured smile and elaborate wave to come inside. He leered down her body.

She stepped away from him. Impossibly, her heart hammered harder and faster. Maybe his behavior at the meeting hadn't been exclusively for Rock's benefit.

"Sir, I was hoping I could ask a favor."

"Of course." He closed the door behind her, stepped back around his desk and sat. "Sit. Sit." He motioned to a chair.

The large slab of wood between them lessened the swell of panic at his nearness, though her heartbeat still surged, thumping hard at the base of her throat. She rubbed her clammy palms on her skirt and pulled the tiny microphone from the pocket as she sat.

Morgan folded his hands on his desk and focused his cold, crystal blue eyes on her. "Would you care for something to drink?" He pretended to be so civilized, perched on the top rung of the food chain, looking down on his prey and feasting on the agony of others. Always with formal manners and an even tone.

She maintained eye contact with him to avoid staring at the hideous scar marring his otherwise beautiful face. "No thank you, sir." Her voice had quavered.

He smiled, almost imperceptibly.

She'd be dead in short order if she couldn't stop signaling how petrified she was.

"So what can I do for you?"

She fidgeted, crossing and uncrossing her legs, so planting the bug would appear to be a fidget like the ones preceding it. "Well." She shook her head and laughed nervously. Jesus. She was a freaking basket case. "I'm sorry to bother you. I know you're a busy man."

"Go on."

She took a deep breath and leaned back in her chair. "I know there's a good chance I won't make it back from the mission." Curling her fingers under her seat, she pressed hard, hoping the adhesive side of the bug was sticky enough. After she let go, she held her breath, waiting for it to fall to the floor. Waiting for Morgan to ask her what she'd just done.

Chapter 6

Rock sat in the solitude of his kitchen, picking up where he left off the night before, putting finishing touches on the pincer mechanism for Jordan's prosthetic hand.

A muffled noise emanated from the receiver sitting on the counter. Finally, someone was planting the bug. He set his work down and walked toward the tiny speaker. Turning up the volume, he listened intently. The bug was activated, but all he heard for some time were the indistinct sounds of the microphone rubbing against something. Finally, the reception became clear. "I know there's a good chance I won't make it back from the mission. The fact became exceedingly clear at the briefing yesterday."

"Laila." Rock pounded the granite counter. "No. She is not doing this." He scrambled to make sense of what he heard. His ordered and rational thoughts exploded, fragmenting into shards of unrelated facts. Was she in the Emerald Zone cell? Or was she simply in the room with someone else in the cell? What else had they asked her to do? This was the errand she had to run? When their training was over for the day, he hadn't even asked her where she was going. He'd been too focused on the changes he needed to make in order for her to be better prepared. His bad. It wouldn't happen again.

"There's really no need for you to worry about your safety," Morgan said in a placating tone.

The parallels between the night Emily died and that moment terrified him. Laila was alone with that lunatic, and all he could do was listen, desperately hoping he wouldn't have to listen to Laila die, too.

"The trucks are invincible. My best people will be protecting you and the pieces you recover."

"Yes, sir. I want to thank you for that."

"But?"

"No buts. It's just—I was hoping I'd get permission to talk to my mother one last time before we leave. I want to say goodbye."

"Your mother is an Amber, isn't she?" His tone had turned curt.

"Yes, sir."

"I don't think there's much I can do to help you since we're currently at a stand-off with Amber and communication with that zone is banned."

"Yes, sir. I understand. I just had to ask in case there was any way I could talk to her one last time."

"Get out of there," Rock growled at the speaker. Morgan was a paranoid bastard, and the longer she stayed, the greater the chance she'd do something to trigger his suspicion. Flashes of Jordan, of the risks she took and the price she paid crowded his thoughts, testing the containment of his fury.

Muffled movements sounded before she spoke again. "Thank you for taking the time to see me."

"You're welcome, Miss Lewis."

The door closed behind her, and Rock tapped his earbud. He'd never programmed her number into his system. Exasperated, he pulled his hand-held out of his pocket and searched her name on the intranet directory. When he found it, he entered her info and tried to contact her again.

She didn't answer the call.

When he heard the beep, he forced calmness into his voice. "Where are you?" He couldn't say more without beginning a diatribe about her lapse of good judgment. He disconnected and paced a trench into his tile floor, mentally detailing the list of flaws in her actions.

Her reply didn't come.

After a half hour, he realized he'd not identified himself, and she probably didn't have his information programmed into her hand-held either.

He commed again, and gave his information so she could reach him. Then he sat on his stool, bouncing his knee. He couldn't concentrate well enough to finish fine tuning Jordan's prosthetic. So he paced.

For almost an hour, Morgan's office remained silent barring the occasional paper shuffling or chair squeaking. "Please contact Sydney, let her know she's needed in my office ASAP," came through the speaker.

Rock stopped in his tracks. Already, the bug was producing useful information. Sydney was a Guard, yes, but he hadn't known Morgan made himself available for one-on-one meetings with her.

Not more than a quarter hour later, Morgan's interior door buzzed. "Conrad, it's been almost a week. I've missed you." Sydney's voice was more feminine than he'd ever heard it. She spoke as if she didn't have a dick dangling between her legs—almost.

Rock stepped closer, startled and listening hard. He turned the volume up as loud as it would go.

"Quit your whining, Sydney, I'm a busy man." Morgan's chair squeaked, a long, earsplitting sound. "Now come around here. Let me get a good look at you."

Footsteps echoed softly through the speaker.

"Take your shirt off. I want to see those tits."

"No fucking way." He almost laughed. Could it be she was a Guard because she was sucking Morgan's dick? A definite possibility, especially if he'd given up raping his prisoners after Jordan's attempt on his life.

"Mmm. Very nice," Morgan said.

Shuffling and the rasp of a zipper sounded. Slurping, sucking and moaning followed.

"Right here, baby," Morgan murmured, his voice husky. "Yes, that's right, all the way to the back of your throat."

Sydney and General Morgan's relationship was a priceless piece of information that revealed he and Laila were in more danger than he'd originally thought.

The encounter lasted about two minutes. All in all, pretty funny. Almost humorous enough to change his murderous mood. Almost.

Laila still hadn't contacted him. He strode to his front picture window as he'd been doing every couple of minutes during the past two hours, and tapped his earbud. "Time." He set his jaw. It was after five.

The stark silence did nothing to calm his simmering anger.

At seven thirty, Laila strolled through his front door and into his kitchen. Eyes sparkling, she smiled at him.

The wild storm brewing inside couldn't be tempered by her smile. As he walked toward her, she caught his expression and the joy radiating from her faltered. He stopped directly in front of her and crossed his arms. Now that she was there, safe, he wasn't sure how to start his imminent meltdown. "Where have you been?"

Her eyebrows lifted, and she cocked her head. "I was at my doctor's office."

His guts clenched. "Why? What happened?"

"Nothing happened."

"Then why did you need a doctor?"

"I didn't *need* a doctor. I just—" She rolled her eyes. "I'm turning twenty six in a few days. My implant was due to be replaced." She gestured to her arm, twisted it and showed the stitches. "I wanted to wait until I was an Emerald before I went so I wouldn't be forced to get a new one."

"Oh." Big news, and unexpected. He pinned her to the edge of the counter, caged her with his arms.

She looked up at him. "What?" she asked softly. She pouted as if she hadn't started their first day of training lying to him and putting herself in mortal danger. Her deceitful innocence enraged him.

"You stupid little girl." He knew the choice of words he'd just growled at her should have been tempered, but his indulgence wouldn't keep her alive. "From now on, you will not—" He'd escalated from soft spoken to a yell within the span of a handful of words. Taking in another slow breath, he continued in a more reasonable tone. "You will not go anywhere near Morgan again."

Her mouth fell open and brows bunched. Cascades of rapid-fire expressions were barely exposed through the mask she put in place. "How do you know where I was?" She attempted to push one of his arms away.

Once he'd made clear he could keep her there as long as he liked, he raised it.

She stepped to the side and began to back away from him. Cautious deliberation reflected in her eyes.

"You have to be fucking crazy, planting a bug in Morgan's office."

"I'm sorry."

With every one of his steps forward, she took one back.

"Please, Rock. Don't turn me in."

"Why shouldn't I?"

She stood there, shaking her head, obviously searching for the right words.

He only became more enraged at her inability to defend herself. "How does it feel to be caught, Laila?"

Her face paled.

"Tell me!" he yelled. "Tell me what it's like knowing you're dead already!"

She backed into a corner, panic widening her wild eyes, and froze when she couldn't go any farther.

She was petrified, and he wanted her to be because scarier people than him were out there. "There's nowhere to run." He came to a stop only a foot from her, and saw the moment her bravado collapsed.

She hung her head. "If you have any compassion in you at all, you'll kill me now," she whispered, lifting her chin to meet his gaze. Tears ran down her face. "Do it. Just do it."

Rock grabbed Laila's arm.

She jumped and cried out, but didn't struggle as he dragged her into the kitchen. The fact she wasn't fighting to get away from a man she thought was going to kill her indicated how much work lay before them. She'd given up on her life already. He wanted to throw something, but picked her up roughly and set her on the kitchen counter instead.

"Don't you ever," he bellowed, "ever give up on yourself, on your survival so easily again. Don't admit your crime and definitely don't ask for death! What the fuck, Laila!"

Her eyebrows scrunched together. Then, she sagged. The crease between her brows smoothed and she released a long breath of relief. "What's happening?"

Rock nodded toward the speaker on the counter. Her gaze shifted from the speaker, to him, and then back to the speaker before she whispered, "You're Resistance?"

He nodded.

"Oh." She wiped her tears with the bottom of her blouse, looking as if she was trying hard not to meet his gaze. "Did you know about me before today?"

"Do you think I'd let you do what you just did if I knew?"

She lifted her chin. "I'm not going to report all my activities to you as if I were a child, and I'll complete the tasks I've agreed to, Rock, without your knowledge or approval. Half of it's done already."

"Half? Uh, no. Your part is done now. Who is your Resistance contact?"

"I don't know who you think you are—"

"I'm the man who's going to keep you alive."

"How could you let me think I was caught like that?" She placed both hands on his chest and attempted to push him away. "Asshole!"

He wasn't letting her go anywhere. "I want you to remember those sixty seconds forever. I want you to remember your terror when you thought you were caught. Maybe that will scare some sense into you. Now, who is your contact?" he asked with thinly veiled fury.

"Stop trying to bully me," she snapped. Her jaw was set.

"God dammit, Laila. It's my job to protect you, and that's what I'm going to do." He leaned in toward her, caging her even more. They were nose to nose. "Even if what I'm protecting you from is yourself." He scowled over her as they squared off, his teeth grinding against each other.

She still looked him right in the eye then whispered faintly, "I gave my word to Jordan. I will not renege, and I will not name my contact."

Then she put both hands on his chest and shoved hard. "Now, get away!"

Rock stepped back, and she immediately hopped off the counter and headed for the door.

"Fuck you!" she screamed over her shoulder as she left. The door slammed so hard, the house's front windows rattled.

"She did not just..." He took a step toward the door then forced himself to stop. The instinct to follow her and spank her ass was nearly overwhelming. His fists balled as he reined in the impulse and took a deep breath, calming himself.

He needed to process.

Chapter 7

Laila stormed through her front door and slammed it shut. The quietness of her home slapped her in the face and her indignation fell away. For twenty-four hours, she'd been an optimist and thought Rock might fill some of the emptiness she carried around inside. He'd just crushed that hope to pieces. She knew better. Hope was a stupid notion in New Atlanta. She ran upstairs and collapsed on her bed.

The part of her that needed filling would always be there. Huddled in a ball, she hugged her legs and cried until she was damp from the heat in the stuffy room, and her hair stuck to the back of her neck. She'd learned years ago sleep was the only relief from overwhelming solitude so Laila gratefully gave herself to the exhaustion gripping her.

* * * *

She'd fallen asleep around dinnertime. Now, she lay awake in the middle of the night. The rest had altered her perspective. She wasn't angry anymore. Even though what Rock had done was cruel, it was a powerful lesson that would never fade from her memory.

She tossed herself onto her back and released an exaggerated sigh into the darkness of her bedroom. She'd done it. A sense of pride in herself brought a small smile to her lips. She'd risked her life for freedom today. Laila pumped her fist in the air. She would never forget this day. Never. She'd run across a quote during her trip preparations. "Our country will remain the land of the free. Only so long as it is the home of the brave." When she'd read it, she'd known bravery would be the only thing keeping her to her promise to help the Resistance instead of running in the opposite direction.

Ironically, she'd forgotten the most important part of the day because of the blow up with Rock. Being an Emerald meant she was no longer required to submit to mandatory birth control. With the removal of her implant, she was free to have children.

Plural.

Her chest tightened, and she laughed at herself. From celebration to near tears in four point two seconds. New record. Then, her thoughts ran full circle, landing on Rock again. That beautiful bastard was the only man she'd ever known who took her breath away.

Her reaction might have been an overreaction to the drama of the day. Rock was raised Amber, and had already been given the assignment of her protector. He expected to take care of her. To him, it didn't matter that they weren't actually on the mission yet.

She pulled her hand-held out of her deep skirt pocket, depressing the button to activate the screen. She spoke Rock's name and waited for the results of her search. The first was a news feed video, detailing his capture of the first serial killer in New Atlanta since the pandemic. He'd killed the woman and received his Emerald designation because of it. The events were high profile, but she wasn't surprised she hadn't heard the story. During the past year, she'd been too engrossed in the final planning stage of the Fine Art and Artifacts mission.

She got out of bed, peeled a curtain back and peeked across the street. A low glow emanated from Rock's front window.

They would be training in earnest tomorrow and would spend the next few months of their lives pretty much attached at the hip. So, avoiding him was out.

She slipped out of her skirt, let it fall in a pool at her feet, pulled on a lightweight pair of shorts and slid her toes into her flip-flops. She padded down the stairs and out the front door. Cricket sounds filled the night and her feet collected dew as she walked through the grass of his lawn. When she tried the knob to his front door, it turned, and she walked soundlessly into his home.

He sat on the couch watching the vid screen, and his gaze darted to her.

She smiled and tilted her head, trying to look cute and hoping to brush off the effects of their earlier clash. "Darn. I was hoping to catch you naked." She waggled her eyebrows at him.

He displayed just the barest of smiles and then waved her over. "Come on." His voice was rough. He'd been on the verge of sleep.

Instinctively, her Amber needs flared to life. The need to be smiled at, touched, hugged, fucked. This man triggered all of them. She plopped down next to him. Thigh to thigh.

Laila had dreamed about having the unconditional acceptance of a roommate relationship in Circle City. Through the years, she'd often wished she had a man watching over her, caring for her like all the other girls she'd grown up with in the Amber Zone.

Rock offered his hand, and she laced their fingers together.

"You have to tell me where you're going before you go," he said. "This is non-negotiable and not entirely because of what you did this afternoon. During your training, we'll create routines that will keep both of us safer. Actions will speak louder than words between us. Sometimes the absence of a routine or a non-response to a normal everyday signal is the only warning you may be able to give. Do you understand?"

She sighed. "Yes."

He shook his head and closed his eyes for a few seconds as if her simplistic view of the world tested him. When his gaze met hers again, it had softened. "Baby, you're in the big leagues now. If he'd found that bug when he searched you, that guardsman wouldn't have hesitated splattering your brains all over the walls."

"I get that. Your little drama drove the fact home loud and clear."

"Good. Now, who is your contact?" His voice was gruff, but she didn't feel any anger in him.

"If you're Resistance, you know I can't tell you." Cells were made up of individuals who didn't know the others in their cell, unless something occurred to make it absolutely necessary. Morgan interrogated with drugs. Many Sapphire Resistance members in drug-induced stupors gave up co-conspirators, decimating a substantial portion of the Resistance in that zone.

"Do you even know the name of your contact here in Emerald?"

"Yes. And if you knew it too, it could mean a death sentence. It's not worth the risk."

He responded with silence.

I'm right, and he knows it.

It didn't seem like the subject was settled as he sat there, stiffly, a million miles away.

She experienced a sinking feeling in the pit of her stomach.

His sinking feeling.

"What is it?" she asked.

Eyebrows furrowed, he looked down at her. "How did you know to ask *what*?"

"Huh?"

"What did I do that prompted you to ask *what* just now?" he asked, over-enunciating.

Avoiding his gaze, she shrugged. She'd almost given herself away.

He grabbed her chin and lifted her face to meet his gaze. It seemed like he inspected every nuance while their eyes were locked until, finally, he released her. "Your risk today has already paid off. Unfortunately, the news isn't good. We won't be any safer from the Gov when we're out of the city. Morgan couldn't let us go. Couldn't let us out of his reach."

"What are you talking about?"

"After you left his office, I got an earful of him getting his dick sucked by none other than Sydney Parr."

"Oh, no." She groaned.

Rock raked his hand through his shaggy brown hair and focused on the vid screen. The flickering light tinted his face blue.

She laid her head against his arm and yawned.

"There's something you need to know," he said. "My father was one of the original Resistance members back when the Repopulation Laws were enacted. The history between Morgan's father and mine seems to have aligned the stars to make us enemies. It's like we were born to finish the struggle they started so long ago."

"Except this Morgan is crazier than his father."

"Yeah. And since he can't outright murder me without severe retaliation, he placed me on the recovery team, hoping something or someone will do his dirty work for him. I've been on mission after mission outside the city walls. It has to be pissing him off I keep returning.

"Now you're assigned to a mission traveling farther from the city than anyone's gone since the pandemic."

"Yeah."

"He's hoping you won't come back."

"His goal may be for neither of us to return, with Sydney on the mission to make sure of it. You have to be very careful with Garret. If Sydney's being deployed on this mission to kill us, he probably is, too."

Rock grabbed the remote off the table and flicked off the video, plunging them into darkness. "C'mere." He shifted them around until he spooned her. With a heavy leg slung over hers, he enveloped her in solid muscle.

"So that's it," she said, "an old grudge started by your fathers? I had a sense something more personal was going on."

"It's not all, but enough of an explanation for tonight. Just be aware Morgan will never leave me alone. If I had the opportunity, I'd kill Conrad Morgan with my bare hands, and he knows it. So, he flexes and flaunts his power in my face every opportunity he gets, knowing I'll never get close enough to make him pay for his actions."

Laila closed her eyes and enjoyed his warm breath ruffling her hair. The slow expansion and release of his chest pressed at her back. His heavy arm slung over her waist cinched her close to him. She felt exceptionally small and perfectly safe.

"So, you can have babies now?" The rumble of his words vibrated against her back.

"Yes," she whispered, feeling if she said it too loud, it wouldn't be real.

"Are you going to run right out and fuck the first man you see?"

Something fluttered inside. *You're the first man I see.* "If that's your way of asking if I'm seeing someone, the answer is God no."

"Not just no, but God no? Why so adamant?"

"Getting me pregnant is all sex with any of these boys outside Amber is good for. And, yes, I mean boys, because men should know how to give a woman an orgasm."

He chuckled. "I've heard their skills are lacking."

"You're being kind. Not one man I've been with since I left Amber could get me off. Plus, every damn one of them treated me like a novelty. Brave men who took a walk on the wild side putting their dicks into an Amber. It didn't take long to realize what was going on. Overall, it was too much effort to put in just to be disappointed once we got our clothes off."

Rock laughed, shaking her body along with his. Laila loved the sound of it.

"How long has it been?"

She avoided the question by turning over so they lay face to face. His hard bicep was her pillow. Embarrassed, she shook her head.

One side of his mouth quirked up. "Come on. Out with it."

"Years."

The silence filling the inches between their faces was deafening.

"Jesus, Laila."

She smiled. "We could be benefriends." Immediately tensing, she prayed for the response she wanted. Putting herself out there wasn't her style, especially when she was unsure if the interest was mutual. She'd felt his desire once, when he'd allowed his mind to wander. It had made him upset. She didn't understand why, yet. "Don't be scared, I won't bite." She snapped her teeth and laughed.

He hooked the nape of her neck and pulled her head closer to his. They were nose to nose. His eyes glittered "You're the one who should be scared, because I do."

He seemed surprised she didn't try to get out of his grip. Her empathic gift flared as he channeled his pent-up sexual desire.

"Trust me, baby, you don't want anything to do with my twisted version of sex."

She wasn't intimidated by his warning. She was intrigued.

He shook his head slightly. "No. No benefriends." Between his grip on her neck, that dark sexy voice, and the fire burning so hot inside him her panties were damp, she'd almost missed his rejection. She waited for more of an explanation, but that was all she got.

He closed his eyes, shutting her out. He was done talking.

She stuck out her bottom lip and poked the hard spot at his sternum. "You're not very nice. In fact, I'm starting to think you're kind of mean."

When he focused on her again, he'd donned a mask of cool indifference. "Baby, I never claimed to be nice."

"Good, because sometimes I don't want nice," she whispered. His clean scent filled her nostrils. His touch nourished her, rebuilt a part that had been broken. The air was charged with her anticipation and his lust. His cock was hard and wedged between them, pressing against her belly.

On impulse, she clutched both sides of his face and kissed him.

Chapter 8

A rough, playful action, the kiss took Rock by surprise, and before he had the chance to react, it was over. She carelessly poked a stick at the beast he'd chained, with no idea what was inside. Even Amber women found his proclivity for extreme sex more kinky than they desired. He relished the challenge presented by this impulsive and unpredictable woman who zigged when he expected her to zag.

The lone fixture burning in the kitchen provided enough shadowy light to see the lovely sight before him. He focused his attention, seeking to read what wasn't said with words. In a flash, he flipped them until Laila was on the couch beneath him.

She gasped. Her cheeks were flushed, and her eyes danced. She was playing with him.

"Yeah, I'm mean." The gravel in his voice was as menacing as he could make it. "And depraved."

Her breaths came faster.

"Demanding."

Her pupils dilated.

"Controlling."

The pulse at the side of her neck quickened underneath his index finger. She hung on every syllable, unblinking.

He leaned in closer. "Domineering."

Her lush lips parted, and displayed the barest peek of her sweet tongue.

"And strict."

Her pupils swallowed up the deep brown of her irises, and her peaked nipples hardened against his chest. He shifted slightly, positioning his lips next to her ear, and whispered, "I'm the kind of man your mama told you to stay away from."

He finished the sentence, and she'd stopped breathing. Their faces were mere inches apart again. "Breathe," he whispered.

Wide-eyed, she inhaled a hearty gulp of air.

Breathing heavily himself, Rock was a hair trigger away from unleashing his lust. "Now, I'm tired. Didn't sleep well last night. Let's go to bed." He sat, bringing her with him.

She squealed.

"To sleep."

She frowned and pouted. He lifted her until they were chest to chest. She wrapped her legs around him, and cupping her cute little bottom, he carried her up the stairs.

He set her on her feet next to the bed and took a knee in front of her. Hooking his fingers at the waistband of her shorts, he slid the material down and lifted each of her feet to free her of the garment. "Lie down." He turned away from her while he folded her shorts and placed them in one of the dresser drawers he'd emptied that afternoon. He removed his T-shirt and jeans, stowed those away as well.

Laila spread out under the top sheet.

He shut off the light and slid in next to her. Covering the ache in the middle of his chest with his palm, he allowed himself to feel more in that moment than he had in a year. His defenses were gone, with this Amber woman, and he was about as wide open to an onslaught of emotions as he'd ever been. He'd always known someday he wouldn't be able to contain them any longer. He'd expected he'd end up murdering someone when they broke free, but this was bearable.

Laila scooted close, burrowing into his side until he turned toward her and completely surrounded her with himself. Her slow, regular breathing followed, and didn't it just figure, he was wide fucking awake.

She'd surprised him today. He didn't surprise easily or often. He prided himself on that. Her courage with Morgan, her reactions to his words—breathtaking.

She needed more than benefriends.

So did he.

The possibility she might be able to give all of herself to him, hand everything over completely and trust, made anticipation thrum through him.

Rock hovered on the threshold of sleep, his thoughts roaming in a lucid dream while his consciousness was completely aware of the woman who slept next to him.

He dozed for a few hours but was fully awake earlier than normal. Above him, high windows displayed the slight fade from black to navy blue in the eastern sky. He'd be generous and call it five thirty in the morning, but just barely.

Laila was beside him, her hair partially covering her face. Her light breaths fanned his chest. Their legs were entwined, his dick hard and demanding attention. Throwing an arm over his eyes, he groaned. He was screwed.

Rock gingerly slid out of bed and padded downstairs. The house hadn't cooled much overnight, and it was going to be another hot one today. Not ideal for Laila's first day of real training, but this would be the first of many hot days of exertion for her. She might as well know what she was getting into.

The lone light burning over the center island in the kitchen beckoned. He sat at one of the high stools and put his earbud in his ear. "Call Dad."

"Two nights in a row?" His father answered the call with a raspy voice. "This new assignment got you in a twist?"

"Hey, Dad."

"Everything okay?"

"Yeah."

"Bullshit, or you wouldn't be calling me in the middle of the fucking night."

Rock chuckled.

"Have you spent time with her yet?"

"Yeah. Her name's Laila Lewis. She grew up Amber."

"Tell me about her."

"She's..." Rock fell silent until he found the right words. "She's intelligent, fun, Amber through and through. She's been soaking up the touch time since she found out I'm from Amber too."

"Pretty?"

"Very."

"Sounds like you like her. You going to take her on in a personal capacity?" Rock could tell his father smiled as he asked the question.

"No."

"Why not?"

Rock's chest clenched and guilt sat heavy in the pit of his stomach.

His father sighed. "You're alive, Rock. You didn't die on that floor. You have to start living again."

"I know. I just feel guilty. Like I'm betraying her by even having this conversation."

"All I'm saying is, it's okay to let go."

"How do I do that?" he asked, louder than he'd intended. He reined in his knee-jerk reaction. "Because I don't know how. Not without making what we had seem less somehow. Less mind-blowing." The sob stuffing his throat made it difficult to speak. "Less gut wrenching. Nothing about what we had was less, Dad."

"I know, son. I loved her, too. But I love you more, and if you have even a slight chance to build something again with someone else, you have to take it. It won't cheapen what you and Emily had. And, Rock, she would have wanted you to be happy."

Silence between them lengthened. Rock tried to lighten the mood. "Well, in any case, it's a good thing I don't have to spend the next couple of months with a troll."

His father laughed. Then, after a few more beats of silence, he continued. "I called Xander. He invited me to dinner tomorrow night. Said he'd invite Journey, too."

"Good. Is he taking good care of her?"

"She's coming out of her shell."

"Give her a hug. Tell her I love her."

"I'll do that. Call me tomorrow, at a decent hour, if that's at all possible."

By then, his father would have the letters he'd left the last time he was at the Resistance drop house. "Will do. Go back to sleep." Rock ended the call and glanced at the clock. Time to get the trainee up. He had a big day planned.

After a half hour of watching Laila drag ass, he sent her across the street to get dressed for their first day of real training. He waited impatiently for her to return, intermittently glancing out the window to see if she was on her way back. When he finally caught sight of Laila crossing the street, she was not the flowing skirt, sandaled, bohemian-looking woman he'd gotten glimpses of before their training started. She was decked out in the standard issue recovery team uniform—black, from the zippered cargo pants and military style boots to the black T-shirt and Kevlar body armor.

He met her at the door and chuckled. "You can ditch the body armor. You won't need it today." He pulled the tabs free and lifted the vest over her head.

"Good. That thing is hot."

He led her to the kitchen, and placed a heaping plate of biscuits and gravy in front of her. "I recommend you eat it all. You're going to need the energy." He packed them a lunch then leaned against the counter, watching her.

She'd put a good dent in the pile then pushed the plate away.

"Ready?"

"I hope so."

During the ride to OZ, she stared out the window. Her silhouette against the morning sun revealed the graceful slope of her neck and the red highlights in her long brown ponytail.

She hadn't smiled once since she'd gotten out of bed that morning. His benefriend rejection might have hurt her feelings. The last thing he wanted to do was add to the strain she was under, but it looked as though he had anyway. He knew what she needed, and would give it to her. But his proclivity for extreme sex and compulsion for the enmeshed relationship he thrived on would only stress her more. By the end of the day, she'd have nothing left, and wouldn't have the energy to worry about anything.

During National Guard shift change, like now, the small Emerald Zone looked like it was under military occupation, with hundreds of guardsmen clogging the roads and walkways. When the guardsmen dispersed, the streets would be empty. There were no pedestrians, like in Sapphire and Amber. The VIPs here drove, or were chauffeured. When they arrived at OZ, he proceeded through the checkpoint gates and parked.

"Why is there's so much security at this compound?" Laila asked.

"There are weapons here. Lots of them." OZ was a huge lot surrounded with chain-link fence topped with razor wire. A handful of one and two-story buildings contained the armory, training and meeting rooms, and the shooting range.

"Oh. Makes sense." They got out, and she glanced at him across the truck bed as he pocketed the keys and motioned in the direction they were headed.

"We're going to the motor pool."

They turned a corner where a row of heavy-duty vehicles were lined up, except for theirs. The armored vehicle they'd be using for the mission was already pulled out of its spot and waiting for them.

"This is our truck." He stopped next to it, helped her into the passenger seat of the armored monster and walked around the front. After climbing into the driver's seat, he leaned toward her, wrapped an arm around her waist and pulled her across the seat so she sat as close to him as possible, her thigh pressing against his.

"What are we doing?" She looked up at him. Still no smile.

"This is your first driving lesson."

"I'm not sure this is a good idea."

"It's a very good idea. I'm going to give you as many skills as I can between now and our go date. If the shit hits the fan, you'll need to know how to drive so you can get yourself back to New Atlanta." He took her chin between his finger and thumb. "Now, don't question your training. I know what you need."

She frowned. "Okay."

They spent an hour sitting thigh to thigh in the hot cab of the armored truck. He taught her all the knobs and buttons, how to adjust her mirrors. Outside, he ran down the vehicle's capabilities as well as simple maintenance like changing a tire and adding radiator fluid. Then he quizzed her until she was easily able to toss the information back at him. He smiled at her self-satisfied expression.

"Okay, good. Now I want you to remove a tire and put it back on."

She stood next to the front passenger side tire, hands on her hips, while he sat on the passenger seat, legs hanging out the open door. She gaped at him, ready to protest, so he leveled a serious stare at her. "I'm waiting."

Several beats passed before she finally rolled her eyes, dropped her hands from her hips and proceeded to crack and remove the lug nuts one by one. It took significant effort on Rock's part not to help her as she wrestled the huge tire from its perch. She lost her grip and tumbled onto her ass then pointed at him and glared. "Don't you dare!"

The effort to keep a straight face was no doubt worth it because she didn't look daggers at him very long. She successfully removed the tire the second time around, brushed dirt off her hands and rear end then looked to him. "I'm going to need some help lifting the tire back on."

"Yes. You are," he said straight-faced, but stayed put.

She raised her eyebrows. "Well? Are you going to help me?"

He shook his head. "If you're changing a tire by yourself, it's a given I'm dead. You need to be able to figure out how to do it yourself."

Her eyes bugged and jaw unhinged. The possibility he could die, leaving her out there to fend for herself, had never occurred to her.

"You also need to learn how to keep that expression in check. You wear all your feelings on your face. Shielding your thoughts and feelings from others is absolutely necessary, if you find yourself in trouble."

"Okay."

Laila looked around the fenced-in lot that held the recovery vehicles and found a cement block and a board behind one of the sheds.

She trudged toward him, dragging the board. Laughter fought to burst from his lips as she blew a stray curl of hair out of her face and glared a hole right through him. He was going to burst a blood vessel with the strain of holding it in.

She set her jaw and got to work, ignoring him. She was feisty and proud. Not the type of woman who'd quit until the job was complete.

By the time she'd maneuvered the tire back on the vehicle, Laila was sweaty and covered with the rust-colored dust that seemed to permeate everything because of the hot, dry summer. She was a sight to see, eyes alight, face red and splotchy. Standing there, with her hands on her hips, she was raging innocence clashing with pure stubbornness. Made him hard all over again.

"Nicely done," he said, jumping down from his seat. He caught her by the wrist, pulled her to him and rewarded her with a smacking kiss on the lips, then set off toward his vehicle.

"What was that for?"

"You did well. You get a kiss." She scrambled to catch up to him. "Let's get some lunch. You're going to need some fuel for this afternoon."

"But—"

"Don't question your training," he said.

Her fists balled at her sides and her lush pink lips pressed tightly against one another.

He slapped her on the ass. "Good girl."

She growled at him and he nearly lost it again. "What are we doing this afternoon?"

"Lunch first. Then, this afternoon and every afternoon until our go date will be spent on self-defense."

"You're going to fight me?"

"No, you're going to learn to defend yourself in all situations. You'll be carrying a side arm and a small knife while we're out of the city. I want you to be passable in the use of both in addition to being able to take a man down with neither."

They sat in the shade of a metal storage shed, eating the sandwiches and fruit he'd packed before they left the house. Sweat-soaked and wilting in the midday heat, Laila looked like she wanted to go home. "Ready to get started?" he asked her.

"Ready is not the word I'd use to describe how I feel right now."

His hard heart melted a little as he pulled her to her feet. Yet, he refused to go easy. He kept her hand in his and walked with her to the path of worn grass running around the perimeter of the compound. Without letting go, he began to jog.

"Ugh. No. Please." She tried to pull her hand out of his.

"I'll let you go if you promise to keep up."

"I don't know if I can."

"You can, and you will." He kept a tight grip on her until she agreed. "It's only a mile today."

"Only? Today? It's eighty-five degrees out here, and I'm exhausted from this morning."

Rock swatted her ass. "Quit complaining."

She put some space between them, but also finished the mile without comment. He loved her stubbornness and strength of character. The challenge teased him.

When they were done, her black T-shirt was gone and the tank top she'd worn underneath was wet and sticking to her back. Her cheeks were beet red, and damp tendrils of hair encircled her face. She was beautiful in misery. Rock experienced a flash of compassion, knowing the brutal pace he'd set. But the training had to progress in order for her to be prepared for the trip.

He brought water to her where she lay flat on her back in the little piece of shade she'd found. "You have fifteen minutes."

"Until what?"

"Until we finish our conditioning."

"What does that mean?"

"Crunches, pushups and squats."

Her eyes snapped open.

He smiled. "The glare again. Cute." He turned and walked toward the main structure, housing the break room. After he'd gotten almost out of earshot, she said something unintelligible. With a wide grin, he entered the building. "Yeah. Feisty and cute."

The fifteen-minute break passed in the blink of an eye, and after giving Laila a new bottle of water, he pulled her up from the ground. She groaned.

"You sore?"

"Dying maybe, maimed perhaps, but sore definitely doesn't cover it."

"The more you move, the better you'll feel." Rock grasped her hand again and slowly led her into the armory and shooting range, where he delivered his first lesson on the assembly, disassembly and safety features of her side arm.

"Can I shoot?" She'd perked up. The hope in her upturned face gnawed at his resolve. He loved that she wasn't afraid. "Please," she whined.

"In a couple of days."

She drooped in disappointment. She was a mess, standing stiffly in her dirty clothes. It was okay, though. Nothing wrong with a little pain and emotion to remind a person they were alive.

Today, he'd lived.
So had she.

Chapter 9

Laila was nearly asleep by the time Rock pulled into his driveway. He walked around the front of the truck, opened the passenger door, and caught her before she tumbled out. He offered his hand.

"Ahh! Stop!" she cried, squeezing his hand hard. "My muscles have stiffened up." She gingerly slid the rest of the way out of the truck, until her feet found the pavement. "Holy shit, you've broken me." She stood there hunchbacked and grasping his hand so hard she felt his knuckles roll against each other. "I can't move."

"Okay, up you go." Rock hauled her into his arms, wrapping her legs around his waist and supporting her rear with his hands, just as he'd done the night before.

Laila experienced a twinge of pain at the mere thought of clinging to him, so she tucked her arms between them and snuggled into his chest instead.

He carried her upstairs, as if she weighed nothing. In the bathroom, he sat her on the edge of the tub. She just sat there, not wanting to make the motions required to take off her clothes. Her limbs were heavy and about as useful as boulders.

Rock turned on the faucet and adjusted the knobs. His T-shirt pulled tight across his magnificent back and his sculpted ass looked delicious in the black mission pants he wore. She smiled for the first time that day. Rock's rejection to her offer of sex the night before had maimed her dignity. For the most part, he'd followed her lead, staying businesslike during training, but when he turned to her, he'd changed, too. Pure sex rolled off him, kicking up her heart rate.

He pulled her up, and stepping back, he assessed her. His blazing eyes moved slowly, from her head to toes while she stood there, hobbled. She was depleted, had absolutely nothing left, and wondered if she looked the way she felt.

With an apologetic look in his eyes, he tenderly helped her sit back down. She slumped, resting her forearms on her knees. "Poor baby," he whispered as he knelt in front of her.

"Please don't make fun of me."

He gently pulled off one of her boots and then the other. "I'm not. Promise." He peeled a sock off and massaged her foot with strong, probing fingers.

"Oh, that feels good." He took his time, kneading with both hands, digging into her arches.

"You knew you were going on this mission. Why didn't you train ahead of time?" Rock's voice was soft, his tone concerned, with no reproach.

"I did. I trained my mind. I learned, planned, and then contingency planned how to get these pieces back in one piece." She groaned again as he let go of one foot and started on the other. "I shouldn't need to train my body too. Protecting me is your job."

He chuckled softly. "Still cute."

She ground her molars together, barely able to contain her ire. She wanted to bite his head off, tell him to go fuck himself, something.

"Up," he ordered with a nudge to her arms. She ignored his direction until he met her gaze and raised an eyebrow.

She lifted her arms slowly.

He peeled her top off and tossed it on the floor. "Up." He nudged her rear end and she stood. He unbuttoned and unzipped her pants, hooked his thumbs at the waistbands of her pants and panties and slid them down until they landed on the floor. A moment later, her bra was unhooked, and sliding off her shoulders to the ground.

He took her hand and helped her into the tub of tepid water. She sat awkwardly, sloshing the water around as her rear landed clumsily on the smooth porcelain of the tub.

Rock grabbed the hand-held showerhead and pressed the button, diverting the spill of water filling the tub to the hand sprayer. "Learning to defend yourself is a huge part of your training," he said softly. "You need to be able to fend for yourself if the worst case scenario happens." He soaked her hair and upper body before returning the water flow back to the faucet.

"What exactly is the worst case scenario?"

"I'm not there to protect you, and Garret and Sydney are trying to kill you." He lifted from his knees and leaned over to grab the bottle of shampoo before sitting on the edge of the tub. He unscrewed the cap and held the bottle under her nose. "Smell."

Sylvia Ryan

It smelled like him. She opened her eyes, smiling.

He sniffed the bottle before he poured some in his hand. "Look up at the ceiling. I'll wash your hair."

For a split second, she was going to tell him she could do it herself, but she thought better of it. He treated her like a queen, literally, and she wouldn't turn away a second of this china doll treatment. Head tilted up and eyes closed, she savored his strong fingers scrubbing her scalp. A mass of bubbles slid down her back as he washed different areas, working down toward the ends of her hair. When he grabbed the hand sprayer to rinse, the absence of his touch made her greedy for more.

He took care not to get any shampoo into her eyes. He was so good, she was sure he'd done this many times before. "Did you do this for the girl assigned to you, your roommate in Amber?"

His eyes softened. "Yes."

"What was her name?"

"Journey."

"Do you miss her?"

He didn't answer right away, and avoided her gaze. She lifted a hand and touched his cheek. His sorrow was palpable even without opening herself up to his feelings.

"Did you love her?"

He nodded. "Still do."

A tinge of jealousy toward Journey darkened Laila's mood while Rock coated her hair with conditioner. She didn't particularly like the fact this man, who so carefully took care of her, had done this with someone else. Not just someone else, but someone else he still loved.

"You shouldn't be giving me a bath if you're in love with another woman." She plucked the soap and washrag out of his hand. "I can finish myself."

He rumbled the deepest laugh she'd ever heard. Then, he leaned in close. "You've got a little brat in you." His deep brown eyes twinkled.

His amusement exasperated her.

He sobered. "Do you want me to stop?"

She looked down at her hands, hating herself for the truth. "No," she whispered.

"I didn't think so." He took back the soap and washrag and coated every part of her above the waterline with bubbles. The gentle cleansing stimulated every sense. The slow glide of the washcloth, the slight breeze of his exhalations floating across her damp skin. The smell of the soap and warmth of the water. She was enthralled by the reverent attention she received from this man.

"Stand up." He gripped her hand to assist her.

When she faced him, he examined every subtlety of her form. From his seat on the edge of the tub, he rubbed the washrag slowly over the curve of her hips and then between her legs, making sure to get between her lower lips. He stroked once, twice over her clit.

She held her breath. Their gazes met. His glittered with desire, but he moved the washrag along, coating her legs.

He nodded at her. "Sit." The word was raspy. He cleared his throat and said the word again as Laila stiffly submerged herself at a snail's pace, disappointed the erotic wash was over.

He grabbed the sprayer again, and she closed her eyes, lifting her chin as he rinsed the conditioner out of her hair.

Taking a deep breath, she opened herself up and searched his energy. He radiated calmness and gentleness. It soothed her.

She'd made a point not to open herself to him for the entire day, as was her habit. She found out at an early age if she let everybody's energy affect her, by the end of the day she'd be a wreck. Plus, she'd been irritated with him most of the afternoon and didn't particularly care how he was feeling at the time. Her mood was beginning to return to normal now that the warm water eased her muscles. She lay back, happy and relaxed while he lifted each foot out of the water and fingered between her toes and along the soles, with the slick coat of bubbles easing the way.

Rock submerged the sprayer head under the water and nudged her legs apart with it. She jack-knifed up and met his gaze.

"You need to get off." His tone was matter of fact. "Lean back."

"No. Stop it."

He did, immediately replacing the sprayer in its base by the faucet. Then, he crossed his arms and turned a stern expression to her. "We can do this one of two ways. You can either be totally honest and open with me, as I will be with you. Or you can pretend I don't know exactly what you need."

They stared each other down.

"Do it," he whispered.

With an aggravated sigh, she lay back against the tub, and he nudged her thighs apart.

"Aggressive much?" She breathed.

"You have no idea," he said straight-faced as he grabbed the sprayer again.

Laila closed her eyes, settled in, waiting for the jet of water to stimulate her.

"Open your eyes. Keep them open."

"Why?"

"Don't question your training."

"This is not training."

He straightened, turned off the water and stood. "Baby, everything's training. Now stand up."

For a few moments, she sat gaping at him, working hard to figure out what the fuck was going on with this man. She was pissed off all over again. He'd rejected her benefriends suggestion, worked her hard with no sympathy or compassion for her depleted body, told her he loved someone else, and now this? She didn't think so. She eyed him as he held a towel open for her to walk into, wanting to tell him off, but she wimped out. Plus, he'd think her a raging bitch with wild mood swings if they ended yet another night with her over-the-top emotions. Instead, she stood.

He wrapped the fluffy towel around her, his big tattooed arms lingering and lifting her out of the tub. He set her feet on the soft cotton bath mat. Rubbing briskly, he dried her hair and then took a thorough route, drying her from head to toe. Rock unceremoniously shoved her head through the hole of a T-shirt and motioned for her to put her arms through. After she'd followed his direction, he clasped her hand and led her to the bedroom. "Sit." He put a hand on her shoulder and pushed her into a sitting position on the edge of the bed then walked away.

She was a second away from lying back and losing consciousness between the luxurious white covers when he returned with a wide-toothed comb in his hand. "If you lie down, you won't be able to get back up again, and you need to eat."

He'd read her thoughts exactly. Unsettled, she swiveled her head to look over her shoulder as he sat at her side and hitched a leg up on the mattress behind her.

"It wasn't that hard. I've told you already you wear your thoughts and emotions like a headline running across your forehead. Keep working on it."

Raking his fingers through the wavy strands, he got out the large tangles, and then combed it out.

She reveled in the feeling of his hands sliding over her long, damp hair.

The back of his hand grazed her neck. The pad of his finger brushed across the shell of her ear. The incidental touches were intimate and made her acutely aware they were sitting on the bed together. What would it feel like to have a man like him want her? He was the embodiment of authority, power and sex all wrapped up into an impossible-to-resist package. Her insides fluttered just considering the possibilities, because when he made love to a woman, she was sure it was as thoroughly as he did everything else.

He finished combing and squeezed the ends of her hair with a towel to absorb the excess water, showing her he'd definitely done this before, too. A fact that added to the torment of her day.

Apparently finished with his task, Rock walked the towel and comb back into the bathroom. On his return, he took her hand, pulled her up from the edge of the bed, and led her down the flight of stairs to the first floor.

"What about you? Don't you want to take a shower?"

His soft eyes smiled at her. "Don't worry about me."

In the kitchen, he sat her on the stool she'd found him in that first night. He opened up the refrigerator. "Spaghetti and salad okay?"

"Yes. Maybe more salad than spaghetti?"

"No. You need protein and carbs, too."

"Why ask me, when you've made up your mind already?"

His head swiveled in her direction. "I'm being polite."

She got lost in her thoughts as she absently watched him prepare the meal, trying to figure out the man. He was intimidating and scary to the rest of the world, yet so tender with her. She considered that he had multiple personalities, but knew that wasn't it. He let her see the real him, not some made-up, public version of himself.

She was content. It was an uncommon feeling. Was this what she'd missed by never being placed in Circle City? This utter devotion and complete sense of safety? Despite the torture he'd put her through that day, the understanding that this was what she'd missed out on by earning a Sapphire designation left her with doubts, on the brink of regret.

Rock turned the burner on under a large pot of water and pivoted. He glanced at her and stopped in his tracks.

Again, she hadn't concealed the emotional expression on her face, and he'd caught it. With just a split second glance, he'd seen it all. And if she'd doubted that fact, his next words confirmed she'd been right.

"What's happening?" That was all he said. He didn't need to elaborate. She knew what he was referring to.

"Rock, I'm sorry I'm so grouchy," she rasped. "It was kind of you to take such care with me. Thank you." He smiled. God, he was beautiful when he smiled at her. Just a heartbeat's worth was all he gave her before he went back to cooking dinner.

Maybe he was an empath too. "How did you know something was happening, you know, just now…with me."

"I've been training myself to read you since the first time we met."

"Read me?"

"Yeah. You know, body language, expression. It's part of my training for this mission. We'll get into the details later. Right now, dinner is served." He held a plate under his nose, and inhaled. Then, he held it under hers so she could do the same.

"Why do you smell everything?"

He set the plate in front of her. "Why not?"

They sat side-by-side, eating the large portions of food. The man could cook, and Laila couldn't keep herself from groaning with pleasure while she ate.

By the time she finished the last bite, she was having trouble keeping her eyes open. It was early. The sun was just beginning its descent toward the horizon. "What time is it?"

"Eight twenty and your bedtime."

Even though she wanted to tell him she could determine her own bedtime, she wasn't going to argue because bed was the only place she wanted to be. Laila slipped off her stool, groaned at her yelping muscles, and took her plate to the sink.

"Don't worry about it. I'll take care of the kitchen later," he said from directly behind her. He took her hand and led her slowly up the stairs. With the bed spread out before her, she sluggishly crawled in.

Rock pulled the lightweight cover over her and kissed her on the forehead.

Sleep came fast and hard.

Chapter 10

While Laila slept, Rock sat on the back steps of his home. The sound of crickets filled the humid air. The nearly full moon lit up the night sky. He scanned the shadows of the tall pines in his back yard, while his mind wandered to places it hadn't gone in a long time. So long, it shook him up.

Not once in the last year had he even looked twice at a woman. He had shut that part of himself down. He thought he was done having that vulnerability and would never again give the Gov the power to completely annihilate him by hurting the woman he loved.

Today, that mindset had fallen by the wayside. He couldn't deny the connection between them, the strong physical pull. They had chemistry. Rock had regained some part of himself that had been lost, but with that, he'd opened the floodgates retaining his emotions. He had allowed himself to feel, and discovered he wasn't as angry or hurt as had been the status quo for almost a year.

His guilt over his sexual thoughts about Laila was front and center now. His body didn't give a shit about any vows he'd made. It reacted to Laila on a molecular level. His heartbeat raced, and lust ran thick in his blood whenever she was near. He'd suffered from yo-yo dick all day. It was maddening…and normal, for him, at least until he'd been made Emerald.

From the age of fifteen, until the night he'd lost everything, he'd gotten laid at least a few times a week. Since he'd been in Emerald, he just hadn't had the urge. He'd even had moments when he thanked God he didn't, because if his dick had been raging during the past year, he would have suffered. There was no fucking way he could have been with anyone else. It would have ripped him apart. A year without touch had made him hard and cold and helped him live through everything that had been thrown at him. He'd been a bomb ready to explode with a desperate, devastating fury for what the Gov had forced his life to become.

He didn't need to live like that anymore. Laila was there, upstairs, right now, in his bed. She wasn't a trick or a trap, just a beautiful woman. She touched him, literally. Inconsequential brushes, hugs, a hand on his shoulder for support. It reminded him that he existed, that he had feelings and needs.

Yes, today he'd definitely regained some part of himself that had been missing.

In the last few days, Laila had gone from barely registering on his radar to being the only thing on it. Today, he'd spent hours watching the tilt of her head, the slope of her neck, the drop of a lilting curl tickling her cheek, and the focus of her big brown eyes as she set her sights on the almost impossible tasks he'd assigned her.

He felt good in her presence. He shook his head, amazed. He actually felt good. Her free spirit sparked optimism in him. An optimism that had him thinking it was possible to love again.

Maybe love was already starting to take root in his soul.

The relationship he and Emily had was more than intimate. The years of her giving herself to him in every way, of experiencing everything together, of being so close communication didn't need to involve words had forged something incredible. They were two halves of a whole, enmeshed psychologically, mentally and the line differentiating between them blurred. Emily had delighted in the experiences of life along with him, up to the jagged edge of acceptability and beyond. It was fucking amazing—and scary—for her. He knew from their conversations and the split second glimpses of emotion that crossed her expression from time to time. He knew because she wouldn't agree to marry him. It was the only part she ever held back, never giving him that one last piece of herself.

Could Laila give him what he required? Just thinking about his growing need and the excitement he experienced when she was near reignited something inside. His drive to form an intimate relationship with her was overpowering.

She had a mind of her own, and he loved that she was smart and strong willed. She was definitely not the shrinking violet type, like Journey had been. No, Laila was more like his wild child, Emily. And, like Emily, training her would be a challenge, but the result would be a satisfying accomplishment earned through respect, trust and consistency.

Sitting there in the twilight in his back yard, Rock understood he couldn't be what he needed to be with Laila while he still maintained a death grip on his grief.

His dad was right. It was time to move on.

A lump the size of a fist blocked his throat, and his eyes filled with tears. He looked up at the sky and hoped if there was any part of Emily that remained, she'd hear him now.

"Em." He wrapped a hand around the nape of his neck and squeezed the rigid muscles there. His throat constricted and his soul screamed as he closed his eyes and imagined Emily's cheek flush against his, felt her curls sift through his fingers. His heart broke.

"I'm weak and lonely without you. I don't think I can stop myself." Silent tears rolled down his cheeks.

He hung his head. "I'm sorry, Em. So sorry."

Rock sat for hours in the sultry night air while he built up the courage to let go of grief-filled promises to his dead love.

He let go of sleeping on the couch to avoid the emptiness of his bed.

He let go of the daily little punishments he gave himself because he'd failed to protect her.

He sat there until his guilt and grief were exhausted. Maybe, just maybe, he could wake the next morning and begin in earnest, taming this new woman assigned to him. He'd mourned the wife and the life he'd never had. Now it was time to take the path that lay before him.

He walked up the stairs to their room and slid into bed. Sighing, he wrapped himself around her. She was like a little peanut, cradled within his frame. Feeling at peace, he slid into sleep.

* * * *

It seemed only minutes later when an anguished groan woke him.

Laila's eyes were open, but she looked stricken.

"What's wrong, peanut?"

A tear slid from the corner of her eye and soaked into her pillow.

His grogginess fled and he sat quickly. "What?"

"I can't move. Everything hurts."

He let go of the breath he'd been holding and smiled down at her. "You'll feel better once you start moving around."

"Did you not hear me?" she snapped. "I can't move."

He left her lying there. Sometimes the most difficult part of training was turning away when all he wanted to do was hold her in his arms. He stopped at his medicine cabinet to get the bottle of Peppermint oil, which would loosen her up and give them a good start to their training today. "Come on, let me help you sit up and take the T-shirt off."

Her gaze fell on the tiny bottle in his hand. Instead of following directions, she asked, "What's that?"

"It's peppermint oil. I was going to give you a rub down to loosen your muscles and then help with some stretches. But, since you chose to ask me a question instead of following directions, you lost the privilege. Lesson one, follow directions without hesitation or question."

He set the oil on the stand next to the bed then glanced at the clock. "You've got fifteen minutes to get downstairs for breakfast." He forced himself to walk out and to the kitchen. God, he hated this part, acting as if he didn't care. But he'd been lenient with Emily, many times unable to discipline her properly when she defiantly did whatever she wanted, disregarding their understanding. It had gotten her killed.

Rock felt lighter today, almost hopeful, as he cooked breakfast. The eggs and potatoes were near crispy, and Laila still hadn't come down. He packed peanut butter sandwiches for their lunches, and was deliberating his next move when she hobbled through the great room and into the kitchen. Still wearing the T-shirt she'd worn to bed, she sat stiffly at the island.

He wondered what she'd been doing up there for the last half hour until he smelled the peppermint.

"I don't understand why we need to go through all this," she grumbled. "I mean, when are we going to have to jog or fight? The chances I'm ever going to need these skills are so slim, it's not worth the pain."

"You think? The Gov has been exiling about a hundred criminals a year to the Onyx Zone. Multiply that by twenty-five years, then add the offspring from the exiled people and you have at least three thousand people living within a fifty-mile radius of New Atlanta. Three thousand people who would do anything to take what we've collected out there. Besides, it doesn't matter how miniscule the possibility. You train because the possibility exists. I don't feel like dying on this mission, and you have to realize that not only am I covering your back, you may have to cover mine. So, I'm going to teach you every skill I can, and you're going to take the training seriously and try your best."

By the time he finished his breakfast, Laila had slowed to picking sporadically at egg remnants.

"Done?"

She nodded.

He collected the dirty dishes and pulled her off the stool.

She groaned.

He hunched down in her line of vision. "Go home. Get dressed."

She stood in an unnatural way, her head tilted slightly to one side, her shoulders bunched. He caressed her cheek. "It will be better soon.

Promise." He swatted her rump. "Now go on. You've got ten minutes," he called before she closed the door. No slam this time. He smiled.

He stowed the dishes in the dishwasher and straightened up. She returned with time to spare, walking as if her body was loosening up. He greeted her with a smile. "Looking better already." He placed a kiss on her temple, led her out to his truck and drove them to OZ.

They started their morning routine with a driving lesson, and he tested her on the gas to additive ratio. He wouldn't let her turn over the engine, but she didn't say shit about it. He mentally celebrated the small victory.

He opened the door to the armored truck and grabbed her around the waist, pulling her out. He held her close so she slithered down his body. Her lush lips parted, and their quick breaths intermingled. Time stood still as her slow slide continued until her feet hit the ground. He let go, and she stumbled. He snatched her up quickly and helped get her feet underneath her again. "You okay?"

"Uhh." The utterance quavered. "I'm good."

He heaved himself up and sat at the opened door with his legs angled out. "Go on and change the tire."

She gaped. "You're insane if you think I'm doing that again." She crossed her arms and kicked out a hip, openly belligerent and waiting for a fight.

"What's lesson one?"

She sawed her molars together before she answered. "Follow directions."

He raised his eyebrows, waiting for the rest.

"Without hesitation or questions."

The staring contest between them lasted about fifteen seconds before she gave in and started cracking the nuts on the tire. She finished the task in half the time it had taken the day before.

"Nice job," he said, kissing her temple again.

He pulled his T-shirt off. Her gaze affixed to his chest, to his nipple piercings. She seemed fascinated by them. "Let's run before lunch today." Before she had the opportunity to display her displeasure, he grasped her hand and started a slow pace, dragging her with him until she gave in and jogged.

He kept a close eye on her. She was overheated and panting. He would have to keep the distance at a mile again tomorrow. Afterward, they sat in the shade and ate lunch in silence. Rock made sure she rehydrated, and allowed her extra time to recover. Then, they retrieved their side-arms from the armory and returned to the shade to review its care and use.

"When are you going to let me shoot?"

"You think I'm giving you a loaded gun when you're this irritated with me? Sorry baby, don't have a death wish. There's plenty of time for that later," he said evenly.

She opened her mouth as if to speak, but snapped it shut instead.

He smiled at her. "Good girl."

"What?"

"I said, 'good girl.'"

"Why?"

"Because you didn't complain when I could see you wanted to."

"A lot of good it does me."

"Exactly."

Toward the end of the day, they made their way into the gymnasium area of the main building. Laila eyed the enormous navy blue mat with the big circle in the middle as Rock took his place inside it. She followed until they stood face to face.

"We're going to train in hand to hand every day."

Her mouth fell open. "I can't fight you. You're twice my size."

"You can. And you will. Today, I'm going to teach you the basics of—" He tapped his temple. "Up here. You're so small, you have to fight smart. Gouge the eyes, knee the groin, kick the knee, hard and preferably in the opposite direction of how the knee bends normally." He put his finger up and made sure he had her attention. "If you choose groin, be careful. Men can be hyper aware of their need to protect their balls."

She laughed, and he stopped to take it in then forced his expression to match the seriousness of the lesson. "If it comes to this, you'll be fighting for your life, and I absolutely guarantee you can win a fight against any man if you fight smart and dirty. If feasible, catch the person off guard by taking the first strike. Put as much force behind it as you can. No sympathy. Got it?"

She nodded.

"If you get a good one in, run. The only time you stay after the first shot is if you don't think you'll be able to get to safety before your opponent gets to his feet and catches you. If a big man tackles you from behind while you're running away, you're done for. Got it?"

She nodded, looking worried.

"Come at me."

With a running start, she attempted to knock him to the floor. He swiped her aside like she was a gnat.

"Get up. If this were a real situation, you'd be dead. You have to get away from the opponent's immediate reach if you go down. Either get right back up, or roll away."

Eyes narrowed at him, she took her place in the circle again. She attempted the same maneuver, and so did he. Rock looked down at her splayed body and realized he couldn't follow his own advice. He had too much sympathy to toss her around the mat anymore.

She groaned as she got slowly to her feet.

"That's all of this for today. I want you to think about your approach. Figure out a better way."

"Fifty kicks to the heavy bag." He pointed to where it hung in a corner of the gym. "And then we'll call it a day."

Like the day before, by the time they arrived home, Laila's muscles had stiffened. She whimpered as she gingerly slid out of the vehicle.

He advanced on her fast, scooped her up and slung her over his shoulder.

She cried out. "You're not helping."

"I know, peanut. I can hear your muscles yelping from here." He laughed and carried her up the stairs that way, finally putting her down on the edge of the tub. He pulled off her shoes and socks while the bath filled with lukewarm water.

She seemed distracted, staring at the filling tub. Maybe thinking of the events from the day before? Had she learned her lesson, or would she be stubborn and denied an orgasm tonight as well?

He assessed every part of her as he removed each piece of clothing. Her breaths were quick and short, and her nipples were puckered and hard. That, along with her weary compliance, made him sure he would see her come today.

As soon as his brain wrapped around that delicious piece of information, his cock filled. Ignoring it, he grabbed the shampoo, flipped the cap, and held it to her nose to smell before he washed her hair.

When he was done, he made her stand. He stood this time as well, starting their washing ritual at her shoulders and smoothing the sweet smelling foam all over her. She lolled her head back, with closed eyes, as she gave herself over to him. She widened her stance so he could pass the washrag between her legs, not knowing his touch without the barrier of the washrag would have to be earned. They weren't there yet.

She groaned as he lathered away from her pretty little cunt and down the fronts of her thighs, moving slowly and building her anticipation.

Finally, he made her sit while he diverted water to the hand sprayer and rinsed the conditioner out of her hair. This time, when he submerged the sprayer in the water, her legs fell open to him, and she moaned at the first sensations of the jets hitting her pussy. Her head fell back, and he studied the curve of her clavicle, her bared neck, and the dark rose hue of her parted lips. For more than a minute, he sat on the edge of the tub, admiring her pleasure soaked face and listening to her express appreciation at the sensation he provided. She was breathtaking, a priceless snapshot etched in his memory for a lifetime. Unfortunately, he had to teach lesson two.

"Peanut."

She opened her eyes but her gaze remained up at the ceiling. "Hmm?"

"Look at me."

She grunted her objection then lifted her head to meet his gaze.

"Don't make a sound." He put his finger to his lips. "Complete silence." He repeated the hand motion.

She nodded and laid her head back again.

Less than a minute later, her body was rigid, coiled and ready to explode. Her thigh muscles quivered, and she gripped the lip of the tub. She cried out as an orgasm rolled violently through her. He immediately removed the jet of water from her spasming core.

Her eyelids flew open. "Ahhh!" she screamed.

He turned off the water and set the sprayer in its cradle. "Follow directions tomorrow and maybe you'll get to finish that orgasm. Maybe even have two." He winked at her, then motioned. "Up."

She sat in the tub, eyes glazed, truly stunned. Then, her brows furrowed and those glazed eyes narrowed. "More training?" she ground out between her teeth.

He leaned, hovering over her until their lips were merely an inch apart. "Everything's training, baby." He gave her a quick peck on the lips.

She stared at him. "This training makes you happy."

He didn't answer, just smiled.

Chapter 11

The end of Rock's first week of tutelage was only an hour away. Laila wanted to jump for joy and scream at the top of her lungs in celebration. She was being overdramatic. It hadn't been all bad. She'd earned luscious peppermint oil massages the last three mornings in a row. She got to start the truck and actually drive it, though it was only a few feet. And as an added treat the morning before, Rock hadn't made her change the tire anymore. On top of all that, she ran the mile without wanting to pass out afterward.

Now, she was going to take Rock down inside the big white circle on the mat. She'd been wholly unsuccessful all week, trying different approaches. But she quickly found that the opportunity to knock that arrogant wall of muscle on his ass, and success in doing so, were two entirely different things.

She'd paid close attention to the moves and tried hard to get them right during drills. She'd tried her hardest to take him down, and he just stood there, brushing her aside, relaxed.

It ticked her off. He didn't even try to appear as if he had to defend himself. Her blood boiled with every failed attempt. She was going to kick his ass.

After a shrieking run and an unceremonious counter move that left her ass planted on the mat, she was livid. He waved her to come again as she picked herself off the floor, challenging her to take her best shot, groin or knee. She accepted the challenge…over and over again, but none of the kicks landed at their intended destination.

After falling face down and breathing in a whiff of men's locker room for what had to be the fiftieth time, she picked herself off the floor.

He waved at her to come again with that smug look on his face.

She was going to scratch his eyes out. Then, in a second of brilliant clarity, everything clicked into place. She lunged at him the way she had dozens of times before, and as he leaned over to swipe her leg away with his forearm, she raked his face with her nails.

It hadn't been a good hit because he'd adjusted his defense at the last minute to protect himself, but one nail hit its mark, scoring the front of his cheek.

When she picked herself off the floor and turned to meet his gaze, he smiled at her, the raised, red line on his face moving with the motion.

"Good girl. Remember, you have to fight smart. You'll be able to tell from your opponent's stance what he's expecting from you. Then, you'll give him something else in the spot that's left exposed."

He waved her to come at him again and took his stance. She examined his positioning and changed her strategy accordingly. As she attacked, he read her move and blocked it, knocking the air out of her lungs as she landed hard on her belly. She stayed down this time.

"I hate you." She flattened her hands on the mat and pushed herself to standing.

"That's okay. I'm not concerned about winning a popularity contest."

They sparred more and she took at least five more trips to the mat.

After Rock called it a day, he picked up his water bottle, took a long swig then offered it to her. "You did well today," he said as she drank big gulps.

"Thank you."

The drive home was silent. It usually was. They needed time to mentally transfer from their formal training interactions to home. Even while it appeared no one was looking, they maintained a professional relationship when they were in OZ. During the eight hours they spent there every day, Rock acted as if there was no relationship, connection or affection. He insisted it be that way. Said it was safer. The ride home allowed her to rid herself of the restrictions and slip into her old self—her true self.

Rock opened the front door and stepped aside so she could enter first. He followed her upstairs then guided her to the edge of the tub.

Instead of filling the tub, he turned the water on in the separate shower.

When he returned to her, he peeled her clothes off the way he did every day, and kneaded her aching muscles while using one word commands to move her to suit his needs.

He gave her the signal for quiet and then a new signal, touching the spots directly under his eyes with his index and middle finger. "Keep your eyes right here," he said quietly and did the motion again.

She smiled, remembering the last two days of him getting her off while she remained totally silent. She'd gotten good at it and was sure she could remain soundless, even in the most difficult circumstances. She should have known that, just as she became comfortable with the skill, he'd change up the game.

She focused on his gorgeous face, his bottomless brown eyes, his lush lips. Looking at him was easy. Locking gazes with the soul she found behind those all-seeing eyes got easier and easier by the day.

She wanted to die when she realized he was stripping himself. All week, he'd showered alone after they'd eaten dinner together. She hated it. The fifteen minutes he was gone seemed like the longest minutes of the day. She wanted to return the favor and slide her hands across his wet skin, lathering him, taking care of him as he did her.

Picturing the glimpses she'd gotten of his body, Laila nearly giggled out loud. Glimpses, ha! More like brief, intense bouts of gawking. She actually looked forward to the torturous running he forced her to do, simply because he took his shirt off. The tattoos were badass despite the fact she still hadn't had the opportunity to read them because he never stood still long enough. And the nipple rings, she loved looking at the nipple rings. Every day, once her gaze landed on them, she found it hard to drag it away. Looking at his form was like looking at art.

He was her incentive.

Today she'd gotten an eyeful of the area between his belly button and the waistband of his pants. The skin was tight over defined muscle that came to a luscious vee somewhere underneath the damn clothes he insisted on wearing all the time. The man was ripped. The thought of being able to finally see everything made her stomach dance.

Now he wanted her to not look at it. Yeah, right.

He cleared his throat, capturing her attention, and raised an eyebrow.

When she complied with his wishes, she got an added bonus, his emotion. Pleasure washed over her as his peace and happiness surged. She guessed it had been a long time since he'd experienced those emotions, and she wanted to be the person to give them to him.

With a hand on each of her biceps, he walked her backward into the shower stall. She kept her eyes focused and locked with his as he washed her. The experience was terribly intimate, as if he saw her soul.

When she was clean, he began washing himself.

"Can I do you?" She felt his satisfaction at her question.

"No. Stay with me." He gave her the eye contact signal again.

She about died when his hands lowered out of her peripheral vision. He was hard. She knew it without having to look directly at it. She just knew.

She realized he had not moved on. His eyes were locked with hers, and he was stroking himself.

"Oh God," she whispered. Suddenly, she could barely catch her breath.

"Stay with me, peanut," he repeated. His words were deep, guttural. "You can do this."

The entire situation sent her reeling. She wanted to beg him for just a glimpse and she was sure he read it in her face.

The seconds were interminable. All she could do was think about what she didn't have, what she couldn't do. She was frustrated, provoked, and every cell in her body wanted to defy his command.

"Relax your muscles."

She consciously made her muscles grow limp.

"Breathe," he whispered.

She did so, slowly.

In.

Out.

In.

She followed his direction until it wasn't just their gazes that were connected. *They* were connected. It was as if she'd fallen into his eyes and landed in his soul. Nothing else existed. She opened herself fully to his feelings. Warmth and affection, happiness, love—they were all there. They overwhelmed her.

Moved her.

Aroused her.

Never had she wanted to freeze a moment and live there forever, until then. This feeling of being plugged into him filled her up, made her whole. It was bliss.

She experienced his release through their connection. His feelings rushed at her, only arousing her more.

She heard herself gasp and saw the change in his gaze. The moment was broken, but it was an experience she wanted more of. It filled up all the empty Swiss cheese holes formed by the loneliness she'd experienced in the last five years. Alleviated the anger left by prejudice. Eased the regret.

The experience was intense and profound. The rest of their shower was a blur. And when it was over, the disconnect between them weighed down her mood. She was quiet, pensive for the rest of the evening. What amazed her most was that he let her be that way, as if he knew she needed it. Maybe because he needed it, too.

At bedtime, they lay holding hands, their heads on the bed where their feet should be, taking in the moon and the vast landscape of stars through the high windows that met the vaulted ceiling.

Laila snuggled close, putting her head on his chest. His chest hair tickled her cheek and the tip of her nose caressed his sternum as he swept his fingers through her hair, letting it fall to her back when he got to the ends.

She peered up at him. His eyes were closed. He was content tonight, almost light. She felt the same. Playfully, she opened and closed her eyes in rapid succession, fluttering her eyelashes against his pectoral, trying to tickle him. He chuckled.

She did it again.

"Laila." This time, there was a clear warning in his tone. He pulled her in tight so her eyelashes smooshed against his chest.

"What's the matter? Afraid if you have fun I won't think you're Superman?"

"I'm fun," he muttered.

She giggled.

Rock loosened his bear hug and tilted his head to meet her gaze. "What?"

"Rock Rodgers. Sorta sounds like the name of a super hero."

He flashed a wry expression. "Okay, Laila Lewis."

"What?"

"You don't see the similarity between Laila Lewis and Lois Lane?"

"Who's Lois Lane?"

"She's—"

Laila flashed her brightest smile at him. "I'm teasing you, Superman."

While they snuggled in silence, Rock resumed his caresses through her hair, starting at her scalp. The tips of his fingers touched the back of her head and neck, and ticklish sensations zinged down her spine.

It was fun, teasing him. She wondered how far she could go before he cracked.

Laila adjusted her position, peeked her tongue through her lips and licked a damp trail on his neck.

"Would you quit? You're making me crazy," he rumbled.

"Sorry," The whispered sentiment was disingenuous, and still she moved her hands daringly over his skin.

"Laila."

She looked up at his face, trying to make a connection and gauge his mood. He showed her nothing, but she felt his arousal mingling with hers.

She ran the pad of her index finger over the ultra-fine hairs that were like peach-fuzz on the outer shell of his ear.

He hissed in a breath.

She suppressed a giggle then scooted up his body a little. His face was expressionless. But he wasn't fooling her. He was hard, and just to make her point, she leaned into him, pressing his cock into the softness of her belly.

"Laila."

"Okay, okay. I'm going to sleep now." She could barely say the words with a straight face as she slithered over him in order to lay her head on her pillow. She flashed her most evil smile as her body rubbed suggestively against him.

"That's it." He swatted her ass, his big hand connecting with the bare skin below the hem of her panties. Then, quite quickly, he wrapped his arms around her, pinning her arms at her sides. In a quick roll and turn, he was spooned behind her. "Go to sleep."

She wiggled her ass against his groin. "Why not?"

"You haven't earned it."

She wiggled again and the play atmosphere between them shifted.

He moved fast, rolled her onto her belly, going with her, until his weight pressed her into the mattress. His hard-on was wedged obscenely between them, and his lips landed next to her ear.

"Listen up, sugar. You're trying to open a can of worms that's been closed for a long time. Let me be clear. I'll watch your pretty little ass. And, I'll like doin' it. And yes, I'm an Amber and I'll never turn you away when you need to be held or taken care of, and I'll keep you safe from everyone.

"But, peanut, have you stopped to ask yourself who's going to keep you safe from me?"

A shiver ran down her spine as wisps of air from his words hit the back of her neck.

"I am not a gentle lover. I'm rough and demanding with my women. It's not for everyone. You need to think long and hard on that. I need both of us to be doubly sure we want to go down this road because once we've started the journey, turning back is not an option."

He tucked her tightly into him. "Now, go to sleep."

She had a hard time trying to ignore the raging hard-on pressed against her rear. This ban on fucking was pissing her off. She didn't understand.

"Is this about Journey? Are you not fucking me because you're hung up on her?"

"No."

God she hated his one-word answers. "Then tell me why. I deserve to know."

"I told you. You haven't earned it."

"I have to earn sex?"

"Goodnight, Laila."

She humphed, knowing she wouldn't get anything more out of him. "Goodnight."

Chapter 12

When she rounded a corner inside the main building of OZ and face-planted right into Rock's chest, Laila's adrenaline spiked. She hadn't held her position as told, and she'd almost been caught tucked away in a dark corner with Garret.

With no time to hide her fluster, Rock asked her what she'd been doing.

"Uh, nothing." He eyed her, then took two steps and looked around the corner in the direction she'd come.

His expression didn't change as he took in the view.. She opened herself to him. His emotional grid didn't explode. Garret wasn't standing there anymore, but her relief was short lived. Rock was suspicious and examined her pupils and breathing, as if with x-ray eyes. His anger intensified, and the energy it took to control his emotions made his eyes glitter. There was no doubt in Laila's mind Rock knew she'd just lied to his face, and as if to confirm, his anger expanded. As he stood there, suspicions growing, his anger hemorrhaged, boiled, bombarding her with his wrath.

He wrapped his hand around her forearm and her ability to feel his fury doubled. Her own gasp took her by surprise.

"What's happening?"

"You're so angry." Trying to gain some distance between herself and the storm swirling around him, Laila caught another breath and stepped away from him.

His expression mellowed. His anger diminished "I would never hurt you, Laila."

She swallowed through a dry throat, uneasy about the trajectory of their current conversation. "I know."

"Then why are you trying to get away from me?"

She felt the blood drain from her cheeks. This was as good an opening as she'd get to tell him everything. The realization had her spooked. Her heart thumped hard as she gulped air. She had to tell him her secret. She'd wanted to tell him. But here? She looked around to make sure they were alone.

"What are you afraid of?"

This is it. Do it now.

He stepped closer, and she stepped back.

She'd never told a soul her secret. So many times, she'd wanted to tell someone. As a child, growing up in the Amber Zone, surrounded by love and acceptance, she'd never sensed the perpetual dangers inherent to New Atlanta. The terrifying stories her mother told to deter her from chatting about her ability to anyone who'd listen worked especially well, even all these years later. She'd be taken away. She'd be an experiment in the Gov's genetic labs. Her life as she knew it would be gone. Those constant reminders were enough for Laila to never tell a soul.

"What the fuck am I missing here?" Rock's tone was grim.

She looked around again. "Nothing," she lied. Another one he saw through.

He dragged her to his truck, tucked her into the passenger seat and stormed to the driver's side. She jumped when he slammed the driver's door. "What is going on?" he asked as he pulled out of his space.

Stalling, thinking, she licked her chapped lips. "I've been meaning to tell you. It's just—" Covering her face with her hands, she shook her head. "I've never told a soul. And I'm not sure I can," she said, more to herself than to him.

He waited silently, proving himself to be exceptional at gauging when to push her and when not to.

Finally she lowered her hands and glanced at him.

"Do it like a Band-Aid. Just let it rip." He didn't look at her, somehow knowing she was a reflex away from bolting out of the moving vehicle. "You have to know by now, your secret's safe with me." His seemingly calm demeanor didn't match the chaotic feelings brewing beneath the surface.

She took a deep, calming breath and let it fly. "I'm an empath. I feel what others are feeling."

Rock's mask faltered as he drilled her with a look of disbelief then returned his gaze to the road. His hands gripped the steering wheel so tightly, his knuckles were white. He shook his head, a slow motion that highlighted his speechlessness.

"Say something."

His Adam's apple bobbed. Now, it was Rock who stalled. "I knew someone else who had the same gift. She kept it a secret, too."

Dread crept up her spine. "*Had* the same gift?"

"She's dead now."

Laila watched the nearly deserted streets of the Emerald Zone whiz by while she digested the ominous information. She knew the answer to her next question but asked it anyway. "Did the Gov get her?"

"Yes." He raked his hand through his hair. "In a way."

"How?"

He remained silent, shaking his head. An undertone of sadness permeated the air. "She talked about it with me. I think I was the only person other than her parents who knew. She said it was all about vibrations. That some people are sensitive enough to pick up the vibration a person's emotions give off." He had a far-off look. "She said we clicked because our vibrations liked each other." He cleared his throat. "Said it was akin to having chemistry." He frowned. "You've kept this from me all this time?"

* * * *

He was sick, unsteady in his own skin, and headed home instead of returning to OZ. He considered calling it a day, but the weeks were passing quickly, and they didn't live in a world safe enough for him to allow that to happen. He'd continue with his plan for the evening despite the fact everything seemed different after Laila's revelation. What were the odds he'd be paired with another woman who had the same gift as Emily? Miniscule. It unsettled him, roused his suspicions.

She waited on the edge of the tub while he walked over to the shower stall and turned on the water.

He'd been anxious to see how she would react to tonight's change. He peeled her clothes off and widened her stance. His attention was colored by his anger and doubt. It was ironic the lesson he'd planned for them this afternoon would crumble more of the personal barriers remaining between them.

"Rock, I—"

"Shh." He put a finger to her lips. She stood, her face raised toward him, rapt, waiting for his next command. His heart softened and cock hardened simultaneously. If Laila was a trap, then let him be trapped. The noose was already tight around his neck.

He looked into her enormous brown eyes and a revelation hit like a comet falling to earth, shaking up his whole existence. He was absolutely and utterly in love. He brushed her hair away from her face and smoothed his thumb over her lush lower lip.

He never wanted her to leave his side. She belonged to him. And owned him. It was too late for her now. She wanted in, and she'd gotten in.

Standing naked before him, she communicated her unease with her expression. She almost looked panicked as he lowered his hand and nudged her lower lips apart. He found the string to her tampon nestled between, and tugged, removing it.

"You think I didn't know?" he said low. His cock was as full as it had ever been.

She shook her head, maintaining the silence as directed.

"There's little that gets past me when it comes to you. Now," he prompted, "get in the shower. I'll join you in a minute." He turned away, leaving her to follow his direction. She had a long way to go if she thought her period was going to change anything. He disposed of the tampon.

She'd done well, so far. He needed to drive home the notion that her body belonged to him. He would do what he wanted, when he wanted with it, and her compliance was expected.

Rock grabbed the razor and shaving cream from the sink and joined her in the steamy warmth of the shower. He pointed the spray toward the wall, directed her to sit and then joined her on the tile floor. Gently he lifted one of her legs until her foot rested on his shoulder and coated it with shaving foam. With long, slow strokes, he scraped the foam away, feeling the smooth stripe of skin left behind, making sure he'd gotten everything. Meticulously, he shaved one, and then the other leg. When he was done, he nudged her legs wider and knelt between her knees. He applied a dollop of the white foam on the hair between her legs. Her head jerked down to look and then up so she could meet his gaze. "Do you trust me?"

"Yes, but—

"No buts."

"Okay, no buts."

"I think your training has been going extraordinarily well." He fingered the cream between her lower lips. "Do you agree?" He waited for the menthol in the foam to stimulate her clit, watching for her body's acknowledgement of it.

"Yes." She said the word in a breathy whisper.

He pushed her knees farther apart, exposing her pussy, beautifully decorated with clouds of fluffy white cream. It looked lickable, like a cupcake piled high with airy frosting. His mouth watered at the thought.

Rock lifted the razor to her exposed, intimate skin and scraped the first delicate swipe, clearing it of hair and cream. He was slow and precise as he handled her, manipulating her lower lips so he had adequate access to scrape the sharp steel against the curves and valleys. Then, as he got closer to what was hidden between, he pinched her clit a little more roughly than he should have, protecting it from the sharp blade he wielded, but also subjecting her to lightning bolts of pleasure and pain. She was flushed and panting as he performed the motions again and again, leaving smooth, bare flesh and an increasingly aroused woman in the wake of every stroke.

He admired her pleasure when she groaned aloud from his manipulations. Her features were serene. She was in this moment with him, feeling it, absorbing the sensations, soaking every one of them up with her senses.

He finished the shave and swiped her now soft, smooth skin with his fingertips. She was breathless and needy, using her eyes to convey her feelings.

"Very good, peanut. I can read you perfectly. Those expressive eyes tell me everything I need to know." He slid his fingers inside her.

She flinched. "Rock, I'm having my period."

"I think we've covered that topic already," he said as he brushed his thumb over her clit and a third finger joined the first two.

"But aren't you," she hesitated, obviously searching for a word. "Put off, by that. I mean…" She stammered then shook her head. "Most—"

"I'm not most men."

She met his gaze, and he didn't recognize the expression, couldn't pinpoint exactly where her emotions were.

"What are you thinking?"

"You're really leaving no barriers between us. It's uncomfortable."

He nodded, smiled. "Yes. Some things flourish when uncomfortable. I like it. I like causing it, watching it." He leaned in, and flicked her clit with his tongue." It makes me want to fuck." Her body jerked. Her pussy clenched his fingers. "My poor little peanut. So eager for my touch. It's taken you a long time to earn it."

Her hips flexed, in tiny, and he guessed, mostly unconscious motions as he slid his fingers in and out of her. This was their reward for the hard work they've been doing. Even though lately, training Laila was like getting an ice cream reward for finishing dessert.

He leaned in and exhaled on her bare pussy, then captured her clit for one torturous lick.

She growled at him, her frustration filling the shower stall. He inserted a pinky into her ass, joining the in and out motion of his other digits. He quickened the deep, thick strokes that had her clenching around his fingers.

"Oh God," she cried.

He withdrew his fingers from her, and she froze. Then he leaned in and sucked her clit, taking the entirety of the little nub into his mouth.

Her body spasmed violently, as if an electric jolt moved through her, shocking her muscles and making them jump. One long, sweet shout followed. An endless note expelled from her until her lungs ran out of air. When she finally sucked in a breath, she cried out, "Stop!" Her chest heaved and her body shuddered as she attempted to slink away from him. He gripped her hip, keeping her there while he watched her pleading expression in response to the intolerable stimulation.

Finally he stopped and absorbed every nuance of the spent and wilted woman on the shower floor. He lifted himself. The hot spray hit his back, shielding her from the direct stream.

Her gaze moved down his body and landed on the ruddy cock pointed at her. She positioned herself to crawl toward him on her hands and knees. "Let me." She rose to her knees. "Please." The pleading in her eyes made his chest ache and, he fought the man inside from grabbing her by the hair and pulling her mouth down to his cock.

Instead, he scooped her up and whispered in her ear as they exited the shower. "God, baby, you were spectacular." He planted a swift, rough kiss on her lips then set her down.

It took only a minute to get a clean tank top on her and boxers on himself.

Rock's earbud pinged, signaling an incoming call just as Laila followed him into the bedroom. He gave her the signal to hold, a skill she still had trouble with, and answered. "Rock."

"Nice to hear your voice when it's daylight out, son."

"Dad. I was planning on calling you later."

"You can still do that. Right now I'm wondering if you're with the young lady, the one you're working with?"

Rock glanced over his shoulder at Laila, who was doing a mighty fine job of holding her spot while he was in the room with her. He repeated the hold signal as he walked past her and exited the bedroom. Taking the steps to the first floor two at a time, he said, "All right, Dad, what's going on."

"After we talked last time, I kept stumbling over the name of this girl. It bothered me for a while. Then, poof, it just pops into my head while I'm getting dressed. Lila Lewis."

"Lila Lewis?"

"Lila Lewis is Laila Lewis's mother."

Rock leaned his rear against the edge of the kitchen counter, facing the direction of the stairs. "You know her?"

"I did. A long time ago…two, maybe three, times," he murmured. After the flu took Rock's mother, his dad dealt with his emptiness in a way opposite to the way he had. His father ran toward women, a lot of women, in an attempt to fill the emptiness inside.

Rock groaned. "Dad, you didn't." It was rare for his father to draw his ire, but this did it.

"Now, hold on. Let me finish. It's not as bad as it sounds."

"God dammit, Dad. That's my—" He cut himself off before he said the next word perched on the tip of his tongue.

"Your what, son?"

Every muscle in his body tensed. "My woman."

A charged silence spread long and loud over the connection. Then, in a gentle tone, his father said, "Nobody knows better than I how hard it is to look forward instead of looking back."

"I know, Dad."

"You did the right thing."

More silence.

"So, uh…I'm so sorry about Lila."

Rock couldn't remain mad at the man who'd raised him. "Okay. Tell me."

"I met her at an open house at your elementary school. She had a daughter, who I now know is Laila, in one of the younger grades."

Rock caught movement by the stairs and looked at the time display on his hand-held. He shook his head. She couldn't even hold for two minutes.

"Anyway, we had a conversation at the school that resulted in a date, which ended up, well, you know. We saw each other a few more times after that. Nevertheless, the rebuilding was demanding and it took most of my time. That, and you. We liked each other, but it was too hard. We were too broken after watching every one we knew die within the span of months. Shit, the entire population was traumatized, and all formed the most fucked up ways of coping. Lila Lewis was just another futile attempt to fill the hole your mother left. As you know, it didn't work. I'm sorry, son."

"You don't have to apologize. Like you said, you were just trying to cope."

"You're a better man than I was. A stronger man."

"How did it end?"

"Amicably. Neither of us thought we'd develop some grand love affair. We just took some comfort where we could get it. We lost touch fairly quickly."

"And once you realized the connection?"

"I paid Lila a visit. I've been visiting a lot of people lately." That was his father's way of telling him he'd seen Xander and received Rock's letter.

"And?"

"And I'd like to speak to Laila, please."

Rock was asking if he received the escape plans mapped out in the letter he'd left at the safe house. But either his father didn't get the point to his broad inquiry, or he was being purposefully dense.

"Now." His tone said you might be all grown up, but I'm still the Alpha here.

"Hold on." Rock pulled the earbud out of his ear and walked to the bottom of the stairs. Laila sat on a step as far down the flight as she could without being easily seen from where he'd been standing. "You didn't last two minutes." She shrugged and shot him an innocent smile. "Are you even trying?"

"Mmmm." She pursed her lips and tapped a finger to her chin, looking serious for a moment, then grinned. "Not really."

He shook his head and offered a hand. "Come on." He walked her to the kitchen and pulled his hand-held from his pocket. "My father wants to speak to you." He hit the speaker button. "Go ahead, Dad."

"Laila?"

"Yes?"

"This is Rock senior."

A smile crossed her face. "Are you a super hero, too?"

He chuckled. "Far from it, darlin'. From what I hear, it's the other way around."

Her spine stiffened and she darted a glance at Rock.

"Isn't that what they're calling the woman who's going to risk her life to rescue all those important pieces of paper in Washington?"

Her shoulders slumped slightly. "If you say so. Nobody's saying that to my face, though."

He chuckled. "I wanted to let you know I saw your mother this morning."

Laila's mouth dropped open. "You did?"

"Yes, and she'd never try to contact you. She's too loyal a supporter of Morgan to break his moratorium on trans-zone calls. And, of course by now you must know that I don't give a shit. Pardon my French. So I just wanted to let you know she's okay and pass on a message."

A sudden rush of emotion transformed his girl. Sadness filled her eyes and her bottom lip protruded, quivered. "Message?" Her voice quavered. "Is she okay?"

"Yes, she's fine. She said she's proud of everything you're doing. Be safe. And, of course, she loves you."

Laila stood, looking at her toes to escape Rock's observation, then whispered, "Thank you."

"You're welcome. It was nice to reconnect with your mom after all these years. We'd been friends when you and Rock were in elementary school. Rock knows the story and can fill you in on the details later. Just know I'll be keeping an eye on her for you. Make sure she doesn't need anything, that she's okay."

"Thanks, sir."

"You can call me Big Rock. That's how people refer to me when they need to distinguish between us."

She snorted. "That means you're Little Rock?" She pointed at him.

Rock scowled at her in return. "Done, Dad?" he barked.

"Now Little Rock," his dad said, "don't get your panties in a twist."

That sealed it for Laila. She laughed so hard she had to cross her legs so she wouldn't pee herself.

Rock disconnected, put the hand-held in his pocket and waited until her laughter died from a roar to gulping, stabilizing breaths. She wiped her eyes and finally met his gaze. Then she started laughing all over again.

* * * *

"Go ahead, get it all out," Rock said to her. "And then we need to talk about your inability to hold in place when I give you the signal."

He obviously didn't find his father as funny as she did. What a shame, because Big Rock had made her day. "Uh, no. I don't feel like it," she said mischievously.

"Too bad." He took her hand and led her out his front door.

"Where are we going?"

"Tonight, we're working on the hold command. I need to know you'll stay where I left you if we have to separate."

"I'll hold when I really need to. Not everything has to be training, Rock."

She glanced up at his gorgeous face every couple of steps, hoping for a reply. She got none. His stern mask was in place. He was in Rock wall mode.

Realizing what he was going to do, she said, "I don't want to stay here by myself. This is silly, Rock. I can hold if I need to."

"Baby, it's not your call. It's mine." He stood with her just inside the doorway to her house. "You need to do this unconsciously. When we're out of the city, there's no room for errors. You have to show me you can do this." He kissed her on the forehead. "I'll see you in the morning." He gave her the signal to hold and walked out her front door.

Her mood jumped from the proverbial ledge, freefalling due to the harsh desertion. He'd transformed her house into a prison, holding her in solitary confinement with just his words. She stood there in the silence, scanning the space. The living room was a modern interpretation of a rustic cabin with hard wood floors and saddle-colored leather furniture. A fine coating of dust covered the surfaces.

This wasn't her home. This space, with its gorgeous furniture and attention to every detail, this lavish luxury, was just a void to her. Since the first day of training, she and Rock spent every night together, and she considered this house the world's biggest closet, nothing more.

Rock wasn't trying to teach her to hold. He was punishing her because she'd been busted doing something she wasn't supposed to be doing. And, he knew she lied to him about it. The man had a memory like an elephant.

She walked out her back door and sat on the edge of the wood deck. The late day shade of the tall pines shielded her from the setting sun. Shadows danced deeper in the trees and insects chirped their twilight song.

Finally beginning to come down from the day, she noticed the little pains she'd accumulated from training and became achingly aware of the emptiness in the pit of her stomach. She wasn't complete unless they occupied the same space. That was her new normal. Sitting alone in the beautiful setting, something that, before, would have rejuvenated her, was a punishment she'd have to endure until she could see Rock again.

She shook her head at the potency of her dependence. Any other time she'd had feelings for a man, they were light and bubbly, like ginger ale. What she and Rock had was more intoxicating, like whiskey, warming her in the center of her chest and making her feel a little off kilter. It was different from anything she'd ever felt.

It was better.

But, along with that gift, came an irrational, insecure fear of losing him. How could she live without this man who made her feel whole, whose presence made her body sing?

There, in the dappled late-day shade of her back yard, Laila spent over an hour keenly feeling the difference between a night with Rock and a night without.

Finally, when she couldn't sit there anymore, she slipped on her flip-flops and grabbed her bag then went out her front door. The slight breeze stirred against her skin. It was a cooler evening than the one before, just perfect for a walk.

Rock's truck was gone from his driveway. That seemed to make her feel even more irrational.

She didn't know where she was going until she found herself entering the Emerald Zone Specialty Store by the entrance to the Emerald housing development.

As she walked over the threshold, an old-fashioned bell announced her. The interior of the cozy space smelled wonderful.

She was taken aback at the sight of the inside. Her gaze landed on items she'd never seen in Sapphire or Amber. There was gold and silver jewelry sparkling in a case to her right. A sales woman stood behind the case, her gaze darting to Laila's Emerald tattoo.

"Hello."

Laila nodded and smiled in her direction. It was cool in the store, like the building housing her office. If she knew she could have escaped the heat by going shopping, she would have done it more often.

"Would you like a cup of coffee, or perhaps some chocolate?"

Laila whirled around. "I've never had either. I'd love to try both, if that's okay."

"Of course." The lady avoided eye contact as she moved from behind the jewelry counter and scurried to a station that held the specialties.

Laila stood for a minute, taking her surroundings until the woman approached with a small cup of black liquid and two small squares of chocolate displayed prettily on the saucer.

"Here you go." She smiled nervously. Her Sapphire tattoo peeked from the end of her sleeve.

Laila returned her smile. "Thank you."

"My name's Rachael. If you're looking for something particular, I'd be happy to show you what we carry."

"No, thank you. I'm just taking a look."

She nodded. "Okay, but we close in twenty minutes."

The old analog clock on the wall displayed it was close to nine, surprising her.

"Our recent acquisitions are displayed on the large center tables. Those are unusual items we don't get often. Everything else in the store are pretty much items we carry regularly."

Laila started to wander, then took a sip of the steaming black liquid in the cup she'd received. Despite the color, she expected coffee to taste delicious. From all the pre-pandemic movies and TV shows, it had been a passion and sometimes an addiction to those who had easy access to it.

That assumption, however, was dead wrong. The stuff was thick and disgusting, with the bitter taste remaining in her mouth even after she'd swallowed.

Rachael must have been watching for her reaction, because seconds later she offered to take the cup. "Most people don't like it," she said as Laila handed it off. "You'll like the chocolate much better."

"It couldn't be much worse now, could it?" Laila said, laughing. "Is there anything else equally craptacular I should stay away from?"

Rachael relaxed and let out a soft laugh. "Yes. The fish eggs are an acquired taste."

"Thanks for the warning."

Laila picked up one of the squares of chocolate on the tiny plate she carried and popped it into her mouth.

"Oh my God." She looked over her shoulder at Rachael, who had returned to her place at the jewelry case. "You were right. This is fantastic."

"I know. I can't even imagine what it tasted like when it was first made."

Laila popped the other piece into her mouth and set the tiny plate down.

She browsed through everything. There were entire displays of wine, champagne and other exotic alcohols, chocolates, cosmetics, scented soaps, shampoos and sprays. She picked up several bottles, sniffing at the multicolored liquids with exotic names like Moonlight and Soft Cashmere. She recognized Rock's scent and looked more closely at the bottle she held. Cruel. She hovered her nose over the bottle again. Yes, she was sure it was the liquid soap Rock used when he showered alone.

In the end, she bought a bar of chocolate and the bottle of Cruel. Not for Rock, but for herself.

The moment she arrived home, she trudged up the stairs and into the bathroom, trying to ignore the fact Rock's truck was still absent from its place in his driveway.

She twisted the knobs in her shower so the spray was lukewarm and lathered herself up, soaking in his scent.

After throwing on a shirt and panties, she descended the stairs and stopped at the bottom. The room was stuffy as hell. She opened some windows, plopped on the couch and turned on the vids. She devoured the entire bar of chocolate in a video induced trance. It was her consolation prize.

Even after she'd fallen asleep on the couch, some part of her brain monitored the night sounds for the return of Rock's truck. She opened her eyes momentarily when the sound finally woke her. It was almost dawn. She frowned and rolled over before falling back to sleep.

Chapter 13

The next morning, Laila wanted to run out to meet Rock when she saw him headed across the street to her house but hung back, relaxing on her couch as if the separation had been no big deal.

He walked in, looking gorgeous, as always.

"Good morning." His gaze roamed her reclined figure, scanned the room then landed on the wrapper of the chocolate bar she'd eaten the night before.

"I told you to hold."

She shrugged. "What makes you think I didn't?"

His arms were crossed over his chest. "Lie."

She didn't deny it. She knew she pushed her luck, but was mad at him for leaving her alone all night. He had to know the sudden detox from him would be hard on her.

He walked through the living room and entered the dining room. "You need to work on your focus. I've come up with an excellent way to help you with it."

He grabbed a dining room chair and turned it away from the table. Rock met her gaze, and his eyes broached no argument. "Panties off," he said as he sat, facing her.

Still wearing the panties and big T-shirt from the night before, she hooked the waistband of the panties and stripped them off.

He patted his lap.

She stepped toward him and turned to sit. Instead, he twirled her around and gripped her nape. "On your belly."

She tried to push herself up, but he weighted her back with his hand. She didn't have the leverage she needed and landed with an "Oomph!" as her chest collapsed onto his thighs.

"Good girl."

"Like you gave me a choice," she muttered.

"We're going to do this focus exercise for as long as it takes for you to keep your primary focus on me."

She jerked at the cool rubbery texture of something poking the entrance of her ass. "Stop!" He removed his hands, and she pushed herself up from his lap "What are you doing?"

The fact he looked shocked she'd stopped him was a good testament to how good she'd learned rule number one.

"I'm putting a plug in your ass." He'd said the words as if it were a perfectly natural thing to do.

A blush heated her cheeks. Humiliation, was an unfamiliar feeling that took her a moment to identify. This was so much weirder than the tampon removal. She put her panties back on. "I need a minute." The words barely past her lips, Laila scrambled up the stairs two at a time. Just outside her bedroom door, she looked over her shoulder.

Rock stood at the foot of the stairs.

She turned back, escaping his gaze and closed her bedroom door behind her. Still needing another door between them, she hurried into her master bathroom, and locked that door. She threw a folded towel over the cold toilet lid and sat, brought her knees to her chest and wrapped her arms around her legs.

During the past six weeks, she'd lost herself and any dignity she'd ever had. Somewhere in the back of her head, she'd thought maybe he would be attracted to her if he saw qualities he liked. Maybe, if she ran farther, fought harder and submitted to his bizarre training practices she'd make up for her mediocrity. She didn't know when, exactly, that thought process had started. Almost from the beginning, she'd let him do anything he wished in the name of training, hoping he'd like what he saw, and maybe, someday, have feelings for her, as she did for him. She'd died a thousand little deaths from all the indifference he'd displayed when given the opportunity to fuck her.

Why did she continue to let him do these intense things to her? She didn't have to think too hard for the answer. She loved him…and the thrill. Their fireworks packed an exhilarating wallop. Add some slightly deviant behavior to the mix and she flew.

Nothing felt better than his happiness, and it surged during his kinky little games and pleasure/pain punishments. In turn, his bolstered hers, giving her happiness squared. She was addicted to happiness squared. She would do anything for happiness squared, and that included everything his twisted mind could think up. She wanted to give back, fulfill his needs, like he did for her.

"Shit," she whispered into the total silence of the room. Where was her line? She didn't have one when it came to him. Especially when it seemed as if he loved her most when she gave everything up for him to control.

Hiding there in her bathroom, she forced herself to face what she'd become, acknowledging she would do anything for this man.

She deflated and shook her head, staying there in the silence for a long time, mulling over their interactions. He was his own contradiction. Sweet and cruel. Demanding and giving. Closed off and yet willing to be an open book to her.

She couldn't imagine not continuing this life they'd crafted together. She was already tangled in these unorthodox bonds with him. Questioning what she was doing at this late date seemed comparable to looking both ways after stepping into the road. It was just too late. She sighed, relaxing a bit. And, that was okay.

She focused on the door. She expected him to come find her. To burst through and tell her to suck it up and get ready for training, but he didn't.

She wanted him to. God, she wanted him to, but his absence was also a lesson. There were some decisions she had to make for herself.

When she finally left the bathroom, it was with a new understanding of what she'd do to keep the man she loved. She rounded the corner at the bottom of the steps and found him sitting in the same chair. That magnificent, scary man met her gaze and smiled at her. He saved most of the disagreeable beast for others. For her, he was mostly a gentle giant.

"I worry that I'm too much for you." His deep, rich voice resonated through the room and raised goose bumps on her arms.

"You're not."

"It's nothing to be ashamed of. I'd be too much for any normal woman."

She walked over, sat on his lap and wrapped her arms around his neck. "Rock, I love you just the way you are."

His beautiful brown eyes softened. "I know what I ask of you is hard." He shrugged. "I want what I want, and I don't like to argue about it. It doesn't mean I love you less, respect you less. What you see is what you get. No games. When I'm angry, you'll know it. I get my pound of flesh and it's over. When I want to spank your ass, or fuck it. I do that, too. I need to be in control. But, you have to know, you have the ultimate power. You can walk away any time you want. And I wouldn't blame you a bit. We'll call it a short, beautifully intense and"—he smiled—"quite sweet affair, if you want to."

He was offering her a way out. She didn't want out. "No, baby. You're not getting off that easy. I plan on being a thorn in your side for quite some time to come. I love you, Rock. And, I'm beginning to understand you. But you have to understand too. Mostly, I love the unconventional aspects of our relationship. Sometimes I don't."

"Okay, but you have to admit that occasionally what you don't like still excites on other levels. How do you know if you don't try? Look how much you've come to enjoy your spankings." He pointed at her. "Don't deny it." She held her hands up. "Not denying, but when I say stop, you stop."

His expression turned serious. "Always have." He held up the butt plug and lube bottle. "Are you ready?"

"As ready as I'll ever be."

"Trust me," he said and gave her a quick kiss.

Laila bent over Rock's lap and dropped her hands to the wood floor. He pressed the cool, slippery toy in her anus, slowly nudging in and back with slight, gentle moves. It graduated in size as he continued to push, stretching her rear farther with each back and forth movement. She wanted to cry out, her lips parting and the yell a heartbeat away from being released, when the ring of muscles in her ass found a comfortable resting place at the base of the plug.

Rock gave her rear end a quick slap, moving the device wedged inside her. "You can put your panties back on."

She groaned and pushed herself upright.

His fiery gaze didn't disguise the satisfaction and lust pouring off him. "Every time you become aware of that plug in your ass, you are to take five seconds to assess your surroundings and lay eyes on me. Now get dressed. It's time to go."

Laila leaned over to pick her panties off the floor and the plug shifted inside her. "Oh, fuck no." She was caught off guard by the constant intrusion of the thing.

Rock gave her a knowing smile, only one side of his lips curling up.

She growled at him, and he chuckled. "I think it's going to be a long day for both of us. Get dressed. I'll meet you at the truck in fifteen." He turned and left her there.

No breakfast? He was definitely still mad at her. "Dammit," she whispered as she got dressed and headed out for another day of brutal training.

After they did their usual morning routine, Laila sat alone, sweating in the shade of a shed, when she spotted Sydney heading her way with long confident strides. Long and lean, she was pretty from far away and gorgeous close up. The woman's jade green eyes were stunning against her dark coloring. Something different this time, though. Her uniform was black instead of the usual camouflage of the National Guard and tailored as precisely as a second skin.

A pin flashed momentary reflections of the sun as she moved. It was an eagle frozen in the moment before a strike, wings spread, talons ready to grab its prey. The lapel pin was the symbol identifying Morgan's trusted inner circle. Sydney was a Black Guard, now. In a zone where being a Sapphire was barely tolerable, that pin went a long way toward improving her pedigree.

Laila didn't understand the fanatical allegiances this new breed of National Guardsmen had to Morgan. To them, it didn't matter that his words and ideas were irrational. Those seemingly intelligent people swallowed ridiculous ideologies to fanatic proportions in exchange for the power and prestige the Black Guard status provided.

As Sydney neared, the combination of smirk and disdain parked on her face made her look as if she were snarling. Laila groaned to herself. The vibe the woman gave off was pure poison. This encounter was going to be unpleasant.

"Where's Rock?" she asked, towering over Laila's wilted body.

"He went inside to use the restroom."

Sydney looked over her shoulder at the main building and then pegged Laila with a blatant look of contempt. "I just wanted to tell him I had a good time last night." Her lips curled in a malicious smile.

"Last night?"

"He must have needed some real training after being with you for the last month. We took a few turns on the mats. I didn't think he'd ever let me go home. It was the wee hours of the morning when I was finally able to get out from underneath him. I'm sore in all the right places." She smirked. "He's good. At everything, don't you think?"

Laila's mouth dropped open at the innuendo. At Sydney's satisfied expression, she snapped it shut.

"I wouldn't know," she said softly.

Sydney smirked. "Well, I suppose you wouldn't. A man like that needs someone more like him. Maybe someone who's not an Amber under all those layers of ink." She looked pointedly at Laila's wrist.

The woman didn't know anything about him. "Rock grew up Amber."

"I know. But look at him, there's nothing substandard about him." She stepped closer to Laila and murmured. "Not like you." Sydney wrinkled her nose. "You're revolting. I can smell you from here. I don't know how he can stand being around you."

Over Sydney's shoulder, Laila spotted Rock's exit from the building. Relief must have flickered in her eyes, because the bitch straightened and pasted on a smile while turning to greet Rock as he approached.

No, Sydney didn't know him at all. If she did, she'd be able to tell how unbelievably angry he'd become when he'd caught sight of her. Eyes blazing and jaw tight, he stopped near them.

A person didn't have to be an empath to know he was very, very pissed.

* * * *

Rock's gaze traveled over Sydney and then met Laila's. He saw her hurt plain as day. Tilting his head slightly, he questioned her without a word, and she cast a glance at Sydney.

He turned his attention to the woman he'd instinctually hated since the day they'd met. Something about her was…wrong, somehow. Prior to Laila entering his world, he'd thought it was because she never bothered to disguise her lust. And, at the time, lust directed at him from anybody other than Emily sickened him. He'd always treated her politely, but avoided her as much as possible.

His life and perspective changed when Laila appeared, but still his intuition red-flagged Sydney.

"Hey, Rock," the woman said cheerfully. Her eyes shone with the lust he'd seen so many times before. It turned his stomach, especially now that he knew who she'd allowed inside her body.

"Sydney." There was no doubt Laila had just been victim to another verbal attack, so he didn't spare her another glance. As he put a hand to the small of Sydney's back, leading her away from Laila, he simultaneously gave Laila the signal to hold.

"Two days in a row, Rock? I think you might be following me."

He didn't reply to Sydney's playful accusation. Rage had taken over. There was no fucking way Laila was going to fall victim to her in any way. It was imperative he stopped the bullshit now.

They were about a hundred feet away from Laila when he stopped and faced Sydney. Satisfaction shone in her expression as she turned to face him. She registered the glower he gave her in return, and her smile faltered. She broke eye contact and crossed her arms over her chest. He saw that action for what it was, an unconscious response in an effort to hide her bad behavior. "I thought I'd made it perfectly clear to you that any communication you had with Laila would go through me."

"You did. We weren't talking, really. I just stopped to say hi."

Rock was almost disappointed in the woman's inability to conceal her guilt. He tried to maintain a calm, even voice through his fury. His head swam with the implications of how much access Sydney would have to Laila outside New Atlanta.

He stepped closer to her, until mere inches separated their bodies. A ghost of Sydney's smirk returned as she lifted her eyes to meet his gaze. She was pretty, and knew it.

"Still with the fuck-me eyes, Sydney. Save yourself the embarrassment. I'm not interested."

She shrank from him. Clearly unused to anyone challenging her.

"Laila has too much on her plate to have you adding your particular brand of bitchy to the mix." He stepped toward her again, making up the space she'd put between them, and leaned in so his livid expression was the only thing she saw. "Since it seems you didn't quite understand my first request to leave her alone, I'm going to make this second request perfectly clear with words you understand."

He held his index finger up in front of her nose. "Number one, she is an Emerald. And as a Black Guard, I know you're aware of the difference in your respective statuses. It is inappropriate for you to engage her unless she asks you a direct question."

He raised a second finger to the first. "Two, our sparring last night was my attempt at assessing whether you're good enough to be on this mission. I'm an Emerald, and it is against the law for us to engage in any type of relationship whatsoever. And for the record, I'd rather kiss a hair-covered, piss-soaked bathroom mop than have any part of my body touch any part of yours in a sexual way. And, Laila is aware of this. So you just made a complete fool of yourself."

He added another upturned finger to the first two. "Three. This is the last time I'm going to have this discussion with you." He leaned in further and she was forced to arch backward to maintain distance between them. Her eyes were wide as he got in her face, showing the full measure of his fury. "If you speak to her or do anything to upset her in any way, I will grind you to dust, and then I'll report your attempts to engage me sexually, and let Morgan deal with what's left. Are we clear?"

Sydney swallowed hard then nodded. "Yeah, we're clear."

"Good. Now get the fuck away from me before I change my mind." With those last words, he turned to where Laila waited for him. Her face was a mask, not giving away any of her thoughts or feelings as he approached. She was getting good at that.

He smiled at his girl. She didn't smile back.

When he reached her, he offered her a hand up. "You ready for lunch?"

She walked beside him to the building. "What did you say to her?"

"I told her to leave you alone. From now on, if she has anything to say to you, she should go through me. If she doesn't, let me know."

"Okay." She was breathless as she scrambled, trying to keep up with his long strides. "She made innuendoes you and her were together last night."

"Excellent. I read you correctly. It was a good test of our training. Unplanned, but effective just the same."

"Were you?" She studied his profile.

He answered her question with silence, because he couldn't immediately find the words she needed. Plus, her doubt didn't sit well with him. It only added fuel to his fury over Sydney's verbal attack.

"You didn't answer my question about you and Sydney last night."

"I came here last night to work out. Or, to be more precise, to get away from you. I needed you to learn to hold, but I was having a hard time letting you. I left so I could stay away."

Laila's heart twisted. "So you were with that bitch?"

"The bitch is fucking Morgan. Do you honestly think I'd stick my dick in her?" Couldn't she feel the absolute love he felt for her? "You should know me better, trust me more than that by now. You're in my bed. That means no one else is. Same goes, the other way around. "We clear?"

Through her empathic connection, she felt the truth. He loved her. "Yes, clear."

Chapter 14

Laila was on cloud nine. It had taken a month, but she'd downed Rock on the mat. Her hand-to-hand moves had transformed from randomly sprinting at him and screaming like a banshee, to more thought-out strategies and softer, increasingly graceful falls. Then, when she'd swept her leg, taking his out from under him, and elbowed him in the eye socket, she'd truly done it. She'd knocked that smug bastard on his ass.

This was the highlight of an already great week. She'd gotten a few messages from her mother through Big Rock. And, she hadn't felt a second of loneliness in weeks. She was giddy, a feeling she hadn't had in years. It energized her. She wanted to laugh and play like a little kid.

"And it just gets better!" she announced with her arms pumped up in triumph.

Rock stood with his head in the fridge. "What does?"

"I'm clean. I'm dressed. And, I feel okay, no aches and pains today. Let's celebrate." It had still been a brutally hot and physically demanding day, but her body was changing. She was leaner, her muscles were more defined and now, didn't protest their use.

"What do you have in mind?"

"I don't know. It's cooler outside than in. I wish we could lay a blanket out on the green in the Amber Zone. Watch the sunset. Lie under the stars."

"I wish we could, too." Then a long, slow smile spread across his face. "But I think I might have the next best thing." He looked her up and down before opening the refrigerator again. "Run across the street, get some shoes on and we'll go."

She didn't ask where. By now, she knew the answer she'd get verbatim: *Don't question your training.* Plus, not knowing what was going to happen didn't faze her as much as it used to. She'd learned to follow Rock's lead and trusted him enough to not be worried about what he had planned.

He was in her living room when she reached the bottom of the steps. "Ready?"

She slipped her hand into his. "More than ready."

They climbed in the cab of his truck, and drove off.

The trip was short, and Laila was disappointed when a national guardsman waved the truck through the checkpoint of OZ. They spent every day there, and it was not fun. She kept her disappointment to herself and met him behind the pickup as he pulled a box and a bedroll out of the back.

He handed her the bedroll. "Come on." In the compound's main building, he took her through the emergency exit at the end of the long hallway and up a flight of stairs. The second story was a sweltering utility area, containing ventilation ducts, water and electricity lines. It was dim and dirty, but still she followed without questioning. When they reached a ladder, he climbed it and pushed open a hatch, revealing blue sky.

He took the bedroll from her. "You go first. I'll hand the stuff up to you."

Laila emerged on the flat roof of the building and lay on her belly to reach her arms into the opening. She grabbed the bedroll Rock handed up to her. When she turned back around to grab the box, he was rising out of the hole with it balanced securely on his shoulder.

Laila stood and took a moment to look around at the three-sixty view. The densely packed skyscrapers of the old city overshadowed the hastily constructed New Atlanta like an old black and white picture propped up in the corner of a green watercolor landscape.

Rock closed the hatch and hefted the box back onto his shoulder. He motioned to the west, then took her hand. They walked the length of the building then he dropped the box and took the bed roll from her.

Normally, her eyes were drawn to Rock when he was near, but she paid little attention to him as he set up an area in which to sit. The Onyx Zone was right there, less than half a mile away.

"It's so close."

"The whole southern border of Emerald is the wall, or should I say, fence. They weren't as worried about security of this border, probably because all the military compounds are right there."

Rock spread out a thin mat and then a blanket on top of it.

"I didn't realize we were living so close to it." Portions of the fence separating New Atlanta from the Onyx Zone were hidden by the encroaching forest, with only glints of razor wire scrolled at the top revealing there was a fence there at all.

He opened the cardboard box and took out two plates, cheese, crackers and a handful of small containers.

"Vegetation has taken over everything. I didn't expect it to be so overgrown."

"It's amazing where some things can put down roots. I've actually seen a tree growing out of a crack in the pavement of a parking lot, and whole neighborhoods completely covered by ivy." Rock got busy making up some plates while her focus switched from the Onyx Zone to the sunset.

He held a hand out. "Come here."

She sat opposite him with the food between them on the blanket he'd arranged. It was a perfect spot to watch the orange-soaked sunset. The air was noticeably cooler up there with an unobstructed breeze from the west fanning their faces.

Laila thought about her mom for what seemed like the hundredth time that day. The last message from Big Rock had felt different, as if her mother had been there, a silent listener to the exchange.

"Do you know anything more about our parents? I got the feeling my mom might have been there with your dad today, listening to my voice."

Rock's expression changed to one of thoughtful consideration. "Probably was."

"They must be hitting it off. You think there's more to this story?" Laila waggled her eyebrows. But, instead of getting a *yeah, right*, she got careful avoidance of her gaze. "What are you not telling me?"

He took a long, deep breath, then avoiding eye contact, pretended to be more interested in the view. "Your mom and my dad have been together."

"What? Oh my God. You're not my brother, are you?"

He laughed. His broad shoulders danced and tiny lines fanned out from the corners of his eyes. "No. I'm not your brother. I don't know what's going on now. What I know about was a long time ago, when we were in elementary school."

"Your dad told you?"

He nodded.

"When were you planning on telling me?"

He glanced at her quickly but remained silent.

"You weren't?"

"Wasn't sure how you'd react." He glanced over at her while she mulled over this new information.

"I don't remember my mom dating when I was a kid. As a matter of fact, I don't remember my mom dating, ever."

"From the sound of it, it wasn't really dating. It was more like fucking. My dad was kind of a ladies' man. He's slowed down in the past decade or so, but back then, he just went crazy trying to fill the hole my mom left behind."

"Do you think they picked up where they left off?"

He didn't answer her question right away, just stared out over the landscape. "Yeah, I do. Maybe it's a good thing he went a little crazy when we first got here. That hook-up so many years ago gave him the gumption to visit her now."

"That entire generation is a little crazy, if you ask me. I don't know if it's survivor guilt, or what, but every one of the original refugees seem to have some kind of issue."

"Including me."

"What do you mean?"

"Some might say my relationships with women might be an issue." He popped a cube of cheese into his mouth then held another one for her to take. She opened her mouth slowly, watching his gaze fall on her lips. "I don't know if you've noticed, but I'm a bit intense and controlling."

"I like how you are."

"Not always," he said with a sexy smile.

She took his hand and twined their fingers together. "Honestly, Rock, I wouldn't want you any other way. This way we live...I'm still adjusting, but you were right. The highs are peaks I didn't even know existed. The lows so excruciating, that, at the moment, I think I never want to feel like that again, but there's something about the brutal expression of who you are that's so honest and undisguised it's precious to me. For the first time in my life, I feel. I appreciate, endure, and savor moments in my life every day. Our time together has been an adventure, and I don't want you to be anything other than who you are."

Laila held Rock's devastated gaze, and her heart swelled with devotion.

He placed his lips lightly against hers. "I love you, Laila." As he spoke the words, his lips moved against hers, the air from those words entered her. It was like a physical transfer of love from his body to hers.

Leaning back, he smiled, squeezed her hand then let it go. From the box beside him, he removed the bottle of hard liquor he usually kept in his freezer. It was sweating from the heat and humidity of the evening. "Crap. I forgot glasses." He shrugged. "We'll have to drink from the bottle. Tonight is more of a feast for the eyes anyway." Rock sniffed the contents of the bottle and took a swig before holding the bottle up to her nose.

"Ugh." She put a finger up to signal Rock to hold on and popped a cracker into her mouth. Then, she chased it with a swig from the bottle. Her esophagus burned as she hissed her next intake of breath. "Damn. Nothing should taste that bad."

She handed the bottle to Rock. He laughed and took another swig. "What about your mom? Are the two of you close?"

"Yeah. She was pregnant with me when she got to New Atlanta. She thinks she was immune to the virus because she was exposed several times and never got sick."

"What's her job assignment?"

"She's cultivated the Wellness Center's herb garden and propagated plants for Circle City for almost twenty years. She was part of the initial group that pushed to beautify the Amber Zone, make it less depressing, more livable. She's got a green thumb like nobody's business."

Not liking the space between them, Laila moved some items out of her way and scooted closer. She rested her head on the outside of his arm, taking in the sun's brilliant descent. It was gloriously beautiful.

She'd changed so much in the short time they'd been companions. She'd learned to drive, to fight, to survive. Those skills were meaningful contributions to her life that would stay with her no matter what their future as a couple held. It was the legacy of their relationship. Wherever they ultimately ended up, her life would be better until the day she died.

The sun was a bright orange sliver just ready to disappear completely below the horizon. She took in a deep breath and sighed. It was a contented, lilting release of air that said more about how she felt than any words could.

"What are you thinking?" Rock asked.

"I'm thinking...I'm thinking I'm a bad ass now."

He examined her face with mahogany eyes that reflected the fiery glint of the sky. "Yeah, baby. You are." Rock wrapped his arm around her shoulders and pulled her tightly to him. His rough fingers caught her chin and lifted it to meet his gaze. His Adam's apple bobbed as he swallowed.

Euphoric from the depth of feeling she sensed from him, she sent hers right back and wished he could feel it, as she did. Even though he didn't have the same gift, they were tuned in to each other, connecting on yet another level. She was addicted, dependent on the sizzle charging the air whenever they were together.

He leaned in and kissed her softly, a tummy-turning brush of their lips. Then deeper. His tongue passed into her mouth as he aggressively demanded what he wanted from her without a word. He'd never kissed her like that before. There was more approval than sexual need in the kisses he usually gave her. The heat of his hand covered her back as he pulled her in closer. With the other, he gripped her ponytail, yanked so her face lifted to him.

The possession of his mouth covering hers submerged her in a place where there was nothing but him. Nothing but his heart drumming against her flattened breasts as he bound her tightly to him. His breaths were her air. His need became hers.

When the kiss broke, she opened her eyes to the hazy blue shadows of dusk.

Rock stood quickly. "Help me put this away before it's so dark we can't see where everything is." He offered her a hand and pulled her to her feet. A minute later, the snacks and plates were stowed away.

As she straightened from placing the last of their dinner remnants in the box, Rock stepped closer and wrapped an arm around her shoulders. The cool breeze was more noticeable when they stood. It licked the sweltering skin on the back of her neck, making her groan with appreciation.

Then, without a word, Rock slowly turned them in a different direction.

Laila scanned the new view, Circle City's tall buildings with rows of lit up squares. Almost every window on every building seemed to emit light. It was similar to the view she had from her bedroom window when she lived with her mom. Her gaze flicked to the area of her childhood home, where her mom was, but they were too far away to see any one-story houses. Still, she continued to search the darker section of the Amber Zone where she'd grown up. "It's beautiful."

Rock stood directly behind her and wrapped his arms around her, rested his chin on the top of her head. They took the scene in. The sun was long gone, and in the darkness, the twinkling lights of the city spread out before them.

"I used to come up here a lot. Just sit and watch the place where I wanted to be. Tonight is the first night I've been up here and not wished to be there instead." He gave her a squeeze. "Tonight there's nowhere else I'd rather be."

Laila closed her eyes and took in their scene on a more intimate level. His arms were cinched tight around her, heavy slabs of warm flesh providing safety and bringing contentedness. His cock pressed into her rear end. She wanted it inside her so badly she thought she'd die from the empty ache.

He grasped the hem of her tank top, pulled it slowly, gently over her head, and then turned her around to face him. His expression changed, hardened. His breathing was harsh, his gaze, a brand as it meandered over her body. He stepped back. With a tilted head and thoughtful smile, he admired her breasts. Then he returned, going down on one knee in front of her.

She laughed at the realization he was as tall as she in that configuration.

"Not even close," he murmured. "You're at least six inches taller."

Laila gasped. When he studied her, he saw every movement of every muscle, and her thoughts were somehow broadcast to him. "You're getting very good at that."

"I'm good at a lot of things." He lazily tugged her shorts down, put her hand on his shoulder, and lifting each foot, rid her of the material pooled at her feet.

Rock lifted from his kneeling position and walked the few steps toward their packed belongings. He pulled out a white washcloth and a bottle of water, twisted the cap off, and soaked the cloth.

She tensed slightly at the momentary cold shock as he laid the drenched cloth across her shoulders. Cool water dripped down the curve of her back. When the rag warmed, he returned to the bottle, soaked it and repeated the process until most of her body was wet.

She groaned at the sweet relief as Rock continued to cover different body parts with the soaked rag. The stiff wind buffeted her cool wet skin. She lifted her chin and breathed in the fresh summer night. The experience was invigorating. Goose bumps rose and sent a shiver down her spine. Goose bumps in the middle of summer; it took her breath away. She gulped in a gust of air.

She hadn't realized the burden of the relentless New Atlanta sun and what it did to her, until it had been lifted, rinsed off her by this beautiful man.

When he'd finished, he smoothed the damp cloth over her forehead, cheeks and neck then rolled it up and wrapped it around her nape.

She stood there for minutes, soaking in the experience, until the wind dried her.

Rock stepped closer and rested his hands lightly on her hips.

"Training?" she asked as he dipped his head to nuzzle behind her ear.

"Tonight, we're making a memory. One you might need someday. Think of it as a reserve of strength for when you need it most."

She'd think of this night often, whether she needed strength or not, because in that moment, in the darkness of OZ, she was cool, happy and utterly, hopelessly in love.

Rock pulled his T-shirt off over his head, revealing his gorgeously tanned torso, complete with meandering tattoos and enticing gold nipple rings. He worked at the front of his jeans and peeled them off. He stepped close, their naked flesh grazing each other's. She took him in hand, and he rumbled.

"You have a nice man-purr."

"Keep listening." He placed his hands on her shoulders and pushed her to her knees. "Show me how much you want my cock in your mouth, and I'll purr some more for you, peanut." His erection loomed in front of her, long and thick, pointing, as if telling her what to do.

She smiled at his bossy penis and gripped the base, cupping his balls with the other hand. Laila wanted nothing more than to show him how much she wanted to be a memory for him, too. She guided the mushroomed head to her parted lips, peeked her tongue out and teased the taut tip, investigating the flare of tight skin.

Rock gripped her ponytail tightly, tilting her head back. Their eyes locked in the deepening shadows of the night. His features were stormy. Intensity flooded her, electrified the air she forced into her lungs. He positioned the crest on her bottom lip, and slipped his thumb into the side of her mouth, using it to keep her jaws open. She groaned as he advanced the massive wedge of flesh into her mouth. "Relax, Laila. Relax your jaw, your throat. I want to see how far I can go." Even in this, he couldn't give her the lead. Pushing forward, he hit her soft pallet.

Rock canted his hips, moving forward and back as she stroked him with her tongue. Hooked like a fish, he held her head still as he fucked her mouth. "Relax your throat, peanut. I want deeper." His voice was guttural, like he was speaking with gravel in his mouth.

Her need to please him overruled the limitations of her body. Concentrating her effort, she angled her head and relaxed her muscles so he could fuck her throat.

"That's my girl," he said as he withdrew almost completely then advanced again even farther than he'd been before.

She had waited an eternity to be this for him. It was maddening how much of himself he held back from her still. She felt like she had something to prove. And she would. He would have to come back for more if she did this the way he needed it.

"Yes, baby. You're beautiful this way," he said, advancing again.

Tears streamed down her face. She groaned, vibrating the head of his cock as he paused at his deepest advance yet before pulling back again.

"Touch yourself, Laila. I want you to come with my dick in your mouth."

She was reluctant to remove her hand from cupping his balls.

He encircled her wrist with a hand. "Do it," he rasped.

With the first wisp of the pad of her index finger over her clit, she quivered. She was primed, ready to explode. Tensing her muscles and controlling it as much as she could, she locked her orgasm down. He wanted them to come together, and she could give him that. She whimpered and knew he was well aware what her issue was.

Rock gripped her hair harder, sped up his thrusts. "I'm going to finish. Just stay like this, baby." He growled his warning before the first spurt of come landed on her tongue.

Laila dragged her fingers over her clit hard and fast. She teetered on the brink, barely able to continue pleasuring herself as she determinedly sucked, and then swallowed. The smooth plane of his abdomen clenched with his release.

Rock was beautiful, with his head tilted to the night sky, brows furrowed, lips parted in a silent shout. When his eyes opened, he sought her out immediately. He beheld her kneeling before him, and then pulled out of her mouth.

She teetered, a bit dazed. Rock scooped her off her knees and laid her on the bedroll. He covered her, holding his weight on his forearms. His face hovered inches above hers. She found herself in this configuration almost daily. Her head buzzed a little as she looked up at him through slightly unfocused eyes. Their quick breaths mingled.

"I need more from you tonight, Laila."

"Okay," she breathed.

"You trust me?"

With a slight movement, she nodded. "I do."

"If you let me do what I wish, I'll bring you to a glorious place where your soul sings and your mind has no troubles. Where I am your world and you wouldn't have it any other way."

"Who would say no to that?" she whispered.

Leaning over, Rock kissed her. His lips were hot and gentle.

A new emotion flared to life from the man who had her caged with his massive body. She'd felt flashes of this alter ego before, but now, it was as if he'd opened a part of his heart to her, releasing the darkness inside.

Rock rolled to her side and propped himself up on his elbow. His touch was a butterfly kiss between her legs, bringing tiny twitches in the muscles of her thighs. She was still coming down from her orgasm.

When he slipped two fingers inside her, his gaze flared. The sticky, wet cadence of his finger fucking sounded in her ears. A corner of his mouth kicked up, giving her a peek of his straight, white teeth against the shadows. "Yeah, baby, you're wet." A third finger joined the first two. She gasped, tensed then moaned as his rhythm included a steady pattern of his thumb circling her clitoris.

Laila lifted her ass off the ground, seeking more of his nimble manipulation. Coiled with tension, she reached for her release, stretched, taut and straining.

"Give it to me," he growled. "Every bit of your attention, every thought. I want it all." He didn't skip a beat as he raised himself up and shifted slightly. "Put the soles of your feet together."

Her knees fell open as wide as they would go. He slipped a fourth finger into her. Her breathing neared hyperventilation. She clenched her ass, trying to raise it, trying to make room, trying to get more. "Please," she panted, her gaze never leaving him. The satisfaction he felt from that one word washed over her.

"Yes, baby. Give everything to me."

He fucked her with his hand, ignoring the attention her clit needed. His avoidance of it made her crazy. Again, she cried, "Please," as she teetered on the precipice of pure rapture, clenching and unclenching her rear and raising into the air, seeking more.

Slowly, gingerly, he slipped his thumb into her. She thrashed her head from side to side. Her body convulsed. Her vision tunneled.

She was in a frenzy when Rock leaned over and suckled her clit. Her muscles flailed as sweet, warm relief rolled over her swollen, hyper-aroused skin. The orgasm was a nuclear bomb, and she wailed at the violent pleasure. His rough hand covered her mouth, muffling the sound.

She shattered into a mindless collection of flesh and feelings, responding to the only thing in her world—him.

Chapter 15

Rock slipped into the locker room, switched out his T-shirt and splashed some water on his face. Preoccupied when he returned to the hallway, realizing Laila wasn't where he'd left her took him longer than normal. He turned a full circle, looking for her. There wasn't a soul in sight.

Dread trickled down his spine. This feeling was a common occurrence, a kind of automatic fear that surfaced when he didn't know where Laila was. With her, a residue of foreboding always clung to him. He recognized it as a symptom of his shame. His failure was tremendous, his scar too deep. It drove his every action.

He froze in his tracks, and those feelings intensified.

She stood on the far side of the gym engrossed in a conversation with Garret. Their heads were close together. They were having a deeper conversation than polite niceties about the weather.

Rock's anger flared. Hell fucking no. She hadn't learned a thing. He stalked through the gym doors, heading in their direction. They didn't notice him until he got within earshot, and when they did, they stopped talking. Funneling every negative emotion into an eye lock with Laila, he said, "Come on. This is not social hour."

She glanced at the National Guardsman standing next to her, and then back to him. "Well, I guess I'm done," she said.

She pulled her hand-held out of her pocket and handed it to Garret. "Put yourself in."

Those three words sparked disappointment. After all this time, she didn't get it, didn't hear his repetitive warning to avoid the Guard at all costs. It took every ounce of restraint to keep from picking Laila up, throwing her over his shoulder and carrying her out of there.

While they waited for Garret to punch in his digits, she scowled and mouthed. "Quit."

He sent his feelings of fury at her, and she blanched.

She got his message. Taking her unit back from Garret, she said, "I've got to go."

Garret grabbed her forearm, stopping her pivot in Rock's direction. "Wait. Is everything okay, training with him?" Garret glowered, baring his teeth and wrinkling his nose as if he smelled something offensive. "I mean…he hasn't hurt you or anything, has he?"

"Laila!" Rock barked before she had time to answer the idiotic question.

Laila turned to him and lifted her eyebrows. "I'll be there in a second." She waved at him. "Go!"

Rock straightened and crossed his arms over his chest. He wasn't going anywhere.

She pulled her arm from Garret's grip. "I'm fine. Listen, I've got to go. I'll shoot you a com soon."

By the time she'd said the last word, her focus was back on him. "What is your problem?" she grumbled, marching past him to the exit.

He followed, his long strides easily eating the distance between them. "Are you kidding? After all the bullshit you had to endure with Sydney, you're making yourself accessible to this guy?"

"It's not the same thing. Sydney wants in your pants."

"And you are naive if you don't think your friend Garret wants the same thing."

He grabbed Laila's arm and whipped her around. "Every time you talk to someone, especially a guardsman, you're exposing yourself to scrutiny. You don't want anybody looking at you too closely or thinking about you too much. It's better to just keep to yourself."

"You're the only person I've talked to for two weeks. It's not like I'm some kind of social butterfly or something." She yanked her arm out of his grasp and headed for the exit.

Rock waited until they were outside before he spoke again. "What were the two of you talking about?"

"Just trip details."

A lie, plain as day. "Then why wouldn't you continue to talk about the details when I approached?"

"Well, uh," she stammered.

"Don't." He opened the driver's side door and slid in.

She looked at him with sad eyes. "Don't what?"

"Don't lie to me again."

"Rock, I…" She hung her head and took a steady breath to calm herself. "Garret is not going to do anything to me. He's nice."

He pounded the steering wheel. "No! That's where you're wrong. None of them are nice. They're deadly, every last one of them."

Their respective doors to Rock's truck slammed simultaneously, and the drive home was silent. It wasn't their usual silence when they slipped from training to home, but the kind of tense silence that made two people feel a million miles apart.

They walked into Rock's house and headed to the bathroom as they did every day. He turned on the shower spray and tried another approach as he undressed her. "I love you, Laila. Any chance you take is unacceptable to me. You lie. You keep secrets from me. I wouldn't do that to you."

"Really? You wouldn't lie or keep secrets?" she yelled. Her face reddened and the tendons in her neck protruded. "Who's the Emily tattooed on your chest, Rock?" She jabbed his sternum. "And while we're at it, why haven't you fucked me yet, Rock? Because if you're not keeping secrets, I'd love to hear the answers to those questions."

She was angry at *him*? Steam billowed out of the stall, hazing the bathroom as Laila opened the glass door and entered, leaving him standing there.

* * * *

Rock joined Laila in the shower stall a few moments later. Her magnificent man stepped forward and pulled her into his arms. He held her close with a broad hand to her back. They stood together under the spray while he adjusted the temperature so it was comfortable and cool enough to feel refreshing after a long hot day of exertion. His tanned chest and nipple rings were in her line of vision. His heart pattered double time beneath her ear.

Even with her naked and in his arms, he was furious. She fell into his black, disapproving gaze. His Rock wall was up, but he couldn't block it all. The interior of the shower, which always seemed so tiny when she was in there with him, was charged with barely leashed restraint. She felt his anger and his lust. Her stomach flip-flopped in the same way as when she'd been a girl and known she was going to be in trouble when her mom got home. She was so emotionally dependent on his approval, it was ludicrous.

He turned her so her back was against his chest. "It's new," he said, holding a bar of soap under her nose and leaning forward to smell it with her. He placed it in her hands, and then positioned his over hers, rolling the bar and creating suds in their joined grasp.

He washed her first with economical and decidedly non-sexual contact. When it was her turn to wash him, she took her time, massaged the bubbles from his neck, across his broad shoulders and down to his narrow waist. She re-loaded with soap and slid her slippery fingers over the rock hard curves of his ass. To escape his focus and maybe get a glance at the cock and balls she washed, she dipped her head.

She didn't know if she could soothe the savage beast or if she even wanted to try. There was something magnificent about Rock when his worry escalated and righteous indignation ruled him. He wouldn't budge from his prime directive, keeping her safe. It was his best and worst quality. Laila stroked her slick two-handed grip to the bulb at the top of his cock. And down again, starting a slow, double-fisted rhythm.

What remained of his Rock wall crumbled piece by piece, and she merged with the man behind the facade more intimately. Her blood pressure rose and her face heated with the influx of his feelings. He was tied up in knots, crushed by her behavior and burdened by tension only gaining in magnitude. She would liberate him from his burden, give whatever he needed to ignite what he bottled up and rid him of the explosion building inside. She wasn't a hundred percent sure how to do that, but he wasn't complaining about her pumping fists gliding over his soapy erection.

"Turn around. Put your hands on the wall and take a step back."

She reluctantly obeyed, flattening her hands against the glass in front of her.

After the soul searching she'd done only that morning, she knew only one response would make either of them happy. "Do what you have to do." Before the last word left her lips, Rock swatted her ass. She yelped her surprise.

"Secrets between us are unacceptable." His palm connected again.

"Okay." She closed her eyes and hung her head. The sharp crack of flesh against flesh echoed inside the glass walls of the steamy cubby.

"I haven't been tough enough." Her legs trembled as his next blow connected. "I haven't given you the consequences I should have." His words sounded as if they were coming from a great distance. "I'm not going to make that mistake anymore."

His disappointment hurt more than any spanking ever could. "I'm sorry, Rock. I wasn't thinking."

"Not thinking is going to get you killed." He continued to pelt her rear and the back of her thighs. Her skin was on fire. Her ears buzzed. She was high. She closed her eyes and the rest of the world fell away. There was nothing except her jumbled thoughts, and the man who stood behind her. She'd gladly withstand whatever he dished out. Then they could move on from that afternoon. She groaned into her dark world. The rhythm of the swats faltered.

"Yes, peanut. You're there." Her punishment ended. She attempted to straighten, but he closed in behind her before she could. His hard body skimmed the back of hers. A bar of soap thudded to the tile floor. Rock inserted a soapy finger into her ass and twisted it around. "I'm not going to allow you to get yourself killed, Laila. It's just not going to happen," he murmured next to her ear. "You ready for me, peanut?"

Laila moaned and then cried out as he added another finger, scissored them and stretched her while gliding his fingers in and out.

He withdrew, wrapped a forearm around her and pulled her farther away from the wall. He kicked her feet apart and nestled his cock at her anus.

She cried, "Please, Rock."

"Please what, baby? Please keep you alive? Please show you the error of your ways? Please help you learn how not to get yourself killed?" He pushed into her. When he was completely rooted inside, he stilled. "That's what I'm doing, peanut. I'm teaching you a valuable lesson. And you need to learn it."

He gripped her hips, the pads of his fingers digging into her flesh, and lifted her until she was on tiptoes, continuing to advance and retreat with his soapy penis. When he began to pump, it was hard and fast, filling her to the edge of pain and then withdrawing until the ringed muscles of her anus traveled over the curiously taut skin around the head of his cock.

He wrapped his arms around her, one hand landing on her breast, the other low on her belly, holding her in place so she didn't surge forward as he pumped into her over and over. Her legs buckled, but his forearms kept her in place.

His lips were close to her ear, and Laila's scrambled mind latched on to his quick grunts accompanying every balls deep thrust.

With one last burgeoning push, he filled her with jets of hot come. He pulled out unceremoniously and let her go. She fell to her knees and searched his face, hoping she would see the approval she so desperately needed. She didn't. Though, most of his stress had washed down the drain, it didn't seem like he wanted to let it go. After every other time he'd punished her, they would revert to their easy intimacy. Tonight, he withdrew from their enmeshed relationship, and she wanted nothing more than to get back into his good graces, to be his "peanut" again.

"Don't lie to me again." He turned off the water.

"I'm sorry, Rock."

"So am I, peanut. So am I." He left her there on the shower floor.

She lay there for a while, buzzed and exhausted, before she finally pulled herself up and stepped out.

Rock grabbed a towel and tossed it to her. "Get dressed."

He had already put his shorts and T-shirt on. "I'm going to start dinner." He turned and left without another glance, leaving her standing there, dripping and stunned.

Her stomach roiled and she had to force herself not to cry. Laila snagged the clean, oversized T-shirt from the vanity, and tugged it on while walking out the bathroom door.

Downstairs, Rock moved around the kitchen proficiently, and none of the malice she'd seen in his gaze remained, until he looked up and found her there. Laila stood stock still as he considered her. His eyes could be so warm and welcoming or frighteningly polar. Today, she needed a parka to bear the look. It was the first time she'd been a victim of the icy stare he gave others.

He motioned for her to sit at the island. "You do realize I pick up on the fact you lie right to my face, don't you?" he asked calmly.

It pissed her off that he was talking to her that way, so calmly, as if she were a mental patient or something. "Yes."

"The dancing around subjects, leading me to other topics, and thinking I don't know exactly what you're doing insults my intelligence." He stepped forward and gripped her chin, raising it so their gazes met. His stare bore down on her, a physical weight pegging her in place. "Why would I make love to a woman who doesn't respect me enough to be truthful?"

Near tears, she pressed her lips together so he wouldn't see her lower one quiver. There was no correct answer to his question.

"And then I ask myself, why is fucking me, a man you have no respect for, so important to you?" He stepped away then, resuming his dinner prep and leaving her feeling detached from him both physically and emotionally. "Until you completely understand who I am, how I am, and what I'll expect from you, you're far, far away from where you need to be before I fuck that pussy."

Her self-confidence wavered. She licked her lips, trying to moisten them while her heart tripped.

"I don't think you know the first thing about love, about devotion, and certainly not about loyalty. You need to get a clue." He swept his fingers through his shaggy hair, looking as if he was trying to stall what came next. With his hands on his hips, he looked around the room, at the ceiling, everywhere except at her and sighed. "I haven't fucked the living shit out of you a thousand times by now because—" He stilled and cocked his head, and then shook it as if in resignation. "I don't want to get you pregnant."

Laila was stunned first, crushed second. In this world, a baby was the ultimate privilege, especially for people who grew up Amber like they had. The words constituted the worst insult ever flung her way and hurt her more than any physical wound ever could. "Would that be so bad?" she whispered.

"Yes. Right now, I'm more concerned about making sure you're one hundred percent informed about what I want from you before I even consider that. I thought you were almost there, that you got it. But now, I'm not sure."

"What else could you possibly want from me?" Her raised voice was high and thready. "I've already told you my most important secret, spent every second of every day with you. You take my fucking tampons out for God's sake, Rock. What else do you want?"

"I found out about your secret only after I'd practically figured it out anyway. And, you're still holding other things back from me. I'd bet money the information you're holding on to is enough to get you killed."

When she didn't deny his statement, he took another step from her and raked a hand through his hair. "By holding back on me, you're telling me you're not all in. You're not ready."

"What I keep secret is barely anything. I am ready. I just don't know how to prove it to you."

"You prove it through actions, and your actions shout loud and clear that complete trust between us is"—his face turned icy—"lacking."

In that moment, Laila realized just how fed up he was.

"You've got to be able to do the simple shit before we can move on to the rest. Once you're mine, you're mine, every last fucking molecule of you, however and whenever I want. And right now, you have no idea what that entails because you can't commit to openness and honesty between us, let alone anything else more significant. I'm not planning on changing who I am or what I want from you. It's you who has to adjust, if this is going to work. So, no, you being pregnant right now is not a good thing."

Laila's heart squeezed.

"This is me being honest. I'll always be honest with you."

Her throat tightened. Oh fuck no. She was not going to cry. "I'm sorry. I didn't know you'd thought this out so well."

"Now you do."

Laila was speechless.

"It's not just the Resistance secrets holding us back. This relationship will not progress until you let your guard down enough to have an up-close-and-personal conversation with me. Share our histories, our hopes, our fears. You know nothing about me." He pressed his palm to his chest. "Do you realize, you've never asked me when my birthday is, or how old I am? You've never asked me what my favorite food is or, better yet, walked around the counter and cooked with me."

He was right. She had been holding back more than just a few tidbits of information. Her five years of being a social pariah and the only person in her world had screwed her up in subtle, unnoticeable ways layered one upon another. She'd been living life alone inside her head for so long, she'd become disconnected.

He knew everything about her, had taken the time to study her, ask her questions. He'd put so much effort into getting to know her, truly know her, he could accurately decipher her body language and practically read her thoughts, including how she felt in any given moment.

She loved him. Why hadn't she made any efforts to do the same?

"At this point in my life, it's more important for me to connect here"—he tapped his temple—"than here." He cupped his junk.

Before she could say anything, he shook his head. "Don't get mad. Just think about it. What I want for us could be earth shattering. I won't settle for anything less. Not even for you."

He was going to tell her he didn't want her anymore. Simply considering having to return to her life, the way it was before she'd met him, made her feel as if the floor was crumbling beneath her feet. He'd become such an intrinsic part of her life. The thought of losing him, of losing their constant connection, scared her.

Laila gathered her dignity, lifted her chin and with a mangled heart, walked out of his house. The trip across the street was a blur. She checked behind her as she reached her front door. There was no sign of Rock. He hadn't followed.

She'd hoped he had.

She stepped inside, locked the front door behind her and took the stairs to her bedroom. The late day sun slanted into the room, lighting up the floating dust motes and splashing bright quadrangles of light on the pale yellow duvet covering her bed. She nose-dived onto it, and hugged her pillow as the spongy mattress shaped itself to her curves.

She'd been too focused on what she hadn't been getting, his dick, and what that meant and the *Emily* tattooed on his chest and what that meant.

Eyes closed, she tried to make sense of her current circumstances. He wasn't wrong. Her years in Sapphire had taught her to keep her mouth shut. Any poorly chosen word could be used against her, or twisted by changing the inflection, altering the tone. It was a short jump from prejudice to hatred and too easy for anybody to whisper her name in a Guard's ear.

That's how Sapphire and Emerald operated. They were a society of sycophants, robots scared to be who they truly were for fear of rubbing someone the wrong way. The consequences could be deadly. They all were so incredibly tense and scared, it altered the way humans interacted with each other. There, a room full of people was still an isolated place. It was sad how they'd evolved through some kind of warped version of survival of the fittest, where the fittest were those who conformed. What once was a species that felt free to express themselves, love one another, and had the courage to fight for what was right had boiled down to this society of terrified souls trapped in a shell of conformity.

Fear paled every experience, muted joy, impeded love. How could a person love when they were too afraid to show themselves to someone else? Her distance was instinctual. It was self-preservation.

The strategy was exhausting, and she was very, very tired of all of it.

Laila dozed in the space where the mind lingers between consciousness and sleep until she gave in and let sleep take her.

Chapter 16

"Do you like the life we're living here, Laila?" Rock's words pulled Laila out of her slumber. She poked her head from beneath the sheet, still groggy from too little of the restless sleep she'd been able to manage. He stood in the bedroom doorway, looking as if he'd also tossed and turned throughout the night. Maybe soul searching, like her.

"It's time, maybe past time for me to put all my cards on the table and show you how this relationship will work, if it works at all."

Panic crawled up her throat. She beat it down and spoke as calmly as she could. "What do you mean, if it works at all? Rock we've come too far—"

"No. I'm more controlling than I've ever been before, and I was a fuck of a lot back in the Amber Zone. I'm not so sure you can accept me this way."

"You know I can. I love you, Rock."

He shook his head. "I know I was hard on you yesterday. You have no idea, peanut, what I'm capable of, what I find exciting. It's time you find out." His troubled gaze fixed on something over her shoulder. "If you know what I am, what fucked up shit I need sometimes just to feel anything at all, all the deviant shit I'll need from you, you can make a more informed choice about whether you want to be with me." He sat on the bed with his back against the headboard. She shifted and laid her head in his lap, looking up at him. "But first, I need an answer. Do you like your time with me?"

"Yes. Every minute. I crave it when we're apart."

"Do you think about the things I do with your body after we're done, re-living them, over and over?"

"Yes."

"So do I. Whether I'm in the thrill of the moment, or remembering it later, it's in those times I feel most alive. I do what I want. Touch what

I want. And yes, do things for you that you can do for yourself." He grasped her hand and squeezed. "I've *lived* these past weeks. And so have you. Every moment with you reminds me life looks beautiful, smells beautiful and feels beautiful. I want to give that to you too. I want you to feel things you've never felt, taste whatever I chose to put on your tongue and experience every physical sensation. I'll wake you up just to watch the sunrise, and do things to your body just so I can hear your cries. I'll give you your highest highs, lowest lows, and together, we'll experience every range of emotion doing it."

"To me, this"—he motioned between them—"what we have between us, is living. It's who I am. If you're waiting for me to let up, to watch you less closely, to stop taking care of you, it won't happen. I will always be this way." He peered down at her, a sad smile on his face.

"I'm scared, Rock. I've been alone, building walls for so long. I'm scared I'll give you everything and lose myself. I'm scared what will happen to me if you really know me inside and out. What if I'm not what you want? I'm scared I can't give you everything you need."

Rock's expression softened. A sad smile curved his lush lips. "I thought you'd figured it out already."

"Figured what out?"

"You're not alone. Fear, Laila, is what makes me who I am. My utter terror of losing you…" He shook his head, cleared his throat. "It rules me. I was already extremely protective before, when I was in the Amber Zone. Now, it's so much worse. It's fucking ridiculous." He let out a sigh of resignation. "I can't stop it. I've tried. I was miserable."

"What you want from me is a difficult way to move through life. Yes, it's exciting, exhilarating even, the way you have of keeping me slightly off balance and guessing your next move. But—"

"I know it takes a herculean effort to be what I need." He cupped her face and his loving expression melted her fear. "I promise the reward of what we're building will be beyond all of your most fantastic expectations. I can't put into words how special it is to share a bond as strong as the one waiting for us. The only way to understand it is to experience it firsthand."

He fell silent and seemed to fall into a memory. She searched his face. He was worried, but his expression didn't show it. "There will be times when you absolutely hate me and that's okay."

"I could never hate you."

"Let me give you a true and honest taste of my most intense urges. It could ease your fears of the unknown, at least in the physical part of our relationship. I won't hold back. Consider it a crash course."

This was it. They'd leave this room with everything, or nothing. What if she couldn't be what he needed?

"All I ask for is your trust. I'll never give you a reason to doubt me. And the connection, it only gets stronger…better with time. Give everything to me, Laila, and I promise you'll be loved, cared for and never have a day of boredom for the rest of your life."

He waited for everything he'd said to sink in.

"I've already made my decision. Did it yesterday. And, for the record, there's not much I wouldn't already do for you."

Relieved, Rock took in a breath. "Yeah?" He stood, bringing her to her feet and pulled her into his arms. "You need to trust me in everything, Laila."

"I do trust you, Rock." The whispered words were a fundamental truth, and she held his gaze so he could read it in her eyes. Carnal energy radiated from him, crashing into her like the waves of a storm. She didn't sense any menace. No, the energy that swamped her as he stepped into her personal space was pure sex.

He stood so close, her chest skimmed his each time it rose and fell with the deep swells of air she rapidly sucked in and forced out of her lungs.

She'd wanted Rock to make love to her since the day they'd met, but this wasn't the Rock she pined for. There was something or someone in him now she'd never fully seen. This different man, this force of nature, was in control. She froze in full fight-or-flight mode. He'd become the dangerous unknown. Laila swallowed through a dry throat made tighter as Rock curled his massive hand around the front of her neck, gripped it firmly.

"You still trust me?"

Even though he completely overshadowed her, she didn't feel scared. She felt small. His heavy-lidded black stare gleamed with desire.

"Yes. I trust you."

A slow, almost diabolical smile transformed his face.

"Wait for me here." He turned and left the room. His footfalls were slower and heavier than usual. He'd said his peace and hadn't been turned away. The composure she sensed from him now was at complete odds with the thrill shooting through her veins and electrifying her senses. The racket inside her body made the stillness of the bedroom disconcerting.

Rock returned five minutes later with an armful of items, and dropped them unceremoniously on the dresser by the door.

"Come here." He held a faded red bandana in his hand.

Laila kicked up her chin as she approached him. Her stomach performed a dizzying waltz within her.

Rock circled her, placed the soft fabric over her eyes and tied it tightly. His clothes rustled with his movements, and she anticipated his touch as he approached her again.

"Last chance to back out," he said next to her ear, making her jump.

"Bring it on," she whispered. He was her Rock. She could withstand anything he wanted her to, as long as he was with her. Her throat tightened as she worked through her heightened emotions. In that instant, all she wanted to be was his Laila. God, she was dumb with the drive to please this man. Anticipation was a presence in the room, hanging heavy in the air, its weight conspicuous against her skin. Its potency made her lightheaded as it threaded through her blood.

His hands had been absent from her for at least a minute. Laila straightened and her muscles tensed. "Rock?" The calloused pad of a finger ran from the nape of her neck and bump, bump, bumped over her vertebrae down the length of her spine. She shivered.

Yes, she'd endure anything for this man. That vow was easy to keep as Rock's hot mouth closed around a nipple. She threw her head back at the relentless suckling and nipping until he pulled free of her breast with a pop. She waited, breathless, for his next touch and he teased her with the absence of it. A cool breeze wafted over her wet areola. She gasped as the air tightened her already hard nipple and raised goose bumps on her skin. Then, cool metal exerted gentle pressure on the distended peak. Whatever it was continued to tighten until it was attached to the bud of her nipple, which swayed slightly from the movement of whatever dangled.

She groaned. "It hurts."

He gave no indication he'd heard her at all. Suddenly, the process began again on her other nipple. The suction he applied with his mouth was almost painful. Then the breeze that seemed to travel down her spine instead of over her incredibly hard nipple. He took his time placing the clamp, and then he set it in motion so the swaying of the weight teased her flesh.

He kept her guessing, unexpectedly touching her in different places with his tongue, with his fingers, with the rasp of his whiskers. Then, he stepped in close behind her, and his fat cock wedged between them. His muscled arms surrounded her as he skimmed his hands over her abdomen and between her legs. A quick swipe to her clit, and then his hand was gone.

He bent her over the bed, until her breasts landed on the cotton duvet and covered her with his body. He breathed loudly in her ear and his significant weight crushed her into the mattress, squeezing the air from her lungs. "Don't move."

The massive body on top of her disappeared. His warmth at her back dissipated. She couldn't hear him, couldn't see. She felt him towering over her and imagined him there with his arms crossed over his chest, absorbing the sight of her bent over the bed, exposing her private places.

"I've held back so much of myself because of the mission," he said. "And because I wanted to be sure. You have been bad, so bad. Not just once, but on several occasions. I let it go." He nudged her feet even further toward the corners of the bed. Her skin thrummed underneath the brushes of his fingers as he tethered her ankles. "But now, I'm sure. And you say you're sure. Are you still sure, Laila?" he asked as he pressed her into the mattress with a gigantic hand on her back.

"Yes," she breathed.

He guided her arms over her head. "Keep them there," he growled close to her ear. She grasped the smooth sheet under her hands and held on tight. "Good girl. I have a backlog of discipline waiting for you." His lust had come alive when he'd spoken the word discipline, and activated hers. "When you make the disappointing decision to disobey me, to keep secrets from me, or put yourself at risk, you will have a punishment waiting for you in hopes that maybe you'll give your actions more thought the next time you're tempted to put yourself in harm's way."

He nudged the hard flesh of his cock between the cheeks of her ass, and pressed his chest to her back. "It's my reward for having to suffer your disobedience as much as it's deterrent for you. Sometimes, peanut, I'll punish you just because I feel like it, but on those occasions, you will be the ultimate winner, I promise." His breaths were labored and humid against her ear.

Rock pulled away, leaving her instantly chilly. A slight panic bubbled. "Rock?"

One of his fingers found the pucker of her ass, and he grunted softly. His fingers were between her cheeks, and then he inserted something small and cool into her anus. It only took seconds for the thing to start stinging, and then the burn began, making her want to curl in on herself. "What did you do? What is that?"

"It's just ginger. Don't worry, it won't have any lasting effects."

She groaned. "It's uncomfortable."

"You deserve it, don't you, Laila? You deserve to be punished for exposing yourself needlessly to the enemy."

"Yes." She cried out. "It burns. Please." She squirmed, unable to keep still with her insides going up in flames.

"Yes, love. I'll make it better. But not yet. The next time I catch you talking to Garret, I will make this punishment seem like playtime. Are we clear, Laila?"

"Yes, clear." She moaned. "Please!"

"Please what, baby?"

"Out! Please."

He inserted a finger into her rear and pulled the small thing out. Within seconds, she felt as if the ginger had never been in there at all. "Thank you." Her words were drowned out by the crack of his hand meeting her rear. The first impact was a sting, quick and sharp. Laila cried out in surprise and then again as his second swat heated her butt. She tried to roll away from him. An instinctual reaction to what she knew would become infinitely more pleasurable after a few more blows. His swats stopped, and he said in a warning tone, "Move again and I'll restrain your arms too."

Laila stilled and withstood the steady impact on her rear and the back of her thighs. She gripped the sheets desperately in an effort to tether herself to the room, but the spanking still took her to another reality. One where it was easy to let go of her worries. One where she could just…be.

"Listen, Laila. Listen to the music we're making. The crack of skin against the soft purr of your cries as the background. It's a beautiful sound, baby. One you'll long for someday."

She moaned in response.

He chuckled, and continued, seemingly unfazed by her retreat into her own existence. The violent pairing of his palm to her ass seemed to carry less sting. Then, just as suddenly as it began, the spanking stopped.

Her ears rang with a high-pitched tone and tears escaped her eyes, dampening the soft cotton sheet under her cheek. The rest of the world didn't exist. Nothing existed, except the sensations of the moment. Her thoughts were muddled, but one thing was clear. Rock radiated satisfaction and pleasure.

Her pulse throbbed, subtly pushing the skin covering her carotid with each thump. Her hands were unusually cool, her adorned nipples impossibly hard and trapped uncomfortably between the mattress and her body.

The pads of his fingers smoothed along the curves of her body, giving her chills. They blazed a trail up the inside of one leg and delivered feather-light touches over her engorged lower lips. God, she wanted him inside her. "Please, Rock."

"Shh. I know, baby. Now you know, too." He pinched her clit. "It's a suffering you need to understand, since you've insisted on defying me."

Rock's voice seemed far away. She hadn't heard him right.

"What?" Never in her life had she been so desperate. "Rock," she implored him. "Please." Her nails tore at the sheets.

"Please what, baby?"

"Take me now, please," she said between sobs.

"Remember this moment. Burn it into your brain, baby."

He was between her thighs, pouring more liquid on her ass. The crown of his penis nudged her there. He penetrated her in a super slow forward thrust until he was all in.

She floated, full to bursting, like a balloon.

He withdrew and pushed in again. "Fuck, yeah. You deserve all of me. Tell me you want all of me, baby."

"All of you." Her spoken words left her mouth, unbidden.

His cock retreated from her ass just long enough to stick a vibrator in her pussy. Then, his thick cock entered her again.

Rock curved around her. She felt as if she held all his weight. He pulled her ponytail, bringing her head back and exposing her throat. Wrapping his hand around her neck, he squeezed, making it difficult for her to take a breath. His lips were next to her ear. "Ask me for air, baby."

An act made almost impossible with his hand around her throat and the full weight of his body on top of her. She dragged in a breath and moaned. She had difficulty ripping her attention away from the vibrator bringing her to the brink of orgasm. Wheezing in another gulp of oxygen, she whispered, "Air. Please." He released her throat, withdrew his cock and thrust into her again. "Oh God! Rock!" She was suspended, so close to her climax. Her muscles froze. Rigid and strained, she was helpless, unable to do anything but focus on the orgasm just outside her grasp.

Dragging in another breath, she exploded with a bone-jarring climax that curved her body, giving him more of her ass. Her muscles shuddered and quaked through the longest, most intense orgasm she'd ever had. Only as the climax faded did she realize she was wailing.

Rock pounded her with piston speed and hammering strength. He dug his fingers into her hips. "Fucking beautiful," he cooed next to her ear. Then his hot seed flooded her ass.

Waves of love from this man and for him filled her heart. The life-altering moment was sweet and sacred. As close to the divine as she'd ever been.

A sob wrenched from her soul and came out her mouth. She was in ecstasy. She was home. The sudden relief and rightness of it ruined her. When she recognized the certainty she wouldn't have to be alone anymore, the certainty that he'd never leave her, she cried her relief. The keening sob she released sounded faraway as she drifted.

Rock was satisfied. He removed her blindfold, and she opened her eyes to the bright light of late morning bouncing off the yellow walls of her bedroom.

Filling her line of sight, he ordered, "Talk to me," as he unfettered her limbs.

"Uh." She blinked several times, trying to get her bearings. Rock's intense gaze roamed over her face.

"When you took away my ability to see, other senses became stronger." Her words were garbled. He straightened her from her bent over position. She was bone weary.

"Sorry for this, Meant to do it earlier," he said as he unclipped her nipples.

"Ahh!" Pain struck as the flow of blood started again.

Rock scooped her up, deposited her gently on the bed, and covered her with the light top sheet. He left her briefly then returned with a glass in hand. "Drink," he said, holding a glass to her mouth.

She was parched, and drank the whole glass before she lay back down and rolled to her side.

He climbed in behind her and cinched her close to him, conforming his body to hers. "Still mine?" he whispered into her ear.

"Mmm, always," she said as she drifted off to sleep.

Chapter 17

As Laila entered the women's rest room down the hall from her office in the Peacekeeper's Compound, she heard the sound of babies crying. It was faint but unmistakable. She turned right, toward the sound instead of entering a stall.

She stooped and listened intently. The crying came up through the vent blowing cool air.

It was an automatic action on her part to leave the bathroom and follow the sound. She opened the door of the emergency stairwell and listened again. Yes, definitely babies, plural, coming from below.

She descended the concrete stairs, trying to quiet the echo of her footfalls. The drab green walls in combination with the fluorescent lighting gave the stairwell an eerie vibe. Arriving at the first floor exit, she peeked her head out and found the building's lobby, quiet and empty. She popped her head back into the stairwell and looked around.

Tucked under the last flight of stairs was a door clearly marked as an emergency exit, stating an alarm would sound if opened. With her ear pressed against it, she heard muffled cries and happy squeals of older children. She stepped back. There shouldn't be children on the Peacekeeper's Compound. She stared at the emergency exit for only a few seconds more before she impulsively pushed the door open. No alarm sounded.

She stepped into the little vestibule and hopped past another door propped open with a chair. The stark white corridor was lined with doors. The sounds of children behind them filled the space. She crept forward, passing childlike scenes of animals and cartoon characters lining the walls.

This place looked like a daycare. Farther down, she passed a wall covered with construction paper kites obviously made by small hands. A child's name was printed on the tail of each. She made a quick count of rows and multiplied. Almost a hundred were displayed.

Next, a half-windowed wall gave a view of infants lined up in cribs. She peeked for a handful of seconds and watched the backs of two women wearing identical blue dresses moving from baby to baby, changing diapers.

A door opened further down the hall and her attention was ripped from the scene. A young boy, grinning a gap-toothed smile pushed through it, followed by another and another. The little men wore the same outfits and all had brilliant blue eyes and hair whiter than any she'd ever seen. Laila ducked into an unlocked door as a young woman followed the line of boys. Scanning the bunk bed lined room behind her, she released a breath of relief. She was alone. What the hell was she doing? She needed to get out. Popping her head quickly into the hallway, she found it empty. She made a beeline toward the emergency exit door and shot through it as quietly as she could.

Taking the steps two at a time, she reached her floor, and flew through the door to her office. Her heart thudded and blood whooshed in her ears as she hustled around her desk and sat. A couple little tasks for the Resistance, and she thought she was a spy. She was either brave as shit or totally insane. She had little experience with brave, so yeah...insane. She unclenched her fists from the arms of her chair. Her breathing eased up to the point it didn't sound like she'd been running. She had not been seen. She might be okay.

A faraway sound of a door closing had her tensing again, muscles rigid, poised to fight if she had to. But no one came.

All those children, mirror images of each other. And the dormitory lined with little beds and dressers. She tried to piece together who they were and why they'd been there and came up with zip.

Her little jaunt rattled her on a day she didn't need any surprises.

Everything had been so perfect when she'd left Rock. She fingered the choker he'd locked around her neck before they'd separated for the day and concentrated on re-gaining the cool confidence she'd built. However, that wasn't going to happen. It was almost time.

Laila left her tiny workspace as the sun set. She met Garret a quarter mile away, just outside the wooded area that lined the fence surrounding New Atlanta. They silently walked the tree line together.

Darkness solidified as they slid through the night, keeping the dark woods to their left. The air was considerably cooler than it had been, and

Laila was thankful. After a long, crazy day of juggling tasks and preparing for mission departure the next morning, she was running on fumes.

She and Garret didn't speak. She figured he was probably just as scared as she was. But she needed his protection, and his presence would prevent other Guardsmen who might see her out after curfew from bothering her.

She scanned the streets ceaselessly. They were deserted, as usual.

After walking almost an hour, they slipped easily into the Sapphire Zone through a well hidden part of the fence where the chain link was no longer attached to its pole, making it easy to peel the metal back and slip through. It seemed like she'd lived an extra lifetime since she'd been in the Sapphire Zone. In reality, it had only been a few months.

They continued to lurk in the shadows, skimming the city's outside wall and avoiding main streets and guard posts.

When they neared the rendezvous point, Garret forged ahead, and she followed in his wake through the overgrown vegetation to the fence line delineating New Atlanta from the Onyx Zone.

"Laila?"

She couldn't yet see the speaker. "Yes. Come on."

The woman approached. She eyed Garret, who wore his Guard uniform and had his rifle tucked under his arm. "You Garrett?" the shadowy woman whispered.

His eyes widened. Laila knew his thoughts. Anybody in connection with the Resistance who knew his name was dangerous to his wellbeing. He scowled at her. "Who are you?"

She approached him. "I have a message from your mother."

Garrett's spine straightened, an infinitesimal reaction to the mention of his mother. "She made me memorize and recite it in front of her before I left for the mission. She wanted to make sure I'd get it right."

Garrett smiled and his shoulders sank slightly. "All right."

She stepped forward, cradled both sides of his face and looked directly into his eyes. "I am gone from New Atlanta, my son. Jordan's relocation center will know where I've gone. Live safe and be well until we meet again." Then she went up on tiptoe, angled his face down toward her, and kissed him on the forehead. When she let go of his face, she stepped away and grasped Laila's hand.

Garret smiled down at her. "Thank you."

"You're welcome."

"We've got over an hour to walk," Laila whispered. "I have to let go of your hand. Holding hands is a dead giveaway you don't belong here."

Their hands slipped apart and they walked side-by-side out of the tree line. Garret closed ranks behind them.

They slinked silently through shadows and residential streets, until Garret split away from them without a word when they were near her home. The mystery woman's head swiveled endlessly as she stared wide-eyed at the magnificent houses sitting back from the street, like lazy giants hiding among the tall pines.

"Will we be going by Rock's house?"

The hair on the back of Laila's neck stood on end. This was wrong. This woman should not know Rock was an operative in the Emerald cell.

"You know Rock?"

She nodded.

"How?" Laila knew the answer to her question by the woman's change of energy. She became serene. The worry in her features smoothed. Her small, almost secret, smile followed a wild blush.

"I'm Journey. Rock was my roommate in Circle City."

Laila's stomach dropped. "Oh." The first day she'd spent with Rock, he'd told her he still loved this woman. She was a mouse. Her meek voice and non-threatening aura would trigger every one of his protective instincts.

Just thinking about Rock touching this woman like he touched her made her more than jealous. She felt violent, wanting to take Journey down with one of the moves Rock had shown her on the mats. "I was hoping I might get the chance to see him tonight," Journey said sheepishly.

"I don't think he's home." Soon they approached Rock's house. "Sorry." Laila pointed at the dark, empty structure. "His truck isn't there."

Journey deflated. "Oh." She looked pitiful, like she was going to cry.

Laila softened. "I'll tell him I saw you."

She pointed to her own driveway on the other side of the street, and they walked together in the shadows to her back door. They entered the house without turning on a light, and Laila guided Journey to the basement. She flipped on the lights. "We can talk freely here."

"How is he? Does he seem happy?" Journey asked.

"Uh, happy is not the word I'd use to describe Rock. Bossy seems more accurate."

Journey giggled. "Then, yes, it sounds like he's happy. Sometimes it's hard to tell what you're going to get with him. I'd heard he still wasn't doing well, but it's been almost two months since I've seen Big Rock." Journey tilted her head and looked Laila up and down. "It seems like things have changed." Journey's gaze landed on the choker around her neck. She took in a quick breath, her jaw dropping open. The mousy woman slowly lifted her hand and fingered the heavy chain Rock had given her. "He loves you," she said, lowering her hand and meeting Laila's gaze. "I'm so glad." She said the words in a sweet, soft voice. Journey had a gentle soul. It was her vibration, and it seemed absolutely impossible to dislike this little girl-woman.

"His father told me he's been inconsolable and lonely since Emily died."

"Emily. The name tattooed on his chest, Emily?"

Journey pursed her lips. "He hasn't told you?"

"No."

"He will."

"Why don't you tell me?"

"It's not my story to tell."

Laila was about to say something brilliant to try to get Journey to spill, but she didn't get the chance.

"You're still a little confused, aren't you?"

"Confused?"

"Yeah. About Rock. Not totally sure what's going on…. Con-fused," Journey said slowly.

"Yeah."

"When I landed on his doorstep," Journey said as she walked into the little nook that held her cot, looking at the items Laila'd left to help her pass the hours. "I didn't know it at the time, but I had won the lottery. It took almost a year to truly trust what I'd fallen into."

Journey looked at her speculatively. "Has he fucked you yet?"

"Not in the traditional sense, no."

Journey smiled, and Laila interpreted it in the worst possible way. Maybe she could scrape up a little dislike for the woman.

"Let me give you a piece of advice. Stop trying. Just accept what he gives you."

"I'm not sure I understand."

"He needs to make the decisions. If you love the man, which it looks like you do, you just have to go with it. Just submit and see what happens."

Laila's stomach twirled at the thought. She'd done that just recently.

"He already thinks of you as his, or you wouldn't be wearing that." She motioned to the chain tightly encircling Laila's neck.

"Do you have one?"

"No. Never. I was his roommate. He took care of me, loved me. But he wasn't in love with me. "I'll spend the rest of my life looking for someone who will love me like"—she pointed to Laila's choker again—"that." She shrugged. "So far, no luck." She picked up a book Laila had left there. "Thank you for this. I don't think I've held a paper book since I was in elementary school."

"You're welcome."

Journey sat on the end of the bed. "Just remember that man is happiest when he's taking care of his girls, or in this case, girl. Surrender and he'll take you places you didn't even know existed." Journey smiled. "You're going to end up doing it anyway, so you might as well cut to the chase."

Laila smiled back. "That sure, huh?"

Journey nodded. "That sure."

Laila intentionally brightened her tone. "I didn't know if you'd be staying here or taking the speaker and going somewhere else, so I covered the windows down here. No light shows to the outside."

Journey lifted her arm and showed off a sapphire tattoo so new it hadn't stopped bleeding. "As soon as I find out who I am, I'll be leaving. I'm taking a woman's place in Sapphire, assuming her identity. She's leaving to start a new life in Onyx, and I'm starting a new life, too. I'm not sure of the details yet so I'll be staying here until I'm contacted." Journey sighed, and her expression fell. "You're leaving tomorrow." Her eyes were sad. "It would have been nice to have a sister again."

"We will be back, Journey. You'll see both of us again."

Journey gave her a polite smile and didn't reply.

"What?"

She shook her head. "Just in case. I need him to know something." Journey's eyes watered as she drew in a breath through her nostrils and let it out of her mouth slowly. "It's personal. I totally understand if you don't feel right about it."

"You can trust me to deliver it."

Chapter 18

Rock didn't like being apart from Laila, even if it was for only a night. Since her final preparations kept her working late, he'd found himself back at OZ, giving the trucks the once over. He loaded the gasoline additives himself as an added precaution in case someone was working against them. Now, he lay on his bedroll with a bird's eye view, making sure there was no sabotage, and keeping an eye out for Laila. A part of him hoped she was having as much difficulty being without him as he was. Maybe she'd make the trip to the compound late at night instead of early the next morning. Either way, the fact he was getting no sleep unless Laila was beside him was becoming glaringly obvious.

Her presence had become a habit. It didn't matter that he knew where she was and had reasons to be away from him. No. It didn't matter at all. He touched his earbud. "Call Laila."

She didn't answer. He waited a full minute before he touched it again. "Com Laila." He paused. "Are you okay?"

He waited. He'd instructed her to sleep with her earbud in tonight since they'd be separated. His chest became incrementally tighter with each silent minute he waited to hear back from her.

Finally, when he couldn't stand the silence any longer, he stood, giving up his vigil and deciding instead to make sure Laila was okay. Even if she only slept through his attempts at contacting her, making sure she was safe was imperative if he wanted to get in a few hours of sleep before leaving the city.

The drive to their neighborhood was quick, and he pulled into her driveway. Her front door was locked. He didn't hesitate and shouldered it hard until the jamb gave way and the door flew open.

He took her stairs two at a time. "Laila? It's just me," he warned. By the time he reached the top, though, he knew she wasn't there. The house gave off the ambiance of vacancy, the sheer silence of emptiness.

He strode across the street to his home and entered through the front door. He checked both upstairs and down. She wasn't there either.

The speaker that had been reporting the goings on, or lack thereof, in Morgan's office for the last two months was gone. He stared at the empty spot. His heartbeat boomed in his chest, and dread, descended, cloaking him with a darkness so complete, he wasn't sure he'd feel the light of day on his face again.

He stood in his kitchen for an hour, on edge and trying not to jump to conclusions about her wellbeing. As with most people born Amber, staying positive was a daily struggle. He'd never been the kind of man to look at the glass as half full, but tonight, he tried. Just because he wasn't with her, watching her, protecting her, didn't mean she would be dead in the morning, right?

He shook his head. God, she was so much like Emily. A mischievous spirit with a Technicolor soul. The heart wants what it wants, and Rock was never attracted to women who were too easy. There was no satisfaction in achieving their level of intimacy if all of it was simply handed to him. A relationship like theirs meant so much more when it was worked for, earned through trial and error, sweat and tears. This was certainly the case with Laila.

Unfortunately, this particular trait of hers left him tied up in knots. He hadn't slept, and knew he wouldn't. Not there, waiting for her to show up. And, if he didn't sleep before they left the city walls, he'd be putting them both in jeopardy.

Rock strode across his yard, got into to his truck and headed back to Oz. He'd at least try to cram in a few hours before their go time.

As he drove to the compound, he could barely breathe through his tight chest and sudden rigidity of his muscles. He didn't know whether to be distraught or furious at her disappearance, but the intensity of all the negative emotions clamoring for expression left him mindless and aggressive, like the barely leashed attack dogs the Guard used to terrorize the population.

When he finally lay on his bedroll underneath the stars again, he reviewed his day. He was certain she wasn't being defiant to gain his attention. Not on such an important night.

She hadn't been angry the last time they'd been together. They'd made love after he'd given her the choker. She had been nervous, however. At the time, he had chalked it up to anticipation for the start of the mission. Now he knew differently.

There was only one option that made any sense to him whatsoever. She was finishing her work for the Resistance. If this was true, whatever she was doing was dangerous, and she didn't want him involved. He sorted through a blitz of possible scenarios, each worse than the one before. His blood pressure rose, the rapidly moving blood heating his cheeks.

He'd told her she was finished with her Resistance work. He was dismayed and proud she was able to hide the fact she wasn't. She'd learned well the skills he'd taught her. A smile flickered through him, and his heart swelled with intense love for the woman who tried to protect him. She would rather sacrifice herself and suffer his consequences than put him in a dangerous position.

Sweet, but wrong. Very, very wrong. The rest of his early morning hours contained a non-stop struggle to gain rest when his mind couldn't slow down enough to allow sleep.

As night turned into day, unfamiliar workers streamed in through OZ's checkpoint. They set up a stage with a podium centered in front and chairs behind. Morgan was making their departure into a spectacle. It fit his pattern. Morgan's portrayal of himself as Mr. Patriotic was what made him a shoe-in to take over for his father. It had been and still was his cover, although nobody believed it much anymore.

Rock continued to check the time, waiting for Laila to show up, while a flurry of activity centered around their trucks.

Concern transformed to torment after the sun was fully up and their departure time drew close. He was on the verge of panic-fueled rampage when, finally, he spotted her walking toward the checkpoint to get into OZ. He checked the time again. She'd cut it way too close. They were scheduled to leave in less than half an hour.

When the Guard waved her through, he collected his bedroll and slung it over his shoulder. Before leaving the roof, Rock looked north, toward the Circle City's tall buildings. He'd spent so many hours on that roof, staring at the place he'd so badly wanted to be. Knowing he would never be back, he burned the moment into his brain and said a final goodbye to everyone he'd leave behind there.

When he reached the ground, he wasn't sure where Laila had gone, so he moved to the trucks where they were lined up and waiting to leave.

He finally caught sight of her exiting the main building, geared up from head to toe, including the Kevlar vest he'd taken off her their first day of training. His heart ran the emotional gamut. Relief, anticipation, anger—they were all there vying for center stage so they could play out.

One of the video stream reporters stepped up to Laila, shoving a microphone in her face. She was gracious, answering questions for a few minutes, until Morgan approached her and led her up the few steps to the stage. She sat in a chair behind him, along with Sydney and Garret.

Morgan, dressed in his usual military uniform, said, "Good morning," into the microphone, and the small crowd silenced.

This event was staged more for the video feed than anything else. Morgan couldn't pass up the opportunity to tell the people of New Atlanta how much he cared about this country.

Rock tuned out the General's blabber and focused on Laila. She looked uncomfortable, twisting her hands while they rested in her lap. She smiled when she caught sight of him and that seemingly innocent action triggered something in him.

Instantly, he was angry. She sat there and fucking smiled at him as if she hadn't been out all night breaking her promises. She thought she'd pulled one over on him, snuck behind his back. Like Emily had.

With that thought, his rage found its stride, and his patience found its end.

She flinched under the cold stare he pinned on her. The slight smile and pink cheeks she'd had when she first exited the building transformed into pale trepidation.

Minutes later, the small crowd was clapping in response to Morgan's send-off. Laila shook Morgan's hand and descended the steps, heading toward him.

She took a steady breath and schooled her expression into a pleasant smile as she approached. "Good morning."

He glared at her, sending her every ounce of disapproval he possessed.

"Please, this is a big day for me, Rock."

He ground his teeth together, and then he nodded. "Hold." He turned and pounded the pavement to the lead truck, where Garret and Sydney waited.

"We're a go if you are," Rock said to Garret.

Garret gave him the thumbs up. "Copy that."

Rock returned to their truck and got in on the driver's side. Laila, however, did not. With both hands dangling from the steering wheel by their fingertips, Rock lowered his forehead to meet them and sighed. "Now you hold?" he said into the empty cab, scooted across to the passenger seat and jumped out the passenger door.

"Come on." He held a hand out to Laila. When she advanced, he gripped her around the waist and lifted her into the cab.

They didn't say a word to each other as they proceeded through the Emerald checkpoint and out of New Atlanta. Rock intended to stay that way. He knew if they spoke now, it would dampen this experience for her, and this expedition was something she'd been working her whole adult life for. No, he would not do that to her.

The strange satisfaction he got from knowing he could discipline her later was absent. Rock swore a silent curse. He was flustered, which was even more disconcerting because it was an emotion he didn't experience often. He needed time to process. Luckily, they had nothing but time.

Her proximity didn't help rid him of his irritable mood. It only made it worse. She smelled so vanilla-ish—delicious, like a cookie. His mouth watered. Rock forced himself to stop, to shut down. No miscellaneous thought. He was good at that particular skill.

Laila made a couple of futile attempts at conversation, but he shut her down quickly and made it apparent he wasn't interested in talking. What followed was hours in that cab. Hours he used to plan.

Her behavior warranted punishment. Something that would make his feelings known, yet not completely derail her and cast a negative pall over this pivotal day in her life. It took him a while to weave what should be a significant punishment into something that wouldn't ruin the fulfillment of her dream. They were almost to their first destination, when he'd decided how the night would play out.

Chapter 19

With the burden of Laila's Resistance responsibilities lifted, her relief was staggering. She would no longer be forced to lie to Rock. Finally, there would be no secrets between them, at least not on her end. She took in a deep, lung-cleansing breath and blew out the last of her tension from the night before. Now, she could concentrate on her life's work and what came next.

As they sped down the overgrown road, leading away from New Atlanta, Rock's wall was up and fortified. He'd found out she, again, wasn't where she was supposed to have been. Still, she had no worries. He loved her unconditionally and last night would blow over.

On several occasions during the drive, she tried to open the dialogue between them, wanting to smooth the waters. Rock's responses were short and curt. She had a lot of silent time to think about the hours of conversation with Journey. She was ashamed of her initial catty reaction when she'd found out about the woman's former relationship with Rock. After talking with her longer than she should have, Laila realized the woman was genuinely sweet. She spoke softly and obviously cared a lot about Rock's happiness. By the end of what ultimately turned into a heart to heart conversation, the sun had risen and her jealousy was re-cast, with respect taking its place.

Journey lost everything when Rock was transferred to Emerald, and she risked it all for the opportunity to say thank you for the years he'd taken care of her. And, though she never admitted it, she was there to say goodbye, too. Laila didn't know why Rock hadn't told her he was leaving New Atlanta. It didn't make sense because he'd pushed hard to develop the connection between them. They'd built harmony, a meeting of the minds and hearts. It was a rush she never wanted to live without.

Laila took in the scenery as Rock put the miles behind them. Dense vegetation, separated by vast parking lots, vacant retail stores and restaurants, skirted the highway. They passed under a faded profession of love spray painted on a bridge. *Jack and Brie 4-ever*. The sign remained after a quarter century while the lovers never had a chance. Entire traffic jams of cars were pushed to the side so their armored trucks could drive past. She glimpsed animals she'd only seen pictures of, like deer and pigs, and imagined what it must have been like to drive that road pre-pandemic.

Hours passed and her thoughts circled, landing on Rock again and again. She feared last night might have been his breaking point. She'd been more trouble for him than anything else. Maybe he didn't want her anymore. And even though she'd made the right decisions, she feared she'd have to live a lifetime with the consequences. Especially now, after her conversation with Journey, she actually had confirmation it wasn't so bad giving everything to him.

She laid her head back and closed her eyes. Opening herself to him, she felt nothing, just the Rock wall. He did that frequently since he'd found out her secret.

After an entire leg of their journey spent with his total disconnect and blaring silence between them, she realized she'd rather feel his anger than nothing. He sat so close without a touch or a word. It was as if a piece of her was missing. By the time they reached the secured rest stop just outside Greensboro, she was bereft. Even though he sat next to her, she missed him.

The rest stop, where they would spend the night, was secure, surrounded by chain link fence, and topped with barbed wire. This was the standard stopping point for the first day when the recovery missions were traveling long distances to the north.

Rock, Garret and Sydney went about securing the trucks and checking the fence, making sure there hadn't been a breach. Before long, a fire blazed and the last fresh meat they'd eat for a while was thrown on a grate over the flames. Neither Garret nor Sydney seemed to notice Rock was being, well…himself.

She still had important messages from Journey. He wouldn't be expecting them and therefore wouldn't wait to hear them before he left for the drop-house. She knew it was near this place. He stood about five feet away tending to the fire with a charred stick, ignoring her.

Garret set a cement block down near her. "Come on. Sit." Then he placed another one near the first and sat on it. A disgusted snort erupted from Sydney then she walked away from the group.

Laila became engrossed in a conversation with Garret about the art and artifacts they would retrieve in DC. Rock watched them as they sat close together, focusing on each other. She felt his possessiveness. He didn't hide it well, or he'd lowered his wall a little.

After they ate, Rock walked Laila back to the truck. Maybe he'd settled enough to talk. "Rock?"

He gave her the signal for silence. When they reached the back of the truck, he gave her the hold signal and deserted her without saying a word.

Her gorgeous man was shunning her, she realized, as he left her there and returned to the security detail. Supposedly, Garret and Sydney were lead on this mission. Providing security for the recovered items was considered most important. Though Rock's only assignment was to protect her, he had a way of commanding authority no matter who he was with, Garret and Sydney included.

Rock returned to Laila and met her gaze for the first time since they left New Atlanta. He looked tired. "I'm going to be leaving for a bit. Stay by the truck. Garret and Sydney will be covering my protection duties."

"Rock you can't just leave me here with them."

"Do not disobey me right now," he snapped.

"But we have to—"

"Don't." He picked up two large black duffels with his left hand and swung them over his shoulder. "I'll be back in less than an hour," he said, giving her the sign to hold as he walked toward a residential area that rested just on the other side of the interstate.

Laila eyed his retreating back, and then she glanced over her shoulder. The gate allowing exit from the rest stop was not directly in Garret and Sydney's line of sight. They wouldn't even know she was gone. She slipped through it and trailed Rock as he prowled silently through the overgrown vegetation encroaching into the streets of the forsaken neighborhood.

He turned down the driveway of a house that looked much like every other one on the street. A faded garden gnome with a red pointed hat stood in a curling bed of ivy next to the front door. She tracked Rock down the driveway toward the rear of the house. As soon as she passed the back corner, a hand wrapped around her throat and an arm snaked around her waist. He slid in behind her, gaining control over her in a split second.

She gasped. He'd scared the shit out of her, dumping adrenaline into her bloodstream. It pumped fast and hot through her veins, heating her cheeks and making her jumpy.

Grasping her wrist, he led her up the steps, through the back door and kitchen, releasing her when they reached the living room. "Strip."

She snapped her head around to look at him.

Rage lit his eyes. "Do it now!"

Nervously, she unfastened the button to her black mission pants.

He stepped forward. His rough tugs got them off her legs mere seconds after she rasped the zipper down. "You lied to me." His Rock wall was lowering, and she began to feel the barely leashed anger that had lain behind it all damn day. "Take your shirt off, or I am going to rip it off you."

Laila quickly grabbed the hem of her shirt and pulled it over her head.

He roughly unhooked and stripped her of her bra. "Kneel."

She hesitated again and he delivered a sharp openhanded smack to her rear. She sucked in another gulp full of air.

"Either tell me you are no longer mine or kneel," he said between his teeth. Handcuffs dangled from his hand. He was furious. The anger buffeted her in waves. He was going to handcuff her so she was helpless against him. The thought gave her an unanticipated biological response— pleasure. For a split second, she hedged, knowing her reaction was deviant at best and pathetic at worst. Swallowing, her parched throat squeaked loudly. Then she knelt.

"Turn." He motioned with his hand so she faced away from him.

Still on her knees, she awkwardly turned around.

He roughly pushed her forward. "Forearms on the ground, ass in the air." He was completely out of her line of sight, but she heard him settle in one of the chairs behind her.

Silence descended between them. It was a suffocating silence, a blanket thrown over her, trapping the explanation she wanted to give and making it impossible to calm herself while the wall of rage loomed behind her.

"I'm a heartbeat away from having a fucking brain aneurism right now."

"Ro—"

"I did not say you could speak," he roared.

She trembled from the mega wattage of adrenaline her body pumped into her bloodstream.

"I have never been so disappointed with one of my girls."

"Rock—"

"Don't speak to me," he interrupted. "I will tell you when you can speak."

The sinking feeling, the kind that comes right before something awful happens, plummeted to the pit of her stomach, rearranging her insides on the way down.

Time ticked by slowly. Despite being cushioned by the carpet, her knees and elbows ached. After at least an hour, she desperately needed to move. The room grew darker, and still, he sat behind her, silently becoming less angry with time.

It was pitch black before Laila heard him move again. She didn't feel his anger anymore. He'd been waiting for it to dissipate.

Finally, she heard him rise and rummage through one of the duffels he'd brought with him. He set a candle on the coffee table and lit it. He stood in her line of sight, and she focused on the flickering vision of him in his black uniform. He white-knuckled a crop in his right hand.

She groaned both yearning for and detesting what came next.

"I want one word answers to my questions. Do you understand?"

"Yes," Laila whispered. The slice of air she heard gave only a split second of notice before the crop landed across her ass.

"Were you doing Resistance business?"

She released a breath and dealt with the sting. "Yes."

Then, the slice and telltale stripe of pain registered on her thighs. It took her breath away. "How long have you known about your mission last night?"

"Rock —"

"That is not an answer," he thundered. "Answer me!"

"Months."

"Why didn't you tell me?"

"You were safer and saner not knowing."

He yanked her ponytail, lifting her cheek off the back of her hands. "You've got this all wrong, peanut. I protect you. It's not the other way around." He let go of her ponytail and stepped back. More rustling around in his bag, and then the first burst of pain from the metal tips of his flogger bouncing off the backs of her thighs.

"I'm sorry," she cried and then whimpered, "I'm sorry."

He seared her thighs again. The whip of the tips slicing the air was her only warning before the pain exploded. "What are you sorry for?"

She scrambled for the right answer. "For...for—"

Thwapp.

"Now you're just making things up. You're not sorry."

"Yes. I'm sorry I didn't tell you where I was."

"I don't have to be looking into your eyes to know you're lying to me," he said calmly. "You would do the same thing all over again." *Thwapp.* Another hail of metal tips bounced off her rear end. He leaned in close. "Wouldn't you?"

She shivered from the hot breath of his words landing on the back of her neck. "Rock—"

"Wouldn't you!"

"Yes."

Thwapp.

"Why?"

"Because I didn't want you to risk your life."

"And there it is. That same problem over and over again. After all this time, there remains your 'I want' instead of the 'I'm yours' I need."

Thwapp. A cry of pain burst from Laila's lips.

"Which is it then? I want or I'm yours? Which do you ultimately choose?" *Thwapp.*

"Please, Rock. I'm sorry. It's done. My work with the Resistance is done."

"Which is it Laila, I want or I'm yours?" He boomed the question as something flew across her peripheral vision, landing on the other side of the room with a crash.

"I'm yours," she whispered, her voice quavering with emotion.

"Then why would you risk the one thing that would destroy me if I ever lost it?" He was right at her ear again. She squeezed her eyes shut, holding her breath and waiting for what was next. Only half of her consciousness was there with him. The other half flew, her senses soaring inside. A feeling of euphoria overwhelmed her.

"Get back into position." She heard the flogger bounce on the carpet behind her.

Then…nothing.

Stillness enveloped them. His mood changed gradually during that quiet spell.

Laila rested her cheek on the top of her hand, getting a bug's eye view. The atmosphere in the old house held an odd loneliness, as if the room was patiently waiting for its people to return. After at least an hour, Laila had relaxed into the position. Her muscles loosened. She took a long deep breath, and on the exhalation, they loosened even more. Then she noticed how clean the house was. She smelled the faint lemony aroma of cleaner, and wondered how often the Resistance visited this drop house. More than she'd thought since they'd taken the time to maintain it.

"Emily felt the malevolence in the woman who murdered her. She'd mentioned it to me in an offhand remark once, but I dismissed it as girl shit. Nothing I needed to be concerned with.

"That woman, under Morgan's orders, murdered her right under my nose." He paused for a handful of seconds, and Laila felt his despair. "I listened to her get stabbed as it happened, and I've heard it in my head a million times since." His voice was gravelly and choked with emotion.

Laila wanted to hold him, comfort him as he relived the tragedy.

"Part of me died that day. Losing someone when in a relationship as enmeshed as ours was"—he swallowed hard—"is barely survivable. At the very least, it shakes a man right down to his soul. Only sheer force of will helped me carry on."

"Rock." She lifted herself from the floor."

"No. Stay there." His panicked words prohibited her from seeing him vulnerable. She understood. He couldn't be that, not even with her.

"And then, there you were, a disease I caught the first time you slipped your hand into mine. But because of what came before, I knew what would become of me if anything happened to you. I would not survive it, Laila." The rustle of his clothing signaled his movements behind her. "I would die anyway. Don't you fucking understand?" He dropped to his knees. "If I lost you, I would die anyway."

Shame twisted her insides, and silence overfilled the space between them. "I'm sorry," she whispered.

His answer was the familiar rasp of his zipper. "You will never do anything like this again." He moved closer until he was behind her, covering her with the sleek planes of his chest and abs. He eclipsed her, settling his full weight on her frame. She strained to keep herself from flattening onto the ground as he snaked an arm around her and cupped his hand over her mound.

"I'm going to fuck that pussy tonight." His fingers explored where the crest of his dick slowly entered her, fondling the place they connected. She moaned more loudly with each invading inch of him until he stuffed her to her limits.

Finally. Finally. Finally. She groaned with joy at the feeling of him making love to her for the first time.

He circled her clitoris, rhythmically skimming with his fingers. "You are mine," he rasped in her ear. "And I am yours."

"Yes."

With no more secrets between them, there was nothing left holding her back, and it seemed like what they'd been missing had finally slipped into place. She'd never loved so much or felt as loved. She'd shatter into a million pieces without him as well.

The moment seemed more significant because he read every nuance of her thoughts just as well as she read his feelings. He knew her weaknesses in both character and behavior. He knew the good and the flaws and loved her still. It was so very freeing.

The long smooth glides of his cock were the only thing in her universe as he withdrew and then thrust over and over again. Her body surged forward with every forceful advance.

She was, literally, reeling, weak kneed and shaky. She cast her senses out, seeking him in a way no other woman could, needing an anchor. Snapshots of sensation registered in the haze. His hand gripped her hip, each finger bruising her flesh. His teeth scraped along her shoulder. He bit down and then sucked, rolling his searing tongue over the sensitive spot left behind. Lingering there with his mouth, he sucked, marking her as he withdrew his cock and thrust again. Every sizzling pull tugged her insides and made her painfully aware of her heavy, lower lips straining against his girth.

Rock grunted with his next thrust.

This was wrong. It wasn't how she thought it would be. There was no romance, no gentle caresses or sweet words.

Increasing his speed, he fucked her at a furious pace. Their bodies slapped together, the rhythm regularly punctuated by each huff of air pushed out of her from the force of his thrusts.

She'd been sliding forward slightly with each aggressive surge. He roughly hiked her ass back up into the air, snaked a hand around her again and maintained firm pressure on her clit.

"I'm close," she cried.

"Then go, baby."

She hovered in that place, that incredible, almost-there place where nothing existed except them. His ecstasy battered her.

"Fuck, baby." He rammed harder, faster. Hot come flooded her, ran down her legs. Then, she fell, crying out long and hard. Wild convulsions wracked her. With her lungs empty of air and her mouth still open in a soundless shout, Laila collapsed to the floor, a mindless sweaty heap. She rolled to her side.

"No, baby, you're not done." He rolled her onto her knees, into the position she'd spent her whole evening in, and stuck a vibrator inside her already too-sensitive vagina.

She jerked upright. "I'm done, Rock," she shrieked.

He guided her back down on all fours. "You're done, when I say you're done."

She groaned, exhaustedly trying to move away.

He cracked her ass. "Stop!"

She obeyed.

He ran his hand along her spine, curled it over the curve of her ass. "That's better, much better. I know what you need." He trailed his fingers through the damp trail of semen on her inner thigh and ran them up, stopping at her anus. He teased her there with short penetrations. "I'll always know how to take care of you baby." He sidled closer behind her, pressing the vibrator deeper inside with his body and wrapping his arms around her again. He started with just the slightest of touches to her clit, caressing it. Soon, she was coiled again and ready to explode. She teetered there, right on the edge of her orgasm. Every muscle tensed. Every cell flooded with exquisite bliss as she reached for it and finally climaxed again. She shuddered with waves of a more dulcet pleasure. The experience was mind-blowing and seemed to go on forever.

Rock chuckled. "That was beautiful, baby."

She opened her eyes. He'd moved to her side and watched her with the flame of a single candle setting fire to his eyes. "Don't you move."

The vibrator continued. It was too much. An indignant cry was perched on the tip of her tongue, but she held back, refusing to continue the power struggle she'd been stubbornly grasping onto since their first day together. This time, she stayed in position instead of giving in to her bad case of noodle knees.

"Good girl." He pulled the vibrating torture device from her.

A lightning bolt rippled through her as his fingers pressed into her. "Go ahead, baby. Grip me hard." He wasn't done.

This was her punishment. "Rock, I'm sor-ry," she sobbed. She tried to collapse, but he hiked her up to her knees.

Tears trailed from the corners of her eyes, landing on the tops of her hands as he knelt behind her and fucked her with his fingers. The force of it made her sway on her knees. His hot breath cooled the sweat on her lower back. She groaned at the fleeting relief.

The vibrator clicked on, and Rock touched it to her clit. Uncontrollable spasms wracked her. Laila wailed in response to the obnoxious pleasure. She seized and bucked as she gulped quick sobbing breaths.

She raised herself to her hands and knees. He covered her hands with his, curling his fingers into her palm and pinning their joined hands to the floor. "Your pussy's so sweet, peanut. It's wet and swollen, your little clit poking out, wanting more," he said as he pistoned into her. "I bet all I have to do is blow on it to set you off again."

His sweat fell in droplets onto her back as he tirelessly pleasured himself to another orgasm. "Fuck, yeah, baby." His heat flooded her. His hands squeezed reflexively with each jerking spurt inside her. He pulled out and rolled to his side. "Stay there." Her quivering thighs were a wet, sticky mess. She could barely catch her breath.

He was next to her. She met his gaze. He didn't look happy or content. Her punishment wasn't over.

"This was what you wanted, wasn't it?" he asked.

"What?"

"Fucked, baby. You wanted fucked."

"Yes. But—"

"No buts. Tonight, I'm going to give you your fill."

He retrieved the vibrator and inserted it inside her again.

"It tickles."

"It will pass."

"I thought you didn't want to get me pregnant," she said, grasping for anything to distract him from his intent.

He chuckled. "I don't care anymore." His tone was curt. It was difficult to care because the vibrator inserted deep inside her didn't tickle anymore. Pleasure built more quickly this time. Her muscles tightened. Her inner muscles clamped down on the device.

"Rock." She met his gaze.

"What, baby?" His response was cold.

"I'm sorry. My Resistance commitment is over. It won't happen again. I promise."

"Good."

"Ahhh," she cried. "Please take it out."

He smiled, and his inner gratification exploded. "I love when you beg baby, but my answer is no."

For a split second, she considered removing it herself. No. She was determined to be what he needed. She groaned and closed her eyes, trying to escape his intense scrutiny and the unmistakable pleasure twinkling in his eye. She attempted to lock down the building orgasm, resist the pull of it, but after the maddening overstimulation, it was a losing battle. She would be his spectacle, a wailing, quivering bundle of bones and flesh, at his mercy.

She came again, violently, collapsing onto the carpet as the pleasure rippled along her spine, making her cells sing out. She rolled to her side when her climax slowed to a shudder.

"I didn't say you could move." He forcefully positioned her on her knees and circled around her until his cock was near her mouth.

"Make me hard," he said, pushing the blunt head of his penis into her mouth.

She tasted and smelled remnants of their previous encounter as his cock grew against her tongue. She pulled hard all the way to the tip. Then she dipped her head and took him down to the base with the tip of her nose resting on his tight abs, the crest moving farther to the back of her throat as he grew. When she sucked him out to the tip again, Rock pulled out of her mouth with a pop.

He circled behind her and filled her again with a rough surge of his flesh. He fucked her hard and fast. It didn't much matter, though. It would have been impossible to come again.

"This is what you wanted, baby—your pussy fucked? You got it."

She was rigid with sensitivity. "I'm sorry." The stimulation was almost intolerable, as he held her ragdoll body still and drove into her until he came with a shout.

When he let go, she dropped to the carpet, half-conscious, but his words at her ear penetrated the haze. "The punishment is knowing, for the rest of our lives together, the first time I was here." He dipped a finger between her lower lips and slid it along her slit. "You made this about having to re-establish our relationship instead of heightening it to highs we've never been to before. I'm disappointed in you, Laila."

Laila couldn't respond, couldn't move. She just lay there, letting his words sink in and drifted off to sleep.

* * * *

It seemed only moments later when she opened her eyes to the rising sun. With Rock spooned behind her, she enjoyed the settling cloud of peace that finally surrounded them.

Not long after, he stirred.

"I have something to tell you," she whispered.

"I don't want to know any of it," he murmured. "It's over. We need to look forward, not back."

"I gave my word, Rock. I have some things to tell you."

She rolled over in his arms until she faced him. Her head rested on his bicep. He rhythmically caressed the curve of her hips around to her rear and back again.

Eyes fixed on his face, she waited to proceed. He ground his molars together and nodded slightly.

"I gave the speaker from your kitchen to a woman. She'll be assuming the identity of a Sapphire who's leaving New Atlanta through the tunnel."

"Journey," he rumbled.

"How did you know?"

"She's the only woman in New Atlanta who'd want to give me a message."

"She's changed her tattoo to Sapphire. She'll be working in the Emerald Zone. Something big, she said. But that's all she could tell me."

He looked at her skeptically. "Doesn't sound like Journey."

Laila nodded. "That's what she said you'd say. She's gotten more involved in the Resistance."

Rock tensed at that tidbit of information. "I was afraid of that." He took in a big breath and ran his fingers through his hair, probably trying to release some of the anxiety that suddenly saturated the space around them.

"She wanted to see you before we left but had to settle for sending a message instead."

"Okay."

"She said to tell you thank you and she's grateful for everything."

"When Journey first came to me, she was painfully shy." He paused and tilted his head as if leafing through words that fit better. "Shy is not quite the word I'm looking for, but close enough." He rubbed his jaw, rasping his fingers over his stubble. "She came a long way under my care and, it seems, even further in the past year. She's been working for the Resistance leader since I've been gone, but I had no idea she could do what she did last night."

"It seems like she's grown into a confident, courageous woman. Because of you." He got to his feet, bringing her with him and handed over her clothes. Rock shook his head. "I didn't do anything. Just took care of her, loved her.

Rock pulled two envelopes from his bag, and she followed him to the kitchen. He tossed the envelopes on the table. One was labeled *Dad*, the other, *Journey*. He angled his head to meet her gaze. "I was like a papa bear raising up a baby bird. But I would never presume to take credit for her successes. I just gave her a safe haven so she could grow into herself."

"It looks like she's doing that."

"Yeah." His expression turned serious. "But assuming a Sapphire's identity, very risky."

"The woman she's replacing just got designated. New job assignment. New apartment. Nobody will know Journey's not who she says she is. It'll be okay, Rock."

Laila sat to put on her boots and got a glimpse inside his open duffel. She saw all the toys in it and glared at him. "You knew I would follow."

"I was hoping you wouldn't."

Rock pulled out the prosthetic hand he'd built for Jordan and left it next to the envelopes.

"Journey said she ran across a pit full of dead men outside the Emerald Zone."

"Not surprised."

"I also saw something weird yesterday." Laila told Rock of her discovery of the children on the Peacekeeper's Compound, and he took the time to jot a quick note to Xander before they walked out of the drop house together.

The glorious morning sun kissed her face and worked on burning away the dew. When they arrived at the rest stop, Rock left her by their vehicle and headed toward Garret and Sydney's truck.

A moment later, Garret walked around the back corner of theirs. "Where the hell have you been all night?" he snapped in a low voice. "I had to cover for you with Sydney."

"I'm sorry. It couldn't be helped." Laila said.

"You should be. Don't put me in a position like that again." He walked away without another glance, his anger still rolling off him.

Rock entered the driver's side of the armored truck, and Laila laid her head on his lap.

"Day two," he said before putting it in gear. The inside of the cab was warm, and they were moving at a good clip. The steady undulation of the truck combined with the white noise of the engine lulled her. For the next hour or so, she dozed.

The truck slowed noticeably. "Get up," Rock said as he briskly rubbed her arm.

She righted herself. The truck ahead of them was stopped with a fallen tree in their path. Garret was already at the back, pulling a chain saw from the open door. She looked past where the men were working, worried the loud growl of the chainsaw would attract unwanted guests. The paved road was still visible through the encroaching vegetation and debris. The area seemed deserted, but the longer it took to clear the tree, the more her anxiety built.

As the minutes passed and her worry for Rock's safety spiked, the mission took on seriousness as a new dimension of this journey became clear. Rock risked his life so she could experience her life's dream.

Her suspicions that he was not returning to New Atlanta seemed to be correct. He'd deposited his two duffels into an SUV, joining at least twenty more of the same, before they'd left the drop house. It must have taken a year's worth of trips to accumulate all of them.

For a moment, she considered whether he might be leaving supplies for someone who lived in Onyx, but then she remembered the toys packed in one of the bags. Those weren't for somebody already out there. They were for him. That was why Journey risked everything to see him. She'd known.

Laila didn't know whether to be angry or worried. Sure now that Rock was not returning to New Atlanta, she wondered why he hadn't said anything to her about it yet. He wouldn't deliver her to New Atlanta and then abandon her to start a new life. Would he? Would he leave her on her own, like he'd left Journey? God, she was unhinged by the possibility.

The entire morning and afternoon were filled with identical fits of starts and stops. With not much else but the scenery to capture her interest as they hopped their way north, she had a lot of time for those thoughts to wreak havoc with her sanity.

Chapter 20

Rock pulled up near the front of the capitol building and put the truck in park. Laila's knee bounced up and down as she leaned forward and visually explored what she could through the limited angles of the windshield and passenger window. He followed her gaze. The capitol looked in remarkably good shape, considering it had received no maintenance for twenty-eight years.

When her hand reached for the door handle, he reined her in. "You can open the door so you don't get too hot, but don't get out until I give you the okay." Her groan made him smile as he got out of the truck and worked with Sydney and Garret to set up an electrified security fence. He felt her intense frustration burning through his body armor and landing heavily on him. After he finished the inner fence, Rock walked a larger perimeter and triangled the camp with laser alarms that would activate if someone or something crossed them.

When he finally helped Laila out of the truck, she was talking before her feet hit the ground. "First we need to scout the first few items on the list. They are priority. According to the intel Morgan had from his father and my research, when the Gov realized the collapse was imminent, they moved the Declaration of Independence, Constitution, and Bill of Rights from display in the National Archives to a secured room underground." Laila smiled at him. "Let's see if they're still there." She started walking toward the archives building.

"Whoa, girl. Hold up." He reached for her, grabbing the edge of the flak jacket she wore to jerk her backward. "You're identification and conservation. We're scouting and security," Rock said, motioning at himself and the other two.

"You follow us, not the other way around," Garret said from behind her.

Rock focused over her shoulder as Garret said, "Sydney and I will go find the items and make sure it's safe to bring you in. Then you can come."

Rock nodded his agreement. Laila grabbed his arm, pulled him away from the other two, and whispered wildly at him, "You have lost your fucking mind if you think I'm going to stay here while they go traipsing off, fumbling around priceless historical artifacts."

Rock laughed. "You need to take a breath, peanut." He paused. Their gazes locked, and he realized, in this, he couldn't say no to her.

He sighed. "You have to wear your side arm. Be ready in five minutes."

Almost an hour later, Laila found the documents in the pitch-black darkness of a maze of underground rooms. "This recovery will be the easiest of all the artifacts if the titanium and aluminum cases are still intact." With a flashlight, she meticulously inspected the cases housing the documents. "They seem to be pristine and should be easy to transport to the armored trucks by hand," she said to the three shadows lurking behind her.

The quartet made three trips from the archive building to the trucks. Rock covered Sydney and Garret as they carried the cases. Laila helped by opening doors and shining light when necessary. The sun was low in the sky by the time all three were secured in the back of the lead truck. Laila stood, studying the last document secured. "The actual U.S. Constitution. It's hard to wrap my brain around."

Rock stood behind her, also looking at the three-hundred-year-old document. "Too bad it doesn't mean anything anymore. In this century, not all men were created equal." He turned and walked away.

The following week was filled with the retrieval, packaging and transfer of priceless art and items of historical significance. Laila meticulously cared for and packaged John Trumbull's painting of the signing of the Declaration of Independence. But other items on the list, like the Hope Diamond, and printing plates for US currency were either missing or destroyed by vandals.

As Laila admired the next painting she would be preparing for transport, she felt Rock's sexual need, surging out of him and saturating the area they occupied. It had been over a week since the over-consummation of their relationship. He radiated a constant simmer she couldn't get away from, adding to her angst at a time when she was already on edge about his still undisclosed plans to leave New Atlanta.

During the first days of the mission, she'd waited for him to tell her. Initially, she was confident that, when the time came to leave, he'd take her with him. But days passed, and the sometimes tedious work she did to prepare items for transport gave her significant time to think of other, less positive scenarios. She dwelled endlessly, wondering why he kept her in the dark. She daydreamed of all the possible things, life changing, future-altering things that would happen if she were to run away with him. It would be crazy, having significant ramifications on her life, including never seeing her mother again and leaving her life's work behind.

By the end of the first week in DC, she'd found herself emotionally withdrawing in anticipation of the news that someday soon she would have to say goodbye to this man. It was incredibly hard. He often sought her gaze, pinched her chin between his thumb and forefinger. She found it hard to close even one door he'd opened during the two-month inventory he'd taken of her. *When I was sure he loved me.*

He did love her…right? This one secret between them changed her entire perspective on their relationship, and she got a good taste of how it felt to be the person waiting, hoping when the secret was revealed, it wouldn't tear her world apart.

Since they arrived in DC, they hid their relationship twenty-four hours a day. She felt so far away from him. The sudden, prolonged disconnect had opened her up to doubt and depression that kept getting stronger as the days passed.

After over a week of waiting, there was a change within herself. The blues and insecurity were morphing into something uglier—anger.

She sighed, fingering the chain around her neck and refocusing on the painting in front of her. He hadn't touched her since that first night, the night of her punishment. Every night since then, they'd lain side by side in their bedrolls with the inches between them feeling more like miles. She'd spent hours lying awake, listening to his even, rhythmic breathing and feeling uneasy about the footing of their relationship. She ached for his enormous frame to surround her. She missed him, missed the routine. Over and over, she thought of his soapy hands sliding over her skin, washing her like he'd done every afternoon since the very first day. The loss of that simple ritual left her feeling detached from him. She missed every single thing they'd spent the last sixty days building. A week ago, she would have said their love was built on bedrock. Now she wasn't so sure.

She woke near dawn with his vise-like arm around her waist, pulled into the curve of his body with his dick wedged nicely between them. In sleep, his body sought her out, but the erection pressed against her ass was a consolation prize. Something he'd given in sleep. It meant nothing to him but everything to her. Lying awake in his arms, her punishment haunted her. What would their first time together have been like if she hadn't had to finish her Resistance obligation the night before they left? The natural thought that followed squeezed her chest tight. Would she ever get the chance to find out? She needed his touch so badly she barely contained her arousal. Her body was ready for him, her panties damp as she spent almost an hour longing for his rough palms to rasp over her nipples. She never got it.

A cold, bereft place expanded inside her. This, compounded with her mind's machinations about whether he would soon leave her wore her patience thin. Something seemed terribly wrong. She wanted to cry or scream most of the time now, feeling muddled with frustration and fear.

They'd spent the last couple of days stalled in the National Gallery of Art. She glanced over her shoulder at the man who, for days, had watched her complete the painstaking work of preparing Renoir's *A Girl With a Watering Can* for transport.

She tried to wear him down during the hours spent alone with him. She did everything in her power to stoke his need in seemingly innocent ways. His hunger for her spiked every time she brushed against him, and his gaze was on fire when she leaned over, giving him a glimpse of the lace bra covering the curve of her breasts. Nevertheless, he still gave no outward reaction to her provocative teasing, even when no one was around.

It could be his way of distancing himself. That meant he would return her to New Atlanta and leave her there.

"What are you thinking? I've never seen that look on your face before."

Rock's words sucked her back into the present. "I was actually thinking about you."

He raised his eyebrows as if surprised at her answer. "What about me?"

"I can't figure out why you're working so hard to stonewall me."

Rock straightened and replaced his expression of interest with his Rock wall. "I'm not." He began to turn away and walk to the chair by the doorway. Laila grabbed his arm, stopping him.

"Is it me? Is there something about me that isn't attractive to you anymore?"

His expression darkened as he cupped her face. "God, that couldn't be further from the truth." His hand lingered on her cheek. A look of sadness, or maybe regret, clouded his face. He twirled a wayward curl around his finger then he dropped his hand.

"Then why haven't you told me you're not returning to New Atlanta?" The words were squeezed through her constricted throat. She was a moment away from bawling like a pathetic idiot.

He straightened, obviously surprised she knew. "I'm not sure yet how I want to proceed. I'll tell you once I've decided." His tone had been sharp, the words clipped.

"What exactly needs to be decided?" She waited for his answer, heart thumping hard in her chest. He'd find the right words. He'd tell her he'd never leave her. This worry she'd been carrying around with her would seem like a silly tangent her mind had traveled.

He glanced over his shoulder in the direction where they'd left Garret and Sydney. "When I know, you'll know, and that's all I have to say on the subject right now."

Laila looked down at her toes. It was not the profession of love she'd been hoping for. She deflated. "Okay. I get the message. I'll leave you alone."

Rock squared his jaw and stared down at her with a cool mask of indifference. She waited for him to say something else, but got nothing. For an instant, she felt his struggle, and then that was gone, too. She didn't feel the connection she craved, only a vague sense of isolation. He had closed himself off.

Laila turned her attention back to her work, essentially turning her back on him. She closed her eyes and inhaled deeply, trying to get a grip on her emotions. How the hell did her dream, her heart's desire to be on this mission turn into something else entirely? She was miserable and very tired of the bipolar roller coaster ride of hope and rejection. She'd had enough.

The simmering anger she'd been harboring since she woke up that morning advanced to a rolling boil. His detachment made her crazy and exposed her insecurities, making her feel desperate and pathetic. Fury rose within her. Her face heated with the rise of her blood pressure. She pulled in a long breath. She had never been so mad at anyone, ever.

Rock moved behind her. Then, his hand landed on her shoulder. He turned her around and sighed. "Laila—"

"Don't fucking touch me," she warned through clenched teeth. "I never want you to fucking touch me again." She jerked herself out of his grasp and walked away, never looking back.

* * * *

Rock's attempt to stall his decision had unintentionally hurt Laila, but he hadn't known it until just now. He found her where Garret and Sydney stood at the front entrance of the museum. Laila stood close to Garret with her head tilted up, looking at him and smiling. Fucking smiling, when just a moment ago she'd shot him a look that made him flinch.

Sydney looked down on his sweet girl with sheer hatred in her eyes. He'd not seen the woman look at Laila like that before. He swore under his breath and knew he'd made their lives more dangerous by putting Sydney in her place all those weeks ago. Blood rushed full bore through his veins. His temper rose and his thoughts roared, demanding Laila be moved away from Garret and Sydney. Standing there, watching Laila's silhouette in the open doorway, Rock came to the harsh realization that, for the first time in his life, he was stuck. He was off his game, scattered and indecisive. There was no right answer to the dilemma of where to keep her as safe as possible while he set up their home. There were only varying levels of danger.

The unknown of traveling and establishing a home base was overwhelmingly more dangerous than being an Emerald in New Atlanta. Yet, he hadn't been able to tell her he'd be leaving her there. Probably because he knew they'd both languish without the other. As the days progressed and the withdrawal from their constant connection affected her, he was glad he hadn't. His tentative decision, to leave her in New Atlanta, began to vacillate again. The more time elapsed, the more she deteriorated.

He didn't want her to suffer when they were apart, and she would. She already suffered from the distance between them even though they'd still been in each other's presence twenty-four hours a day. The only thing that had changed between them since they'd left New Atlanta was the intimacy. And on this, he wouldn't budge. If Sydney and Garret knew they were in love, it would only take a minute for Morgan to know too, after they returned to New Atlanta. That would be a dangerous position for Laila, especially with him still in Onyx, setting up their home. It was actually safer if Sydney and Garret saw they weren't getting along.

Rock followed Laila as she left the two guardsmen at the doorway. Her long brown curls bounced along with her determined strides. He caught up to her at the truck. She let out a disgusted huff and tried to walk away. He caught her easily and trapped her against the flat metal side of the armored vehicle, placing his hands on each side of her body and closing in on her.

"Laila."

She wouldn't look at him.

"Peanut." He caught her chin and directed her gaze to meet his. "I don't know if you'd be safer in New Atlanta or with me."

Laila's grief-stricken expression declared her emotional state loud and clear. Her eyes traveled over his face until their gazes locked again.

"So you'd leave me?" she whispered.

"Right now, I think leaving you is probably the safer option of the two." He continued to withhold his emotions, not wanting to overwhelm her with his turmoil. But even that backfired, because his statement was so devoid of emotion, it seemed to add to her distress.

Her brittle composure snapped like a twig. "Please don't. It doesn't have to be this way."

"Yes, it does," he said gently. "There's no future for us in Atlanta." He stared down at her, reading the emotions as they flashed quickly and jumbled across her features. Her jaw dropped as she stood staring at him. "I can't believe what you're saying to me right now."

He stepped in closer. The planes of their bodies skimmed against one another. With his lips close to her, he rumbled, "I'll set up a safe place and come back for you."

Laila shivered as the air from his words wafted over the curve of her ear. "Please don't leave me, Rock. Please." Her plea broke his heart. Tears trailed down her cheeks. "Please."

He looked over his shoulder and caught the approach of the two guards he'd left behind at the museum. "Now is not the time for this discussion."

"So when is a good time, Rock?"

"I don't know, but now isn't it."

"I hate you for doing this to me," she seethed. Laila swung her arm in a wide arc, and Rock caught her wrist, stopping the slap aimed at his face. He growled, squeezing her wrist tightly. "I know this is hard, but I'm right here. You have to trust me, trust what we've built." His words were a low rumble, meant to soothe as much as caution. But when he looked in her eyes, he realized they'd done neither.

"Let me go!" she yelled as she attempted to yank her wrist out of his grasp.

"Hey!"

They both turned as Garret walked toward them.

"Step off, Garret. This doesn't concern you," Rock stated coolly. From the corner of his eye, Rock saw Laila ever so slightly shake her head. She was signaling Garret to let it go, treating him as if he could read her. And, he could, because Garret stopped in his tracks.

Rock turned away from Garret and Sydney, who'd just joined them, and strode in the opposite direction, dragging Laila behind him.

"Why are you giving him signals?" he hissed as he put distance between them and the man who was quickly growing to be his nemesis.

Garret caught him by the shoulder and swung around. "Let her go."

Rock released Laila's hand and stepped into Garret's personal space. "You need to go away before I snap your neck."

Garret took a step toward him. "You could try." The words were barely out of Garret's mouth before Rock rushed the man. Garret landed with a thud on the pavement, taking the brunt of the fall with Rock's weight on top of him.

Laila yelled for him to stop, grabbing at his Kevlar vest, pulling him back. She whispered in his ear, "He's Resistance, Rock."

Rock stopped at those words, and Garret got in a good jab to the side of Rock's face before Rock had the chance to scramble off the man.

Laila was on her knees next to Garret, presumably telling him the same thing. Sydney caught his attention as she advanced toward them, looking at Laila with contempt.

The best way to play this scene out was to leave. Nothing else could be said between them with Sydney present. He glanced at Garret and knew he would protect Laila from any aggressiveness on Sydney's part. He also knew it was better if Sydney thought he and Laila hated each other, so he turned from where Laila sat next to Garret on the pavement and strode away.

When Rock looked over his shoulder to assess the situation before he disappeared out of sight, Laila stood there, jaw dropped, staring at him while Sydney helped Garret from the ground.

He gave Laila the signal to hold and kept walking.

Chapter 21

They'd lingered in their temporary encampment in front of the capitol for fifteen days, the last of them spent in a state of tense give and take between all the members of the team. Now, several days out from the incident between him and Garret, Rock was relieved to be heading back. He'd have to tolerate very little of the two Guards during these last hours of driving before he walked away. Even though he and Garret were on the same side, there was still no love lost between them. He wanted to flay Garret alive for leading Laila into dangerous missions while they were still in New Atlanta. His heartbeat thundered, raising his blood pressure. "Fucker," he mumbled under his breath.

In an effort to fill up Sydney and Garret's truck, Laila hurriedly readied a few items not on her original list for travel. He was happy for her. She considered the mission a success with the retrieval of eleven items from her recovery list. An hour later, Rock's dour mood only intensified the pall cloaking their departure. The interior of the cab was thick with unexpressed conflict. Laila looked out the passenger side window. The slant of the morning sunlight set her aglow as they pulled away. She was beautiful even with sadness shadowing her features. As the miles from DC accumulated behind them, the words left unsaid between them hung in the air of the cab. It was a familiar, melancholy silence. One of missing and loving, and of reassurances they would see each other again. Rock didn't even have the strength to pull her out of the funk settling around them. He was too deep in it himself.

If things went as expected, they'd say goodbye to each other tomorrow. They'd avoided the topic since the blow-up when he'd made his final decision to leave Laila in New Atlanta. He'd spent most of his days shielding his own devastating emotions so they wouldn't send her plummeting into a more serious depression. But now, in the privacy of the cab, they could speak freely without having to worry about being overheard. "I'm taking you back to New Atlanta."

"I know," she said, still watching the world go by. "You've been shielding your emotions from me. It tipped your hand."

"It's only for a few months."

"Okay." Her slumped shoulders and sad eyes made him want to make it all go away. "If you don't come back, I won't even know what happened to you."

"Yes, baby, you would. Because if I don't come back for you, I'm dead. And if that happens, Laila—" He reached over and grabbed her forearm, getting her attention. Her gorgeous brown eyes were filled with tears. "If that happens, you'll move on. Find someone who will love you and make you happy. I want you to have a happy life, with or without me."

She didn't acknowledge his words, just broke eye contact and stared out the window again. They sat as if they were already separated, everything having been said. The misery-lined silence choked the small space.

He squeezed the little fingers lying limply in his hand. "It will be okay."

She didn't acknowledge the statement, just laid her head back on the headrest.

The brake lights on the truck in front of them flicked on. As soon as Rock got a glimpse of the roadblock ahead, he switched into survival mode.

"Laila!"

She snapped alive.

He slammed on the brakes. "Ditch on your side." She met his gaze, and he saw her confusion. "When I say go, jump out. Don't hesitate. You understand? Keep your legs bent and roll with your momentum."

She popped the door open, looked down, and froze.

Gunfire rang out.

"Go, go, go!" he shouted a split second later. His heartbeat thundered as she tumbled into the dense vegetation clogging the side of the road. An instant later, he did the same.

As he jumped, an explosion sounded.

He found Laila quickly and pulled her to her feet. "Are you hurt?"

She looked down at herself, taking stock. "I think I'm okay."

He took her hand. Together, they ran into the dense overgrowth.

"Was that our truck that exploded?"

He gave her the signal for silence and led the way as they continued to run through the forest skirting the road. Their clothes pulled at them, snagging on branches and thickets, slowing them as they tried to maneuver.

Laila tripped over a fallen tree and face-planted into the forest floor, almost taking him with her. In an instant, he caught her by her flak jacket and lifted her onto her feet again. "Let's find our pace, peanut. We need to be miles away from here." He slowed until they found their rhythm, weaving and jumping over fallen trees and rocks in the shade of the woods.

"I'm out of breath. I can't go anymore," she wheezed after thirty minutes.

"Yes, you can." He snatched her hand and continued to drag her through the brush grabbing at them. "Just a little while longer."

He slowed their pace as they neared a clearing. A suburban neighborhood with tightly packed identical houses spread out in a shallow valley below them. Rock stopped at the edge and surveyed the wide-open space. The houses were half hidden by overgrown weeds, making them look like gigantic turtles sunning themselves in tall grass. The air was choked with humidity and the rolling rumble of thunder sounded far in the distance.

He turned to Laila. She was red-faced from the run in the increasing afternoon heat. "We can't go down there. It's not safe."

"Why not?"

"See the paths?" He pointed. "There and there." Her gaze locked on the worn trails cutting through the tall grasses and weeds to the front doors of three of the houses. "Might be where the attackers live." Rock took her hand again and shepherded her back through the tangle of vegetation.

They walked through the densest areas of the woods, using the brush as cover, keeping parallel to the road. Thunder boomed, vibrating his chest with the force of it. Laila glanced up as if to check the sky. "It's much closer." Under the dense canopy, they couldn't see the encroaching storm, but the forest grew increasingly dark and eerie. The birds quieted and the only sounds were the crunch of their steps on the forest floor. The wind picked up, whipping her ponytail to the side. A deluge of bucket-sized drops fell loudly through the leaves. Within minutes, they were soaked to the bone. Still, they walked, keeping a steady pace.

The substantial downpour lasted an hour, and when it finally stopped, the air was cooler. Soon after, Laila's teeth were chattering. Her eyes met his and she flashed him a radiant, blue-lipped smile. Her wet hair stuck to the sides of her face, and her saturated clothes hung heavy on her frame. In the excitement, she'd lost her sadness, and her beautiful, teeth-chattering grin melted him. It said more about her character than any word or action he'd seen since their first day together.

Rock stopped and pulled her to him. Their flak jackets emitted a soft, bubbled squish as he hugged her. She shivered in the circle of his arms. "Can you keep going?"

She kicked up her chin. "Yes."

"Good girl. We have to get as much distance as possible between us and them. In about an hour, I'll start looking for a place to stop."

"I'm getting hungry."

"It shouldn't be too hard to find something to eat after we find a safe place to spend the night."

She looked up at him with her enormous trusting eyes. "Okay."

He took her chilled hand in his and squeezed it. "Everything will be all right." Rock kissed her and started walking again.

A misty drizzle settled over the forest. There were no wild places like this in New Atlanta and even after a year of missions in the Onyx Zone, the atmosphere was a little spooky and a bit unnerving. Just as Rock was beginning to wonder if they'd find a place to rest, they walked up on a hole-in-the-wall truck stop and diner. He tried opening the heavy glass door guarding the store and registers. It was locked. He unsheathed his knife and broke the glass with the hilt then pulled Laila inside.

"This area should be safe. Nobody's been in here since the pandemic."

They split up, looking through the little store filled with dusty aisles of candy and still-bloated bags of chips.

"Here." Rock grabbed a pink oversized T-shirt with a cartoon cat and *I'm not rude. I have catitude* scrawled underneath and tossed it to her. He picked one with a blue UNC Tarheels logo on the front for himself.

"Take your clothes off. We'll hang them to dry." He stripped off his wet clothes.

She watched him undress with admiring eyes and a tilted head, just like she did when looking at the art she loved so much. He leaned, lowering his head so it was in her line of sight to snap her out of it. "Strip." He pulled the dry T-shirt over his head and hung his wet clothing off the side of the checkout counter, listening to the splat of Laila's hitting the floor.

"Come here." He held out his arms, and she stepped into him, folding her arms between them and nuzzling her cheek into his chest. To him, she was as small as a child with her dainty form completely surrounded by his body. "You did good today." His voice was husky, revealing the emotion he finally allowed himself to feel.

She nodded, saying nothing. He knew his girl. She was feeling him, maybe trying to gauge where he was emotionally so she would know how much trouble they were in. "We're not in trouble here, baby. Everything's going to be okay." He squeezed her tighter and stooped a bit to meet her gaze. "Okay?"

"How are we going to travel? We don't have any additive for gas."

"I'll go back tomorrow and check if they left any additive in the trucks. If they didn't, we'll ride bikes, or walk. It's easily doable." He lifted her chin so their gazes met. "I don't want you to worry."

She nodded. "Okay."

He released her, and she sat cross-legged on the tile floor, pulling the over-sized T-shirt down and stretching it around her knees.

He went about finding food.

After a quick scan of the aisles, he returned with an armful of cans he let tumble to the floor.

"How you going to open them?"

He shrugged, looking around, and her eyes sparkled. She seemed amused he hadn't thought of it. It was nice to see her old self in there.

He grinned at her and pulled a can opener from behind his back. "Aisle two."

Her smile faded. "Darn. I was hoping to see you bully those cans into submission. Is any of that stuff going to be okay to eat?"

"Yep. All of it, probably." He worked at opening the cans of fruit cocktail and corned beef hash.

"Maybe not Emerald quality food, but edible." He handed her a plastic fork. "Dig in."

They ate like rabid animals, and when their bellies were full, Rock pulled Laila onto his lap. "You okay?"

She sighed. "Yeah. More than okay. It's nice to be able to be ourselves again. No more pretending."

"Never again, peanut." They sat there, glued together, for a long time while he warmed her with his body and assessed the contents of the store for something soft to sleep on. There wasn't much. A shelf contained packages of diapers, toilet paper and paper towels.

When he finally let her go, he gathered a two-pack of paper towels, tossed it on the floor, and kneed the package until the rolls were flattened. He lay down, using the towels as a pillow.

Rock caught her wrist and Laila giggled then squealed as he pulled her on top of him. It took only a moment for her to settle in.

He was content, lying there stomach to stomach, their breaths synced. He rubbed her back. "Sleep on me tonight. I'll keep you warm."

"And you're softer than the floor." She sighed. The sound of it made him smile even though he was drained past the point of exhaustion.

His eyelids were heavy. "Tired, baby," he whispered.

"Then sleep. I'll be right here."

He tightened his grip around Laila and dropped into oblivion.

Chapter 22

A feeling of distress grabbed Laila and pulled her out of her sound slumber. Her attempts at pushing up from her hunky mattress were met with resistance. Rock's heavy arms constricted her movement and held her snugly against him.

She knew something was wrong before she was able to fully untangle herself and get a good look at him. He was on fire. A sheen of perspiration coated the parts of her body that had been touching his. His cheeks were flushed a frightening shade of crimson, and his hair was wet with sweat.

She knelt beside him, and shook him. "Rock."

No response.

"Rock? Wake up." She lowered her lips to his ear. "Open your eyes so I know you're with me."

Nothing.

Laila stood and dressed in her damp clothes and holstered her firearm. Hands on her hips, she scanned the store and then walked through the broken glass in the entryway. She cleared their immediate area as she'd been taught, making sure they were safe before she returned to Rock.

Past where he lay on the floor, there was a short, back hallway. Rock had explored there the night before, but she hadn't. She entered the room marked *Employees Only*. It was a tiny, windowless break room, containing a folding table and chairs, sink, and a little fridge. The bulletin board was full of work schedules and signs warning employees to wash their hands and another illustrating the correct way to lift a box. Laila pushed the table to the side.

They'd be better concealed in there.

Returning to the store area, she found some aspirin and crushed them with the side of her knife blade. Then, a little at a time, she sprinkled the white grit past Rock's slightly parted lips.

Expecting a reaction, she stared intently at his heat-reddened face, but there was no recoil from him as the powdered aspirin partially dissolved on his tongue. She chased it with a few drops of water.

He'd gotten mortally sick in a matter of hours, with symptoms alarmingly similar to those during the pandemic. If this was the same... "Oh God." Her insides plunged into free fall. "Oh no. No. No." She groaned into the dead air of the long deserted truck stop. She was solo once again. Trepidation skittered through the space left empty inside by Rock's incapacity. It was likely she would get sick too. They had swapped all kinds of spit and breathed all over each other in the past twelve hours. She'd already been exposed. Whatever happened, happened. There was nothing she could do about it now. Now, it was time to make sure both of them survived.

With all the training and preparation before they left Atlanta, not one person had warned her the virus might still be viable. But then, the Gov would never get people to work the recovery teams if there was still a risk of infection from a virus that almost killed every man, woman and child on earth a quarter century ago. But, that was just it. The pandemic was over twenty-five years ago. It had probably mutated countless times since then. Just because that virus was deadly to humans two decades ago didn't mean this one was.

She placed a hand on Rock's forehead. He didn't seem to be sweating anymore. His fever was too high, and his body's natural ability to cool itself had short-circuited. She needed to reduce his fever, and knew exactly how she'd do it. Laila scooted a couple of feet, grabbed a roll of paper towels, and went to work. A few minutes later Rock's body was mummified with wet paper towels. Her gaze drifted over him, her heart aching. Thoughts of what she should do next cascaded through her brain.

"Laila?"

She jumped at the sound of her name spoken from behind her. Looking over her shoulder toward the shattered door, she saw Garret. "You scared the shit out of me!"

"I was scavenging for food and water..." Garret stopped in his tracks when he saw Rock passed out on the floor and covered in paper towels. "Is he dead?"

She looked up at him from where she knelt next to Rock. "He's sick. Been this way since I woke up." She swallowed before she let loose her fear. "I think it might be the flu."

Garret blanched and motioned with his arm wildly. "Get away from him."

"No. If it's the flu, I've been exposed already."

"If it's the flu, he's dead already, whether he's still breathing right now or not." He held a hand out toward her. "I can get you back to New Atlanta."

For a moment, she didn't comprehend what he was saying. But the minute she put all the pieces together, she stood up abruptly. "I'm not leaving him here to die alone!"

Garret scowled. "Your false loyalty to this man is going to kill you."

She walked over to where he lingered by the doorway. "No, I don't fucking think so. And, for the record, if it was you lying sick, I'd stay to take care of you, too. It's called decency."

"It's called stupid." His words were curt. He studied her for a few more seconds then he shook his head. "You're making a terrible decision right now."

"I'd rather die here with a clear conscience than live without him anyway."

His eyes flickered with momentary surprise.

"Just go, Garret." She turned away from the door and knelt next to Rock. After a few seconds, she registered his footsteps fading into the distance.

She looked down at Rock, refusing to give up.

They were going to be there for a while. It would be good if they were comfortable. They needed supplies, pillows and blankets at the very least.

Rock was shivering now, but when she touched his head, he still felt heated.

Without looking back, she left Rock lying on the dusty floor and abandoned the store. Stopping where the crumbled blacktop parking lot met the road, she looked both ways. They were in a relatively rural area, and it was a toss-up as to which way to walk. She made a left, away from the freeway, and walked down the center of what used to be a road. Now it was an overgrown, slightly less brush littered path leading away from the truck stop.

Laila walked for almost an hour before she rounded a bend and saw what used to be civilization ahead. There were huge buildings surrounded by vast seas of cement, collections of stores, restaurants, banks and gas stations. She read the sign that hovered at the end of a pole, ending at a pinpoint high in the sky. Super Wal-Mart.

Laila breathed a sigh of relief. Her mother had told her stories about going to huge stores like Wal-Mart and Costco with her grandmother. She set off, knowing she should be able to find what she needed there.

The doors to the hulking building had been smashed in years ago, and the exposure to the weather and wildlife had taken its toll on the interior of the store. Birds protested her entrance, calling their warning to others before flying into the rafters high above her head.

Laila gaped. She had never seen anything like it. The store was so massive, she couldn't see where it ended. Slowly, she walked past row after row of clothes and shoes, coffeemakers and picture frames. It was as if she'd walked into a museum of a different sort from the ones she'd been working in. The store provided a glimpse into the everyday lifestyle of the people who'd lived before the virus.

She thought she had a pretty good idea what it was like back then since she'd grown up on TV shows produced before the pandemic, but she had not been prepared for anything like this. She investigated the entire building, sometimes losing herself in the sheer volume of it all. The areas that had once contained food had been plundered by the wildlife long ago. The only things left were canned goods and some items in glass jars that had not tumbled and broken open during the wildlife feeding frenzy.

After a full circuit around the store, Laila had to pare down the mental list of what she wanted, knowing she could only take what she could carry. She could, however, make use of many items before she left. She darted around the store, gathering what she needed.

Laila stripped in the middle of an aisle lined with plastic jugs of water. She washed, dried herself with a slightly mildewed towel, then ripped open a plastic package of panties and put on a pair before dressing in her black recovery team uniform. After brushing her teeth, she was ready to face the long walk back with the cloth bag full of blankets, a pillow and a few other small supplies she needed to keep Rock comfortable and nurse him to health.

The trip was slow going. She sometimes carried, sometimes dragged the bulky bag along the path to the truck stop. It was turning out to be a hot day and the struggle took its toll on her mentally and physically.

Frustrated after the bag got caught in a tangle of branches, she sat in the shade of a tree, wishing she'd brought some water to drink, when a feral snarl sounded behind her. Fear pricked down her spine as she stilled, and her senses went on alert. Turning, she realized she was a stone's throw away from the animal making the dangerous sound. Her eyes tracked the slow movement of a big dog, or…maybe a wolf, with matted silver hair and drool pooling from its mouth. The animal's tail and ears were flattened against its body and the hair on its neck stood on end. It barked furiously, looking ready to pounce.

Movement behind the animal caught her attention. Laila's fear jumped when she recognized what they were: two bouncing gray puppies. The mama snarled again as soon as her eyes landed on the pups and launched herself toward Laila before she could stand and move away.

Laila went for her gun, but the animal locked on to her forearm. She screamed as the animal's canines punctured both sides of her arm. With her left hand, she pulled her knife and hit the animal's hindquarters with the end of the blade. The dog yipped and in the process, released her arm.

Laila scrambled away then stood when she'd achieved some distance between them.

The animal held its ground, barking a vicious warning, but only advancing a few feet.

Laila grabbed the bag and slung the straps over her shoulder, then pulled her gun. She walked backward, trying to put distance between her and the enormous dog bravely zig-zagging over the terrain, staying close to her.

She yelled, loudly and sharply, "No!"

The animal spooked and stopped in its tracks.

Clumsily, she moved backward through the woods, not wanting to turn her back on it. The animal started following her again. "Nooo!" she shouted long and hard.

The mama slowed, and then stopped. She turned, laid eyes on her pups, and then returned her gaze to Laila. The protective stance said it all. She wasn't leaving her young, but she watched Laila closely.

With a sigh of relief, Laila continued to put distance between them until she couldn't see those steely gray eyes anymore. She holstered her gun, stopped and looked around the now unfamiliar forest.

The puncture wounds on her forearm bled profusely, and she was forced to rip the hem of her black mission T-shirt to use as a bandage. Then, as Rock had taught her, she determined whether she was safe first. With sharp eyes and rapt attention, Laila focused on the forest, turning three hundred sixty degrees, then stood quietly for a full thirty seconds before she relaxed a little and directed her attention to her next problem.

It would be incredibly easy to get turned around in the woods. She had to get back to the path. Rock had taught her to read a map during her training, and it only took a moment to transfer those skills to her situation. She made a ninety-degree right-hand turn, picturing a route parallel to the path she'd been on. It was slow going through the snares of sapling's branches and downed trees as she trekked through the woods.

It wasn't long before she reached the highway.

"Yes!" She celebrated with a fist pump and turned right. The truck stop was visible in the distance. She ran for a few minutes with the awkward canvas bag bouncing on her shoulder, until she reached the building.

She lowered herself to her knees next to Rock. Her stomach turned. He hadn't moved at all. She placed a palm to his cheek, feeling the dry, hot skin of his face.

Hastily, she arranged the blankets and pillow in the back room and returned to him. She rolled him over onto a blanket and pulled, sliding him on the dusty tile floor to where she needed him to be.

His hand closed around her arm as she tried to roll him onto the makeshift pallet.

"Get away from me," he growled.

She turned her gaze away from his face and ignored his words. His grasp on her forearm loosened and then finally fell away. She couldn't help but monitor how he felt, and his sadness made her practically useless.

His gaze was fixed on her face. His features were bleak as he took her in, looking at her as if it was the last time he ever would.

Her heart clenched. "Stop it. You are not leaving me out here alone." Laila put all her effort into holding back a sob. "Now do me a favor and roll your humongous ass the rest of the way onto the blanket."

She helped him as much as she could, keeping the blankets underneath him un-bunched as he did exactly what she asked.

"Laila."

"I'm not leaving, and you're not dying, so just—" She shook her head, throat squeezed tight. She swallowed down the sob forming there. "It's going to be okay, Rock. We'll get through this together."

His heavy lidded eyes made his struggle against sleep obvious. "Love you, baby," he said then fell into unconsciousness again.

Quiet. It was so quiet with only the wheezing of Rock's labored breathing to fill the tiny candle-lit space. Laila sat next to him, studying his profile in the flickering light. "Please don't leave me," she whispered before she began nursing this man who had become her whole world.

She spent four days performing a tedious cycle of tasks, dripping water into his mouth, covering him with cool, wet towels, massage, and aspirin.

All the while, Laila talked to him. Whether he was sleeping or delirious, it didn't matter. She kept talking so some part of him knew she was there.

Maybe then, he wouldn't give up, because she had not given up on him.

Chapter 23

Rock was confused. He opened his eyes for a split second. The light from a flickering candle entered through his pupils like spikes hurled into his brain. Even if he wanted to move, which he didn't, he didn't think he could. Every cell ached as if he'd been badly beaten.

"Laila." His attempt at talking came out garbled from his dry, swollen mouth.

"Shhh. It's okay." She hovered over him, placing a cool hand on his forehead. "How you doing, Superman?" She put a bottle of water to his lips. He drank for his life. His depleted body felt more like a carcass, refusing to complete the most simple of movements.

"I'm here. Just rest…you're going to be okay."

When he'd finished the bottle, she rolled him over and straddled his thighs. Her cool hands moved over his shoulders and back, kneading his sore muscles and easing the searing broiling of his skin. All he could get out was a groan of pleasure before he slipped into unconsciousness again.

When next he opened his eyes, the room was dark. He was lying on his side with Laila curled up behind him. She was talking. Every time he'd become momentarily conscious, she'd been talking to him. He tried to focus on what she was saying, tried to stay awake.

"…I've thought about names. Of course, a boy would have to be Rock like his dad and grandpa. But for a girl, I was thinking Leah. It would be a carryover of the tradition of L names in my family."

He tried to hold on to the consciousness. He was so close to being fully awake.

"Are you still listening?" The soft caress of Laila's exhalation wafted over his bare shoulder. "You're going to be a daddy, Rock."

* * * *

"…you have to remember, anybody is chatty compared to you. So, if you want me to zip it, you're going to have to tell me to."

Rock smiled as Laila's words floated to him through his stupor, and then a gasp. "Are you awake, Rock?" There was a quick shuffle of movement in the dim space. She'd rolled over in his arms. "I can feel you, and you're smiling at me."

A flurry of noisy activity followed. Laila heaved his upper body up, forced pills into his mouth and held a bottle of water to his lips.

"Drink it!" She'd yelled the words, which made him jump out of the sleep he'd been returning to. She was relentless in her attempt to get the cool water down his throat, pouring it liberally into his mouth, forcing him to swallow. When the bottle was nearly empty, she let him lie back.

She caressed the curve of his shoulder and ran her palm down his arm. "How you doing, big guy?" She lay down, pressing her length against him. She continued talking. He tried to process her words. Instead, his mind could only focus on the contact of her body with his.

* * * *

"Why don't you give up this sick act and roll over to make love to me? Come on, big guy. Don't leave me hangin'."

The moist breeze of her words kissed the back of his neck. "Is that all you think about, woman? I'm not a piece of meat."

Laila shifted behind him and left him with a cold spot where she used to be. She rolled him onto his back and cradled his upper body in her arms. The lip of a cup perched at his mouth as her soothing words encouraged him to drink.

"Come on, big guy, drink it all for me." The liquid splashed past his lips, instantly relieving the stale dustbowl of his mouth. He finished the glass and she laid him back gently.

She was ashen. Dark circles marred the skin underneath her big brown eyes. If he didn't already feel like an egg frying in the New Atlanta sun, her anxious expression would have told him how sick he'd been.

"How long?"

"Four days." She grabbed a couple of pills and popped them into his mouth, followed by more water. "I should have known talking about sex would get you conscious." She laughed weakly, trying to cover her worried expression.

"It's my favorite subject," he rasped back.

"It's the virus, I think."

Rock nodded and closed his eyes. "Maybe. Could be West Nile. Either way, you shouldn't risk being so close to me."

"It's a little late for this conversation. I would have gotten it by now if I was going to get it at all. Plus, your fever's broken. I think you're getting better."

* * * *

A couple of days later, Rock was on his feet for the first time in a week.

A week after that, he left the truck stop, planning a short day trip to the armored trucks to see if the attackers had left the gas additive. Since they didn't know what it was, he figured they might not have taken it.

He left Laila behind on this trek, figuring the truck stop was safer than going back to the trucks. Awake for almost a week now, he had waited for Laila to tell him the news he thought he'd heard during his delirious haze. That she was pregnant. Yet, it hadn't come. He knew his woman, and after day one without a disclosure, he suspected she deliberately held back the information. After that, it only took a little while for him to figure out why she didn't want him to know. She still held on to the hope he wouldn't return her to New Atlanta, and knew he would if she were pregnant.

Any lingering doubts he'd had about his decision to return her to the city were settled anyway. She'd been attacked by an animal, and her festering wounds didn't appear to be healing. She was already in more danger than he could accept, especially after the tremendous strain of being pregnant and caring for him while he'd been sick. He wouldn't add to that by dragging her through dangerous country, taxing her physically, when she needed to rest and care for herself and their child.

The hike took hours, and he realized he wasn't close to full strength when he was forced to rest several times during the journey. When he finally reached the abandoned vehicles, he approached them slowly. But after a minute, it was obvious the area was deserted.

As expected, all the plastic jugs containing the milky gas additive were left untouched. He circled the perimeter of the two trucks, which were in surprisingly good shape considering the explosion and collision.

The art and artifacts were gone.

Sydney's burnt corpse still sat in the passenger seat of the lead truck. He stood stock still for several more minutes, sensing his surroundings and listening for the sounds of humans. When he was satisfied, he walked to the cargo hold of the rear truck, retrieved a shovel and began to dig a grave by the side of the road for her.

With only the sound of the shovel slicing through dirt and the hot sun beating on his shoulders, Rock silently acknowledged the fact they'd be back on the road again that day. They would have to say goodbye soon. The thought of it made his chest tighten in apprehension of what came next. The emptiness of separation and what it meant emotionally for two people as enmeshed as they were would be difficult to endure. It was a loneliness so complete, Rock thought he'd rather die than feel it again. He would do almost anything to prevent Laila from having to experience it. Anything but risk her life, and in Onyx, there were a thousand and one paths that all led to the same dark place where death waited.

She needed a doctor's care, checkups and ultrasounds, fresh healthy food, vitamins and calm security Onyx didn't provide. By the time Rock had finished burying Sydney, he'd acknowledged he had to be strong for them both.

An hour later, Rock parked his newly acquired little blue car on the side of the road and headed toward where Laila stood outside the truck stop. She wore her black mission outfit and Kevlar, looking fucking hot, as always. Her smile was radiant as her gaze met his. "It was there, huh?"

He nodded. "Ready?" he barked, his voice gruff.

She nodded, her smile faltering. "Is everything okay?"

"No, baby, everything is far from okay." He took a deep breath and continued with a kinder tone. "We're going to be saying goodbye to each other in less than twenty-four hours, Laila. Nothing's going to be okay for a long time."

He took her hand and walked with her toward their new car.

"But—"

"No buts, peanut." He tucked her into the passenger seat. "Don't make this harder than it's going to be already." He slammed the door in her face and slowly walked around the back of the car. His heartbeat throbbed in his throat while his emotions ran riot. His blood pressure rose as his anger grew to epic proportions. This whole damn situation had no right answers, only shades of danger.

As soon as his ass met the driver's seat, he met her watery gaze. "It's always been the plan. And now, with the baby, you have a lot of things to take care of."

"You know I might be pregnant?"

He smiled at her. "Yeah, baby. I know."

Chapter 24

They stopped less than a mile away from the gates of New Atlanta. Rock joined Laila next to the cook fire and began to say the words that had probably taken him all day to think up. She knew they'd be coming. Pain and dread poured off him, and just an hour before, she'd sensed his resolve and the shoring up of his Rock wall. "Tomorrow—"

"No," she snapped. She put her hands over her ears. "I don't want to hear it, Rock." He pulled her hands away from her ears with firm grips on her wrists.

"Laila." He framed her face with his hands. "Please, peanut. This is hard enough. I need you to be strong for a while longer. Then you can lean on me the rest of your life. I promise." He pressed a soft kiss to her lips. "Come on." He took her by the hand, sat and then lay down on his bedroll, pulling Laila with him. Side by side they lay, looking up at the stars like they had so many times before.

She was a grown woman who could make her own choices. She ripped her gaze from the universe of stars above her and lifted herself on an elbow. "I'm not going back. You can't force me."

He didn't meet her gaze, just sighed with a slight smile on his face. "Cute." He jerked her toward him with the arm she'd propped herself up on, and she landed with a thud on his chest.

"You will go back into the city, and I'll set up a home for us."

"Please, Rock, no. I'm begging you. Don't leave me there without you." Tears swam in her vision and then overflowed the containment of her eyelids. The chasm of emptiness his absence would leave in her life loomed. "I'll do anything. Just name it. I'll crawl to you, Rock. Just please don't leave me."

He pulled her fully on top of him until they lay belly to belly. "Shh, baby." His strong arms wrapped over her.

"It hurts, Rock."

"I know."

The pain. Oh my God. She gasped. It was a vast, vicious despair, ripping at her chest, hollowing it. Her heart broke as she memorized the feel of the soft cotton of his shirt under her cheek and the sound of his heart beating so close to her ear. So awesomely familiar, yet the finality of the moment was agonizing.

"I'll be back. Just give me a few months to find us a safe place to stay and I'll be back for you. I promise."

She lifted herself to meet his gaze and stared down at his face. His eyes were honest, and his emotions pure. He rolled to his side, taking her down from her perch over him until they lay face to face with their legs entwined. The night was clear and crisp. The fire warmed her back and cast flickering shadows into the woods behind him.

"I'm going to miss you," she said, squeezing the words out through her tight throat. For long moments, her lungs remained empty of air, her heart aching within her chest. A part of her was dying. She choked in a sob, tears welling again in her eyes.

"No, baby. Please don't." His voice was deep and hoarse. "You'll be safe there. You'll be able to see a doctor, get vitamins, eat fresh food, rest." He brushed her hair from her face. "If I don't come back for you within six months, I'm not coming at all."

"Six—"

He put his index finger to her lips, stopping her words.

Laila's entire body groaned.

His eyes were endless black as he inspected her features. He was memorizing them, so he could keep her with him for a very long time. She sucked in another sob.

"Laila," he whispered. "I love you."

Then his eyes gentled and he dipped his head, wiping her tears away with his lips. He kissed her softly, sliding his tongue against her lips, a gentle request to let him in.

She tasted her tears. Squeezing her eyes shut, she tried to block out the flashes—empty house, failed career, and lonely heart that awaited her. Another sob escaped as she opened her mouth to him. He gave her the gentlest kiss she'd ever known. He swallowed down the agony expelled with every one of her sobbing breaths, gobbling up all he could take and easing her a little bit.

She broke away. "What are you doing?"

They were both breathless.

"Is it working?"

Her jaw fell open. "Yes."

He *was* swallowing, absorbing her pain. His actions moved her more deeply than any words he could ever utter.

When, finally, the tears slowed, she nuzzled the soft cotton covering his chest and the hum of different emotions rose to the surface. Her fears fled and she reveled in the tenderness and safety of his embrace. The comforting weight of his fingers spanned the width of her back. His cock was hard, digging into her belly.

"I have to have you tonight."

She nodded, still nuzzling her cheek into him.

"I'm going to love on you enough to last you a while." His fingertips slipped under the hem of her shirt. Rough skin rasped against the smooth skin on her back. They continued upward and tugged the shirt she wore over her head, flinging it aside. A moment later, he'd unhooked her bra and it joined her T-shirt on the forest floor.

His palms cupped her ass and squeezed. She moaned, grinding her lower half into his erection. The vibe between them was solemn as he sat, taking her vertical with him, and rolled her over until her back met the bedroll. He hovered above her, searching her eyes, reading her as easily as he always did.

Laila tried to give him a smile of reassurance, but he shook his head. "Don't. There's never been any pretending between us. Now's not the time to start." His gaze traveled from her face to her bared chest, and her nipples responded to his inspection. The genuine smile it brought to his face made her belly flutter and her heartache. Tomorrow was hours away. They still had tonight. She wouldn't let her grief spoil these precious moments.

He inched farther back until his hands had access to the button and fly of her pants. With deliberate care, he stripped them from her and then stood. She stared up at his strikingly gaunt form as he rid himself of his own clothes. The firelight danced an orange glow against his bared skin. "Spread your legs. I want to see what's mine." His voice was gruff, growly.

She let her knees fall open and he knelt between them. Spreading her lower lips apart, he dipped his head and touched the tip of his tongue to her clit. She jumped as a jolt of pleasure raced through her.

One side of his mouth quirked in a sinful grin. Dipping his head again, he captured her clit between his teeth. Subtle pain and a flare of pleasure washed over her with his small bite. Laila sighed. Closing her eyes, she let the outside world fall away.

She groaned at the finger he pushed inside her, and its rhythmic pace joined the beautiful music he played with her flesh. She angled her head so she could watch him. His hot, bright gaze traveled over her as she writhed under his tender treatment. She tensed with the rapidly building pleasure. "Rock, stop. I'm going to come."

He released the suction on her clit with a pop. "That's the idea, peanut." The gleam in his eye and slightly evil smile caused her to giggle.

He paused, his expression turning serious. "I haven't seen you look this happy in weeks."

"In this moment, I'm the happiest and saddest I can ever remember being."

He crawled up her body, bracing a forearm on either side of her head and hovered again, letting only part of his weight press against her. They were face to face, their breaths intermingling. The blunt head of his cock nestled at her opening and a slight cant of his hips was all it took to enter her.

"Having you all to myself is the only thing that's made me happy since you slipped your hand into mine in that hallway."

"Since then, huh?"

He smiled. "Since then."

He advanced and retreated. The long slow strokes into her clasping core brought her close. His gaze never left her, and they connected, really connected, for the first time in many weeks. It was the most natural thing in the world to join with him again on so intimate a level.

"You are mine." The advance of his penetration had been languid as he'd said the words.

"Yes."

"When we're apart, you are still mine." He punctuated the statement with another surge into her.

"Yes," she whispered as tears fell from the corner of her eyes into her hairline. But these were not tears of pain, they were an acknowledgement of the beautiful words she'd longed to hear for those weeks when she'd been so emotionally separated from him.

He dipped his head with the next thrust and kissed her eyes, kissed the wet trails left by her tears. "You will not doubt it."

She met his gaze. "I won't doubt it."

He shoved into her and shifted his weight, grabbing a fistful of hair at the back of her head and baring her neck to him. "If you doubt, you're defying me and denying the special connection we have." He bit her neck, and then said, his moist lips still touching the tender spot. "Don't fucking doubt me, ever." He lifted his head. His eyes darkened, and his expression turned hard. "You dishonor what we have if you doubt. When you walk away from me tomorrow there will be no more of it left. Don't let it return. Promise me."

She swallowed down the lump in her throat. "I promise."

Rock tightened the grip on her hair and gave her the scary Rock stare he usually gave to other people. "Keep this promise, Laila. Neither of us will survive this if we're not sure of each other."

Without blinking, she returned his bottomless stare. "I promise you."

"Good girl."

She groaned at the increasing force of his penetration, expecting her demanding lover to return after the promise was made. But tonight, there were no bonds, no toys or demands, just them, giving every ounce of love they had to each other, with the subtle awareness this might be the last time.

Rock continued to pump slowly and maintained the connection of their gazes as he made tender love to her. His love, pure and powerful, was devastating.

Laila wrapped her arms around him and held on tight, lifting her ass into his thrusts. She was close, but she held off her orgasm, locking herself down until they could come together.

Then, with a growl, he wrapped a heavy arm underneath her and clutched her so close it took her breath away. He picked up his pace with deep, punishing thrusts. She held on, digging her nails into his back.

"Come with me, baby." He wrapped his other arm around her, supporting himself on his knees and clutching her like a rag doll. With one final thrust upward, Laila let go, shouting his name and then wailing her pleasure.

They didn't move for a long while after that. She couldn't get any closer to a person than she was with Rock right then. Neither wanted the moment to end.

Laila fell asleep with Rock still inside her.

When she woke, he was gone. But she felt his eyes on her back as she got out of the little blue car and approached the gates of New Atlanta. It took all her strength to not turn around and run to him.

She focused on the movement she saw at the gates, and relief flooded her when she saw a familiar face. Garrett stood in his guard uniform, rifle in hand, but pointed at the ground.

His expression was grim as she stepped to within feet of him. "You shouldn't have come back here," he murmured before another guardsman stepped from the adjoining building and gripped her upper arm.

Chapter 25

Laila sat on the edge of her bed in her isolation cell. When he returned to New Atlanta, Garret had reported he'd left them behind because Rock was sick. She'd been quarantined fourteen days to assure she wasn't returning with the virus.

She stared at the same white wall that kept her company during the worst two weeks of her life. The total disconnect from the man she'd shared her entire world with was made more devastating by the utter lack of stimulation those white walls provided. She'd become dependent on feeling his constant companionship. The loss of it was absolute, leaving an aching hollow feeling in her chest.

The fourteen-day quarantine period was finished, and she looked forward to getting back to work. She stood as she heard the key in the outer lock, but the guardsman who was supposed to release her from her tiny prison handcuffed her instead. "What are you doing?"

"General Morgan's orders, Miss Lewis."

She was taken to an underground interrogation cell in the Peacekeeper's Compound. Her panic exploded as the clang of the metal door closed her into one of the concrete cells, buried deep beneath the administration building. Morgan was a mole, keeping all his most important secrets underground. After some thought as to why she was there, her anxiety doubled. Journey must have been caught, because Garrett's cover was obviously still intact and the only other person outside the Amber Zone who knew she worked for the Resistance was Journey. Rock would be devastated if he lost her to the Gov, too.

Keys jangled against the metal door. When it opened, Morgan himself walked through. He was dressed in his military uniform and he stood ramrod straight, his gaze roaming over her in a disconcertingly interested way.

He motioned to the table. "Sit." He sat in the folding chair opposite to hers and placed a syringe on the table in front of him. He met her gaze pointedly. Cold dread slithered down her spine.

"Good afternoon, Miss Lewis."

"Sir? I don't understand what's going on."

He dismissed her statement with a wave of his hand.

"I've had two weeks to think about the conversation we're about to have," he said as his piercing blue eyes scanned her face, sizing her up. "As I mulled over scenarios and ideas, more questions rose to the surface.

"Did you know the day before you left on your mission there was an intruder in the building that holds our offices?"

Her thoughts shot to that day. The babies. He'd hit her right between the eyes with a curveball. This was not about the Resistance, or Rock, or why Black Guard Sydney Parr didn't return from the mission.

He nodded as her understanding of why she was there took hold.

"We caught the man, so I wasn't terribly worried about the breach. But the next afternoon, when I reviewed the video, do you know what I saw?"

Laila hung her head, not responding to his question.

Morgan sprang, grabbed a handful of her hair and jerked her head up with it. "I saw the man running away, the posted guardsmen pursuing him, and then a minute later, you, tip-toeing into a restricted area, sticking your nose where it doesn't belong."

Laila blinked a few times in rapid succession while her brain quickly caught up. "Yes. I thought I heard babies crying when I was in the ladies room. Naturally, I tried to find where it was coming from. I wasn't trying to…" Her voice quavered. "I mean…" She took a deep, calming breath and started again. "When I left my office, I merely needed to use the rest room. I wasn't intentionally trying to"—she lowered her voice to a whisper—"spy."

The murderous feeling emanating from the General hit her in the face like a blast from a furnace. Yet, his expression was impassive, polite even. He picked up the syringe off the table and stood. "This is to assure me you're telling the truth." He leaned in closer, placed his lips close to her ear. "I've gotten quite good at this, but I still need you to hold still." He stuck her with the needle and plunged the liquid into her vein.

Seconds later, warmth crept through her chest, up the sides of her neck and heated her cheeks. She took in a long, slow breath. Each muscle became lax simultaneously. Her jaw unhinged slightly as her shoulders drooped. Her next intake of air was even longer, slower than the one before.

"Let's play a little game, Laila. What do you say?"

She blinked, lazily. "Okay."

"I'm going to ask you a few questions. If you give me the right answers, I'll let you live. If you give me the wrong answers, I'll take pleasure in shooting you myself."

He sat back in his chair, studying her for what seemed like several minutes before he spoke again. "How do you feel?"

She felt heavy. Her tongue was thick. The noticeably sluggish mechanics of her body mesmerized her. In sharp contrast, her heartbeat thumped boldly. Her hot, drug-laced blood screamed as it jetted through her veins and random thoughts pummeled her normally ordered mind.

"Do you like children, Miss Lewis?"

Sitting across from him like this, she had a difficult time keeping from staring at the results of the hideous wound Jordan had given him months earlier. Laila swallowed through her dry throat. "Yes."

He beamed at her with his brilliant eyes and disfigured face. "They're perfect, these children, beautiful, intelligent, all diamonds. Every one."

She shook her head, confused. "Whose babies are they?"

"They're mine."

"All of them?"

He smiled. "There's no law against fertilizing the eggs harvested from our Diamond women. I'm doing exactly what the egg harvests were meant for, increasing the number of genetically superior children in our population. Right now, we're outnumbered. There are twice as many Ambers as the total population of the rest of the Zones combined.

"But my children, they're Diamonds. The oldest of them are already five years old. A mere decade is all it will take for us to outnumber them. We already outthink them, but we need numbers, too." He sat back into his chair, smiling brightly at her. "They're all my biological children and under my complete control from the day they're born. My sons and daughters will lead this country into the future."

The full meaning of his revelation took hold. "Who carries these babies?"

He smiled, a sickening smirk. "It's ironic really, because that aspect has gotten significantly easier since the Amber uprising and the standoff at the border. Now, since the women designated Amber can no longer cross the border and live in Circle City, like they're supposed to, they have the choice of being put out of the city, or joining my Birthing Corps." He waved his hand thoughtlessly. "But we can talk about my vision for this country's future anytime. It's not what I want to discuss with you today."

Morgan's expression turned ice cold as he leaned toward her and caught her gaze. "So tell me, Miss Lewis, are you in the Resistance?"

Laila shook her head and then silently congratulated herself. That deception was easy. She smiled at him, and then quickly tried to reverse that expression because a tiny voice deep in the recesses of her brain shouted that smiling was a bad idea.

Morgan's laser-like gaze drilled her. "Tell me exactly what happened to Sydney Parr."

"I reported the truth the first time." She paused and attempted to moisten her lips with her thick, dry tongue. "Her truck was attacked. I presume she was killed." She took another long, slow breath in the utterly silent room when a stray thought flitted through her head. Her lips caught the words and spit them out. "I don't see what's so hard about this, why all those Resistance women gave up their friends."

"You're right, dear. We're just having a conversation."

She smiled at him, feeling like the victor in this game of cat and mouse.

"You know, Sydney didn't like you very much."

"I didn't like her either."

He raised his eyebrows. "Really? Why not?"

"Because she wanted to be with Rock and considered my existence in his life a barrier to getting what she wanted."

The General faltered, closing his mouth on the words he'd been poised to say. He seemed genuinely surprised to hear her say that.

"What, you thought your bend over the desk routine was enough for her?"

His ice blue eyes narrowed on her. The scar looked absolutely wicked as he scowled. "What did you just say?"

Laila's feeling of victory over Morgan and his syringe dissipated when she repeated the words in her head. "I'm sorry, that was disrespectful," she blurted out. Then in an attempt to divert his attention to a new topic, she babbled, "Let's not talk about her. There are so many more important things to talk about other than Sydney Parr's whore..." She paused mid-word, wondering what she was trying to say. "Whore...ness." Looking down at her lap, she noticed the quick flutter of the blouse she wore due to her heart's tremendous thumping underneath. She could not meet his gaze, knowing now she was not the cat. She was the mouse, and she was being herded into a very tight corner.

"Laila, look at me."

She heard his words, but it took her several seconds to process them.

"Now!" he bellowed.

She flinched and lifted her gaze to meet his.

He stared at her for a pregnant moment. "Was Sydney having sex with Rock?"

"No."

"Were you having sex with Rock?"

Giddy feelings teemed within her. Not able to help herself, a wide grin spread across her face. "No."

"You're smiling."

"He loves me."

Morgan frowned. "You said loves instead of loved. Is Rock still alive?"

Of their own accord, her guilty eyes darted away from the man sitting across from her. Then she realized without even answering his question, she'd blown it. "Did I say that?"

"Yes, you did."

She simply was not a good enough liar for this. "I meant loved."

"He left you here, didn't he, Laila?"

She didn't answer, choosing to cower from him instead.

"What a pathetic coward he was to leave New Atlanta without you."

"It's not like that."

"Of course it's like that. Where is he now, when you need him?"

Laila shook her head and ran her sweaty palms on the tops of her thighs.

"Can't you see he made a laughingstock out of you?" He laughed at her and then leaned across the table so his face was the only thing she saw. "Oh, I'm sure he gave you some kind of line, like he'll be back for you someday."

Laila felt flustered and humiliation began to heat her face. "He loved me. I meant to say he loved me."

Morgan sat back in his chair and the corner of his lip curled. He looked every bit the monster he was.

She was scared now.

"So how long until he comes back for you?"

She shook her head. "I didn't say." Had she? She started to search her hazy memory and then realized he was talking to her again. "I'm sorry. Can you repeat that?"

"Oh, come on, Miss Lewis, pay attention."

He was confusing her to the point she wasn't even sure if she'd even given up any secrets.

"Did he tell you about Emily?"

She took a deep breath. Something she could talk about. "Yeah. He told me."

"Does it bother you to have to look at another woman's name while he's fucking you?"

Laila tried to keep a calm demeanor but Morgan's aggressive emotions fed her rising anger. She slammed her hands on the top of the table. "Stop!"

"I'm sorry. That was a bit crass of me. Where have my manners gone?" He signaled to the guardsman at the door. "Please get Miss Lewis a cup of tea."

He turned to her and sat back, relaxed in his chair. "Now where were we? Oh, yes. So, Sydney told you about me fucking her over the desk?"

Laila nodded. "Yes."

"I find that hard to believe since she didn't like you."

"Uh…"

"So that makes me wonder who told you I bent Sydney over the desk."

She frantically raced to come up with a reasonable answer to his question.

Tapping an index finger on his bottom lip, he studied her from across the table.

The door opened and the guardsman walked back in with a cup in his hand, she did a double take. He'd just left a few seconds ago. Hadn't he? She looked at him, at Morgan and then down at the steaming cup of tea set before her with a packet of sugar on the saucer next to a spoon.

"What's wrong, Miss Lewis?"

"Nothing," she whispered. Her hand shook as she ripped the sugar packet open and poured the crystals into the fragrant tea. She took a deep cleansing breath in an attempt to get a grip as she stirred the liquid.

"Sydney didn't talk to you about us. How did you know?"

Laila ground her teeth, resigned to the fact she had to stay silent or she'd end up hanging herself.

"Are you spying on me?" The General motioned again for the guardsman at the door. "Take a team and scour my office. Look at every surface for a listening device," Morgan said, studying her speculatively.

Laila tried as hard as she could to look as if she didn't care.

When the guard closed the door behind him, Morgan said, "Tell me about your family. Where were they from pre-pandemic?

"Florida. Tampa, Florida."

"And what nationality is the name Lewis?"

"Welsh."

"Oh, really?" His expression was skeptical. "Do you have any Irish blood in you?"

"No." Her voice quavered.

"While you lived in the Sapphire Zone, did you ever attend a meeting of the Irish Heritage Club?"

"No," she lied.

He sucked in a shocked gasp then glowered at her. "You're not a very good liar, Miss Lewis." His expression turned lethal with cold, dead eyes and a sneer where his scar bit into his top lip. He leaned over the table and stared hard. "It's funny, sometimes when I go fishing and think I'll come up empty, I land a whale. What are the odds?" It seemed as if he was talking more to himself than her. "You work for the Resistance."

"No."

She said the word a little too quickly and the conspicuous tone of panic indicated she was no longer doing as well in her deception as she'd hoped. Suddenly, she wasn't feeling well. Her stomach squeezed bile up her esophagus. Her tongue was a brick as she tried desperately to swallow a sip of tea. Her heartbeat thudded loudly. Too loudly. She was a moment away from full-blown panic. His lips were moving. Was he talking to her? "What?"

He flashed an evil leer. Aimed it right at her. "You were telling me who else you know working for the Resistance." He waved a hand. "Other than Rock, who we've already discussed, of course." He paused, looking so pleasant. "Was there someone else?"

"I don't think..." She focused hard, trying to remember the last few minutes. She couldn't remember telling him about Rock.

"Miss Lewis."

She came out of her thoughts abruptly and turned her attention to Morgan.

"You were telling me about Sydney working for the Resistance."

Finally sure of something, Laila snorted. "You're trying to trick me, General. I caught you red handed."

He smiled, crossed one leg over the other and settled his hands neatly on his thigh. "So you did."

She desperately wanted to scream and scratch that man's eyes out. She was better than this. Stronger.

The door to the room opened and a guardsman entered. He handed Morgan the bug she'd planted so many months ago. She closed her eyes and made her best attempt to focus inward for a few moments. What would Rock want her to do here?

Kill him. She smiled to herself at hearing the deep rumble of Rock's voice in her head. Killing him was not an option at the moment. But the simple solution to this no-win conversation came to her a second later. It was a simple skill she'd mastered during her training. Silence. She could do silent. She *would* do silent. Laila met Morgan's gaze but this time she was the one who smiled.

Proudly, she didn't utter a single syllable for the hours that followed. During that time, Morgan ran the gamut from civil to violent, but she had learned how to be silent during intense and emotional stimulus. This was a different situation, but the skill was the same.

She'd not even been paying attention to the General when another needle punctured her skin. Soon after, the world was a blur of disjointed snippets of time.

She sat on the toilet in a bathroom she'd never seen before. A woman in scrubs was in there with her. The woman's face swam in her vision, her lips moved.

"Sorry…baby…" The words melted before her brain could remember most of them.

She drifted alone until she saw the woman again. "This will help," she said.

A pinch in the crook of her arm.

Feeling so good. Her head lolled. It was too heavy.

The world transformed. A surreal, hazy feeling threaded through her consciousness. She was flying.

Bright lights overhead. She couldn't move her legs.

"Okay," she heard herself saying in response to nothing in particular. The woman undressed her and dressed her in something open in the back.

Then bed.

"Not jail?" she asked the room.

A woman's voice. "Remember, you're going to be okay."

Then she was alone.

Chapter 26

Rock waited ten days. He had no fucking idea why his father never showed at the drop house, but he didn't worry. Rock Sr. could take care of himself and probably stayed to make sure Laila was okay.

Or maybe he'd postponed until he could bring Laila's mother with him. It hadn't been hard to see his dad had feelings for Lila Lewis.

No. He wouldn't worry.

The three hundred miles from the drop house to his new home had taken two days and was blissfully uneventful, with the exception of a few places where the road was blocked by the takeover of plant life. Once he got off the main thoroughfare, it was slower going. Rock spray-painted fluorescent orange arrows indicating his turns as he wove through the maze of smaller roads leading to his destination.

His parents lived in Charlotte, NC, prior to the pandemic. His father had told him stories of their honeymoon on the North Carolina coast. It was he who mentioned in one of their many conversations that living by the ocean might be easier post-pandemic due to it being a good food source.

When Rock finally arrived at the coast, he left his truck behind to explore the area. His first look at the wide beach and immense body of water captivated him.

He walked to the waterline and surveyed the gigantic houses that stood like sentinels left from a different civilization, their bridges leading from their back doors to the beach jutting like huge tongues. He inhaled lungsful of fresh sea air. His dad had been right. This would be the perfect place to start a family.

He searched for homes with their walkways still intact. Some structures were barely standing, weather battered and uninhabitable. Others had held up much better, zipped up tight with hurricane shutters and decks that appeared to be wood but on closer inspection were some kind of plastic.

He circled three homes that appeared as if they were still in pretty good shape.

Finally, he approached the one that looked to be the best choice. It was an enormous blue-gray home reminding him of old driftwood. It had a circular lookout at the very top, giving a three hundred sixty degree view.

The home was protected with metal shutters covering all the windows. Getting inside would prove to be a challenge. Rock returned to his vehicle and drove to the home he'd chosen. Having unpacked his tool chest and a large battery he'd brought with him, he circled around to the back deck.

As predicted, the house was a bitch to break into and ultimately, he had to do some damage to open the first shutter. Once he'd peeled enough of it back to slip inside, he turned on his flashlight and searched the house, looking for corpses or indications the home was damaged. He found neither. It was absolutely perfect.

Using his battery and converter, he tapped into the shutters' wiring and once the power was connected, the metal rolled up, replacing the darkness with brilliant light and an amazing view of the ocean.

He thought of Laila as he toured the home in the light of day. The kitchen was twice the size of his in the Emerald Zone, and that one had been huge. He imagined her sitting there at the island, chatting with him as he cooked, as was their routine. She was never far from his mind, and as he took in the details of the house, it was Laila he wanted to please. He could live in a hut for all he cared, but he wanted a castle for his queen. It looked as if she'd get it.

He walked through the living area. The room was sleekly modern in white and pale blue, colors reminiscent of the sea. Hanging over the mantle opposite the ocean view hung a seascape in watercolor, with white sand and turquoise water.

Rock inspected the fireplace and found it was in good working order, looking as if it had never been used. On the far side of the living room, he took the hallway to the master suite. The view was the same with another wall of windows. The bed was gigantic.

Rock smiled. The headboard and footboard were brass in curly designs. Perfect for ropes. "Absolutely perfect," he announced to the empty room.

He took the steps to the second floor. A common area gave access to all the rooms on that level and held the spiral staircase, leading to the lookout. There were four bedrooms, one of them decorated for a young boy, with trains and cars littering the floor. Rock climbed the stairs, curling his way up to the next level and emerged into a round cupola. It was about ten feet in diameter and, after spending more than an hour trying to get the metal shutters open, gave a breathtaking three hundred sixty degree view and easy access to the roof.

He imagined their children in there, with toys littering the floor. Yes, a perfect little clubhouse for his babies.

Rock grabbed his toolbox, made his way to the kitchen, and sat at the island, swinging the box onto the light gray granite.

He took out his list. He'd had a lot of time to think about what he'd need to do in order to make the home he chose livable. He'd had to bring the important things with him, not knowing if he'd be able to find what he needed in Onyx.

The list was extensive, but when he was done, they'd have some electricity, a place to go to the bathroom, and fresh water. He'd made the plans and learned the skills. Now all he had to do was put them in motion.

Chapter 27

Laila awoke in her isolation cell and groaned. Her head. She pressed her fingertips to her temples, trying to rub out the throbbing that seemed to center there.

When she forced herself to swing her legs over the side of the cot, she found she was nude. With great effort, she wrapped the sheet around her and walked the few steps toward the door. Grasping the handle, she attempted to turn the knob. Nothing. Still a prisoner.

She scanned the room. There were no clothes for her.

She lay down and limped through her memories of the night before. They were like impressionist paintings, giving her a general sense of what had happened, but the details were missing.

She examined the crook of her arm. Three needle marks. She worried for the baby she was almost positive she carried. Whatever they put into her system last night couldn't have been good for the tiny life inside her.

The third injection had been something different. It had gripped her differently and the following hours were filled with snippets of bright lights, questions, and...she gasped. There was some kind of medical procedure. She remembered screaming, screaming for Rock over and over as she was restrained. They had done something to her. The vague memory spiked her heart rate.

Opening her eyes brought her out of the disjointed memory. She looked around the sparse room again and realized she wasn't in her old isolation room as she'd initially thought. This one had a slightly different shade of paint. No water stains over the door. The rest was the same. Cot, sink, toilet, and four blank walls to stare at.

Laila closed her eyes and allowed her world to crash down around her. Rock would return. Wouldn't he? The drugs, combined with Morgan's insinuation she was naive and stupid to believe Rock would be back for her, had chipped away at her certainty.

She turned to face the wall with her back to the door and vowed to keep her promise to remain doubtless about what she'd built with him. She wondered where he was and what he was doing. It had been sixteen days since she'd walked up to re-enter the gates to New Atlanta. She pictured him, walking through the house he chose to spend their lives in. Something with lots of windows letting in a daily dose of feel good rays of sunlight to warm their skin and their home.

Her heart clenched as the reality of her situation intruded on her daydream. Would he even be able to find her when he returned?

The metal door opened behind her and Laila sat up to face the woman who'd just entered. It was the same woman from her hazy memories of the night before. The blue of her scrubs was several shades lighter than the tattoo around her wrist. Her no nonsense expression pinched her face and thinned her lips. Her hair was pulled back tight into a bun at the back of her head. "I'm Nurse Pritchard." She threw a small bundle of clothes on the end of the bed and spared Laila a glance before referring back to her tablet. "Miss Lewis." The woman picked up Laila's wrist and glanced at a watch, holding that position for several seconds.

Laila stared at her Sapphire tattoo while the woman counted her heart rate. When the nurse allowed her to pull her hand away, something remained, flattened in her palm. She sandwiched it between her hand and thigh as the nurse entered her information.

"Listen closely," Nurse Pritchard snapped.

Laila jumped at the terse command.

"Without dissent, you will eat all the food given you, submit to all medical exams and procedures, and participate fully in your daily exercise program. Aside from your daily work duty, exercise will be the only other time you're released from this room. Please don't try anything stupid. The room is monitored through a camera in the ceiling.

"As of today, you are a vessel. Nothing more. If you think you're too good to carry one of the future leaders of our nation, I will be glad to notify General Morgan, and he, I'm sure, can persuade you otherwise.

"I want to make this perfectly clear." She stepped forward and stuck something in Laila's ear for a second and then stepped away to enter more information. Then, she leaned in close so they were nose to nose. "Being here, being the vessel for a Diamond child is a privilege, and you'll behave as such. If you have any thoughts of running, you need to know you're on the Peacekeeper's Compound in the Emerald Zone with only one way in and one way out of this section of the building. And, as you can imagine, General Morgan's Birthing Corps and the children we raise here are well guarded."

"So, I'm pregnant?"

Nurse Pritchard cocked her head and her brow furrowed. "The procedure was last night." She stood silent for several seconds, looking as if she were choosing her words carefully. "You don't remember?"

Laila shook her head.

Pritchard turned her attention to her tablet again, entering something. "You were implanted with several diamond embryos. In ten days, we'll test you and confirm the pregnancy."

"My baby—"

Nurse Pritchard cut her off and shook her head. "No, not your baby. General Morgan's baby."

Laila gasped. *What about my baby?* An avalanche of despair smothered her as her stomach twisted and the rest of the world fell away. Nothing else was important anymore. She'd failed to protect their child. Laila curled up on herself and sobbed as the full implications of what was happening to her set in.

"Stop it!" Nurse Pritchard grabbed her hair, raised her up to a sitting position, and slapped her face. "I will not allow your sniveling to endanger the new life inside you." She tilted Laila's head to face her by twisting the grip she had on her hair. "Do you understand?"

"Yes," she whispered. Tears still ran out of the corners of her eyes, but the shock of the slap had snapped her out of the momentary emotional free-fall.

"You won't be assigned job duties or an exercise program until we're sure the embryos have been successfully implanted." She entered more information on her tablet and then looked up at the camera, signaling. The light buzz, indicating the cell door was unlocked, sounded.

"I'll see you tomorrow."

Then, she was gone.

Laila curled her fingers around the item in her hand before she rolled over to face the wall again. The fact the nurse gave her so much vital information in the few sentences she'd snapped out was not an accident.

Nurse Pritchard presented as nasty and crude, but the woman was on her side of this war. She didn't need to read what was written on the paper cradled in her hand to know that fact.

The irony, that she'd wound up a prisoner in the place where she'd snooped, didn't escape her.

Because of her, Morgan knew Rock was alive, and she was the bait to catch him. Then, Morgan would annihilate him by revealing it was his child inside her, not Rock's. She would kill herself before she'd let that happen.

She waited to look at the message in her hand, wanting to give the eyes on the other end of the camera time to get bored and look at something more interesting. Finally, she began to move, bringing her hands up so slowly she hoped the movement wouldn't be tracked by the casual observer.

The paper was not the easy half-fold repeated a few times. No, this was round, almost the size of a quarter and oragamied within an inch of its life.

Unfolding the paper puzzle became a game as she lowered her hands into the cradle of her hips and worked sightlessly, trying to unravel the folds. Finally, the small square of paper lay flat between her palms. She held her breath as she tilted her head downward toward her hands and read the miniscule writing.

> *You were already pregnant.*
> *The embryos implanted will not take.*
> *You are not forgotten.*

Journey

Relief clogged her throat, and her nose burned as she held in the tears that threatened. Not Morgan's child. Rock's child. That nugget of information changed everything.

Laila put the scrap of paper into her mouth and swallowed it quickly.

Before long, she realized the activity she'd just completed was the only thing she'd have all day to occupy her mind from its ruminations.

The silence and isolation were mind numbing. After three days, she welcomed the verbally abusive and glaring Nurse Pritchard simply for the stimulation of it alone. The noise of conversation and the tantalizing knowledge that, when the woman left, she'd have a tiny oragamied message of hope in the palm of her hand propelled her from one day to the next.

With the exception of the first one, the notes were never signed. But she knew they were from Journey because they sometimes contained vital Resistance updates. Most of them, though, were messages of encouragement.

Between the highly informative, if not brutally presented, information from Nurse Pritchard and the daily notes, Laila was able to maintain hope. She could lie there as long as she needed to, percolating Rock's child. In a bizarre twist, she realized her baby was probably safer where she was than anywhere else in New Atlanta.

After nine days, Laila looked forward to the appointment scheduled with the doctor.

She would test positive, pregnant. She still couldn't believe it. When Pritchard arrived, they left her room together. The nurse curtly instructed her to keep up as she walked briskly down the long hallway lined with closed doors. The nurse identified the floor as the maternity floor. They traveled one level up. The numbers on the stairwell door indicated they were exiting onto the ground floor. As they stepped from the echoing stairwell, Prichard continued her informative commentary identifying the level as the children's floor. Laila recognized where she was when they passed the exit door she'd so stupidly wandered through months earlier. It led to the lobby…and freedom.

As she was directed into the exam room, she was shocked to find Morgan and the doctor conversing in low tones. When Morgan noticed her entrance, he smiled. Malicious glee emanated in strong waves from his direction.

She stopped short. "Please go in, Miss Lewis," Pritchard gave her small shove to get her moving and closed the door behind her.

"You look surprised to see me," Morgan said.

"To be honest, I am."

He leaned forward in his chair and pegged her with a hard stare. "Let me make this perfectly clear, Miss Lewis. If you're pregnant, you're carrying my child. I am not irresponsible. I love and care for all my children. I'm involved in their lives. I spend most of my time here."

Rock had never been able to figure out why the General spent so little time in his office, and from what Garret had reported, Morgan had not been spotted leaving the building in months. The Resistance suspected his new quarters were housed in the building somewhere. Now, she was sure of it.

She sat on the crinkly white paper of the examining table and the doctor approached.

"The urine she gave nurse Pritchard yesterday indicated the embryos implanted ten days ago took. She's pregnant."

Morgan smiled ear to ear.

"Now let's see if we can find out how many of them are viable. Lie back on the table," the doctor said while he put gloves on.

What if he could tell during the examination the fetus was older than it was supposed to be? Laila readied herself to run away. If the doctor discovered her secret, she wouldn't let them take Rock's baby without the fight of her life.

The doctor lifted the hem of her institutional blue dress and placed the cool disk of his stethoscope on her abdomen, moving it around until he found what he was looking for. He stilled. His brows furrowed. In the interminable seconds that followed. "I only hear one, but this baby's heartbeat is strong. Everything looks good." The doctor referred to his hand-held. "She's finishing meals and resting normally. I don't see why we can't slot her into the rotation. Get her familiar with the routine and how things work around here." The doctor was neither looking at, nor speaking to her. He addressed Morgan. She was considered nothing more than an incubator.

Morgan considered her. "If you behave yourself, I'll inform your nurse that you may interact and help care for the children here until you deliver." He stood and grabbed her chin, turning it so they were eye to eye. If there are any problems from you, I have no compunction whatsoever about keeping you locked in a room for the next nine months. Are we clear?"

"Yes, sir."

The doctor opened the exam room door and Nurse Pritchard stood waiting for her in the hall. She looked nervous, and Laila registered the moment when the nurse realized the exam was over and their deception wasn't discovered.

On the way back to her cell, they passed by two barefooted girls dressed in the same plain shift dress as she'd been given. She'd thought the absence of shoes was an oversight. It seemed it wasn't.

Prichard didn't speak to Laila during the trip to her room. There was nothing to say. Fully aware they both had just cleared a hurdle, no words were necessary.

Days passed and Laila's routine was established.

Her latest message had instructed her to count steps. She was to learn the hallways and their relation to the exit door during her new job of changing diapers and giving baths to the twelve to eighteen month-olds. There was only one exit to their part of the building, and by the end of the following week, she could get to that exit with her eyes closed from practically any place on the children's floor.

The rescue was close. She felt the mix of fear and anticipation in the air. Everybody held their breath while waiting for the opportunity to escape to present itself. Laila was painfully aware how secure Morgan's underground fortress holding the Birthing Corps was. The building was the most highly guarded place in all of New Atlanta. This supremely twisted program was unreachable to practically everybody.

She was going to die there, shot in the back while trying to run away. What was the alternative? If she delivered Rock's child here, how safe would their baby be after it was born with brown eyes and dark hair like his father and mother? Morgan would kill their baby and, most likely, kill her, too. If she was found out, death would be the easy out. The other path, being impregnated over and over again until she wasn't useful to Morgan anymore seemed like a fate worse than death.

She couldn't bear the thought of Rock coming back to get her and finding out she was a prisoner here or worse, that she and their baby were dead. He wouldn't survive it. She couldn't let that happen. He'd made a judgment call, a hard one, returning her to New Atlanta to keep her safe from the unknown. He'd never forgive himself if that decision resulted in her death and the death of their child.

As she thought options and scenarios through, and calculated the odds of her probable demise while in captivity, she realized this was not a hard call. She would get back to Rock, or die trying.

Chapter 28

Two weeks later, Laila was alone in the nursery and very close to the exit of her prison, when the lights went out, throwing the room into complete blackness.

This was it. She placed her hand on the doorknob. Adrenaline screamed through her veins, making her entire body throb. She was one rapid heartbeat, existing in a pitch-black void.

She knew the way. Right out the door, thirty-two steps, turn left. That corridor dead-ended into the exit.

When she opened the door to the nursery, Laila heard the slapping of bare feet on the tile all around her. She wasn't the only woman running for her life tonight. She however, had a definite advantage over the others. She knew the compound, knew where she was going, and wasn't in her third trimester trying to waddle to freedom.

She burst through the heavy exit door, scrambled through the lobby and walked into the night. They'd met no resistance. The group of women moved silently, the ambient light from the partial moon and stars glared brightly in comparison to the absolute black of their prison. Once Laila gained her bearings, she ran toward the front of the line of women who'd exited before her and led them toward the tree line.

The reason they'd not been provided shoes became painfully obvious as they moved through the woods toward the fence separating New Atlanta from the Onyx Zone.

As they neared the fence, shadows came out from between trees and guided them in the right direction.

"Laila!"

She spotted Journey up ahead, waving her to come. Laila pointed out the rest of the shadows to her fellow escapees and waved them in the right direction before she broke away toward Journey. Together, they slid silently through a slit in the chain-link.

"I have a truck waiting for you a few miles away," Journey said. "It has everything you'll need to get to Rock. The map to the drop house is inside. He will either be there, or will have left instructions on how to find him."

"How far away will he be if he's not at the drop-house?"

"He's going to the ocean. The good news is, the road will have already been cleared for you, and it should only take you a day or two to reach the coastline."

Laila stopped. "My mom."

"I have a letter from your mom and one for Rock from his dad." She slung a pack off her shoulders and rummaged through it, pulled out two folded up squares of paper.

"So you're the origami master." Laila put them in the pocket of her hideous institutional dress.

Journey nodded. "Did you give Rock my message?"

"Yes."

"Thank you."

They hiked the rest of the way in silence. Some places they passed were wide open, others heavily forested with rougher terrain. Laila's legs were scratched up from pricker bushes and other brush, and she was sure her feet bled.

When finally, they rounded a corner and she caught sight of the truck, her stomach plummeted. "I'm scared, Journey. What if I can't find him?"

"Then make your way back to the drop house. Someone travels there weekly, and they can take you to Jordan to start a new life. She slipped her hand into Laila's. "You can do this. Stay on this road. It's the same one you took to the drop house before. Refuel there, and there's a map in the truck in case you lose your way."

They stopped at the driver's door, facing each other.

Journey squeezed her hand. "Don't worry. You'll find him. Look for lights at night."

Laila hugged the woman. "Thank you so much." She got into the driver's seat and turned the key.

"Be careful."

"I will."

As Laila drove away, she glanced in the rearview mirror. Journey was already gone.

She drove at a snail's pace for five hours on the dark road. She hadn't turned on her headlights for fear of drawing attention to herself.

As the eastern sky paled, she turned into an out of the way spot to relieve herself, which was a lot easier in that damn dress, and then she got back into the truck. Her gaze landed on a flashlight. She shook her head. She hadn't realized it was there. She could have read the damn letter hours ago instead of agonizing over what it might say.

During the hours of driving in the dark, she'd talked herself into thinking that Big Rock would escape New Atlanta as planned, and bring her mother with him. They all could be together. She fished the letters out of her pocket and unfolded one.

She shone the light onto the writing. It was hers. She slipped Rock's back into her pocket. The paper shook slightly as she read.

> *Dear Laila,*
>
> *I've been sitting here at the kitchen table, looking at your chair and reminiscing the day away. I can picture you sitting there, with your two front teeth missing, saying your ABCs. And just the memory of it makes me smile. I've had so many wonderful recollections today, and you were in every one.*
>
> *I am heartsick that these will be my last words to you. I guess everybody has last words, and I should consider myself lucky to have the luxury of thinking about them in advance and writing them down.*
>
> *I need you to know you're not leaving me alone here.*
>
> *I've been sick for over a year, baby. The visiting nurse thinks it might be cancer. At this point it doesn't much matter. In a few months, I'll be gone.*
>
> *I decided I'd get word to you about my illness after you returned from Washington. My failing health would have been*

too much of an extra burden you didn't need before you left.

I prayed, Laila. Prayed so hard these stupid zones would be history so I could hold you, love you in the same room instead of having the Gov separating us.

What I got was not exactly what I wanted, but maybe something better. I know you're pregnant with my grandchild, and I'm ecstatic you have found a good man, someone to take care of you, to love you.

And, surprisingly, I've gotten the same. I'd never experienced what it's like to have a man love me. Now, for the first time in my life, I do.

Thanks to our Rocks, I am not leaving you alone in the world, and you are not leaving me to die by myself. So I guess what I'm trying to say is, don't look back. You'll have no more ties here in New Atlanta.

Go and live your life. If your Rock is even half the man his father is, I approve. Find him. Love him, and make me lots more grandchildren. I'll be watching them grow up right along with you.

I love you, my baby girl,
Mom

Tears streamed down Laila's face as she clicked off the flashlight and set it beside her on the seat. She stared out the windshield. The sun was beginning to rise and a lone bird chirped its good morning nearby.

Everything seemed as it always was, except she would never see her mother again.

Picking up the flashlight, she shone the beam on the letter again, searching for a date. There was none. The letter could have been written weeks ago.

Her mother could be dead already. Suddenly, the walls of strength she'd built to cope with her captivity and fear crumbled, leaving her vulnerable and raw. Her silent tears turned to wracking sobs. The loss, the absolute and never-changing loss of it hit her and left her emotionally decimated.

She lay on the bench-seat and balled herself up the best she could.

She closed her eyes and remembered like her mom had done before she wrote the letter.

The images and instances that floated around in her mind were wonderful, soothing her enough to lull her into sleep.

The sun was high when Laila awoke. She'd slept until the sweltering heat inside the truck woke her up. She was covered with a sheen of sweat. Her hair stuck to her face, and the material of the bench seat was scratchy underneath her cheek. The woven gray material of the seat filled her vision.

She was calmer than the night before, but she didn't move, staying there in the stifling heat for another minute before she gathered the scraps of herself and hauled them up, ready to drive again.

Laila referred to the map obsessively as she drove the route indicated. This task was made even more difficult by the tears seeping from her eyes. She tried to put her mother out of her mind so she could concentrate, but it proved too difficult. Guilt from abandoning the woman who'd lovingly raised her barreled its way to the forefront. She wasn't there to give comfort or take care of her. She would not see her through her passing.

Stopping the truck for the third time since she'd started the drive, Laila wiped her tears and nose with the hem of her skirt. She was fighting a losing battle with her grief.

Then, she spotted the Onyx Zone rest stop, where they'd spent their first night on the mission. Hope swelled as she hoofed the final few hundred feet to the drop-house.

The back door was unlocked.

"Rock?"

The response of unadulterated stillness told her immediately there was nobody there, but she still checked every room, hoping she'd find Rock sleeping.

No such luck.

Letting out the breath of anticipation she'd been holding, she wandered through the house. The bright shafts of daylight slanting in the window highlighted the dust motes floating in the air. She couldn't find a note or message from Rock.

For a few short seconds, she lost it just a little. She'd never find him if he didn't tell her where he was going. It took only moments for the sense of hope she'd had when she walked through the door to snuff out.

She clenched her fists, and her temper rose. *There must be something.*

She walked through the house, searching more thoroughly through drawers and cupboards. When she still hadn't found anything, she moved on to the garage. A large van, different from the vehicle there the last time she was at the drop house, sat in the garage. However, this one was also filled to the brim with black duffel bags. A piece of folded paper was under the rear wiper blade. She took the yellowed note and opened it.

> *Dad,*
>
> *I waited for you ten days as we agreed. I couldn't wait any longer. I have a lot to do before I return to New Atlanta to pick up Laila. This vehicle is brand new and ready to go with a full tank. Gasoline additives are in the back.*
>
> *You know where to find me. The copy of the map I'm using is between the seats.*
>
> *Rock*

Laila pulled the brand new van out of the garage and then re-entered the house through the back door. Her bloody footprints on the white kitchen floor drew her attention. She laughed out loud. She'd forgotten about her feet.

She searched for water, wanting to wash the cuts so they wouldn't get infected. She found a handful of bottles and a box of crackers in an otherwise empty cupboard. She took the crackers and two bottles and left the rest.

Laila sat on the bottom step of the house's back entrance and carefully washed the bottoms of her feet. She snacked on a few stale crackers left in the box while her mind wandered to the activities that took place the last time she was there. They'd conceived their baby in this house the night he'd punished her by giving her exactly what she'd wanted.

When her feet were relatively clean, she closed her eyes and hung her head, taking a moment. She was so close to the rest of her life.

With her determination fortified, she stood.

"Find Rock, or die trying," she said with determination. With that mantra guiding her, she set off to the east, vowing not to stop until she hit the ocean.

Chapter 29

Laila walked the coastline in the dark, keeping the ocean on her right and peering into huge houses to her left. A couple of hours later, she saw it. A point of light in a house set back from the water.

Her excitement exploded. It had to be him. She cut across the sand toward the bridge that would take her to the home, and stood on the back deck, looking through the wide-open threshold of a sliding glass door. She spotted Rock sitting at a bar not unlike the island in his kitchen in Emerald.

She stepped forward. "I saw your light on."

Rock whipped his head around. Whatever was in his hands fell, clanking to the floor. He advanced on her fast. "I could never get you to fucking hold," he growled as he lifted her off her feet and crushed her back against the wall. His mouth covered hers with a brutal kiss.

He clawed at the hem of her dress, bunching it up around her waist and then tore the institutional cotton panties from her. When she wrapped her legs around him, he groaned into her mouth.

Rock fumbled with the button of his jeans while he held her sandwiched against the wall. It only took a second for his raging cock to spring free, its blunt head nudging against her opening. He looked down at her, eyes blazing. Every horrible event, paralyzing fear and second of misery melted as their gazes locked.

"Hi," he whispered.

She was near tears, and couldn't reply without letting all of it go. Instead, she opened herself to him, and his overwhelming love swallowed her completely.

He sank deep inside her without another moment's hesitation, and then his frenzy slowed. His breathing still came hard and fast, fluttering the hair by her ear with warm air. "Welcome home, peanut." He moved one of his supporting hands from her rear and cupped her chin in his hand, angling her so they were eye to eye.

Then he just stood there, motionless, and read her. She did the same. At least a full minute passed while a cascade of his emotions followed. He'd suffered without her. She was ashamed she'd had even a moment's doubt while she was locked in her white, sterile prison, because his love was there, full force and overwhelming.

His stare delved into her soul. She worried what he would see there. So much had happened since he saw her last. Tears ran down her cheeks.

"You're home, baby. You're safe." He pressed her more firmly against the wall. His grip closed on her nape and drew her head closer. "I'm going to spend the rest of my life making sure you spend the rest of yours happy."

They were locked together. It seemed like every part of her was sheltered by a larger, harder part of him. Laila laid her cheek on his chest and absorbed the moment. She reveled in her heart's recognition of their connection. His presence filled all her empty spaces, turning her fear to safety, her doubt to certainty, and loneliness into a place she belonged.

"It's over. We're free." He whispered into her hair.

Her throat was still overfull with the lump she seemed unable to swallow down. She nodded, just a slight movement. It was all she could do with the death grip he had on her.

Nothing but the faint sound of the ocean and the feel of their frantic hearts beating against one another's penetrated her senses. Everything else was him, would always be him, and she willingly handed every molecule of her being over for his safekeeping. Every hope, every wish she'd ever had was him. Her life became complete during those seconds. She could never dream for more than she had at that moment.

He grabbed a fistful of her hair, angling her head back and kissed her again, but slower this time. His thrusts began as a slight cant of his hips. He was barely moving.

He groaned. "Fuck, baby. I'm in trouble here."

"Me, too." Her clit was pressed firmly against the base of his dick, already stimulated from the prolonged time he'd been inside her.

Placing both hands firmly under her rear, he began pumping in earnest. Hard and fast jabs, impossibly deep and ramming. She hung on for dear life, wrapping her arms around him, feeling the bunch and strain of muscles underneath the slick skin on his back.

"Together, baby. We go together," he growled through clenched teeth.

She cried out as he pistoned harder and faster, forcefully knocking her against the wall.

"Rock?" she cried, seeking permission "I can't—"

"Go, baby. Go now." He slammed into her three, four, five more times as she gave herself permission to let go of the orgasm she'd been reining in so tightly.

"Rock!" she screamed. The pulsing jets of his come only added to the spasms of pleasure rippling though her. She rode the wave, convulsing and quivering underneath the wall of hot, damp flesh surrounding her. The pleasure went on and on until her cries were raspy and her muscles lax.

After some recovery time, he took a knee, still carrying her full weight, until her feet found floor. He looked a lot like Prince Charming, on his knee in front of her.

He frowned as he inspected the dirty mincemeat of her feet. The smock she wore with her name and number patch. His Adam's apple bobbed as the realization his decision to make her go back into New Atlanta had been an awful mistake. Their gazes met. Held. She smiled her reassurance, because at that moment, her throat was stuffed with words that wouldn't come.

He scooped her up and walked through one of the huge glass doors that led to the deck overlooking the ocean. "I'm sorry, peanut," he whispered into her hair. "So sorry."

He carried her over the long, planked bridge trimmed with tall grass on each side. The thundering growl of the ocean became louder as they continued along the walkway.

When he set her down, the soles of her feet met wet, shifting sand. He took a knee again directly in front of her, and he placed her hands on his shoulders, shifting her as if she weighed no more than a rag doll.

Carefully, he lifted her foot and gently stroked it in the advancing and retreating surf. When he was satisfied, he repeated the cleaning with her other foot.

"Does it sting?"

"No. I think they're already healing. I'm okay." She would have been more convincing if her voice hadn't trembled.

Rock remained perfectly still while his emotions exploded around them.

"Our baby—"

"Is fine."

He stood, letting the soles of her feet land in the shallow surf.

One-by-one, he unfastened the plain white buttons of her institutional dress and then pushed it off her shoulders until it fell to the sand.

The process was silent. She didn't know why he didn't talk, but she knew why she couldn't. No words could measure up to the significance of the moment.

Seconds later, his jeans joined her dress on the sand.

She sensed his anxiety. He knew she had terrible things to tell him.

"Tell me." The spike of emotion that rushed at her with those two words nearly broke her.

"I just want to leave New Atlanta behind us."

He stilled, looking at her, reading her for several seconds before he nodded.

He took her hand, and they walked side by side into the pitch-black void of the ocean.

It was over.

As the moving surf splashed the front of her, it washed away the fears and everything else that had come with Being Emerald, replacing it with cool relief and everlasting love.

Meet the Author

Sylvia is a wife, mother, and professional, living in Midwest Suburbia, USA. She reads voraciously and loves to lose herself and fall head over heels for the alpha males in her favorite novels.

When she gets the chance to shed the prim and proper persona of average wife and mother, her secret identity, Sylvia Ryan, emerges. This alter ego strives to write original ideas in extraordinary settings for her readers to remember long after the book has been read. Her dream is to transform her racy thoughts and naughty nature into tangible works of erotic fantasy for others' secret identities to enjoy.

Turn the page for a special excerpt of Sylvia Ryan's

Being Amber

Both danger and sex are inescapable in the Amber Zone.

Jaci Harmon was born a Sapphire, but after she's summoned to receive her final designation, the testing reveals she carries a gene slated for eradication. Within a day, she's sterilized and dumped in the Amber Zone, where the damaged are corralled away from the rest of New Atlanta. Scared and alone, Jaci would rather die than face her future as an Amber.

Born in the Amber Zone, Xander Dimos is a product of a lifetime spent under the oppression of the Repopulation Laws. Decades of suffering have taught the Ambers to make the zone a place where touch, sex, and unconditional acceptance ease the pain of their fate. Jaci has a lot to learn about her new home, and it's Xander's responsibility to guide her through the differences and the dangers safely.

With the simmering undercurrents of sexual chemistry growing between them, and in the midst of discovering the Gov's true motives, Jaci and Xander must overcome his secret and accept their love as undeniable… even if the time allotted to share it is short.

On sale now!

Chapter 1

Year 2075

The tightness in Jaci's chest nearly suffocated her. She closed her eyes and took a deep breath, trying to calm the nervous flutter in her stomach. She rubbed her damp palms on her jeans while her gaze darted around, taking in the barren walls of the cubicle. The pervasive pall of the Designation Center was bleak, right down to the ugly green tint of the fluorescent lighting.

She wondered how many people sat where she sat right now with their hearts beating in their throats and breaths coming quick and shallow. How many lives had been irreversibly changed right here? Goose bumps rose on her arms as the acute apprehension building within her exploded. The information contained in the large white envelope she held would impact every moment of the rest of her life. Once the designation was given, there was no turning back. The results would be her color until the day she died.

Hands shaking, Jaci opened the flap and pulled the top sheet of paper free from the envelope.

Dear Jaci Harmon,

As the result of score assessments in all three major areas of testing you have been given the designation of Amber…

Her breath caught in her throat as her vision narrowed to the underlined word.

…If after reviewing all accompanying paperwork, you have any questions regarding your designation, please com the contact listed on the back of this form.

You have been given the job designation of Painter. Your reporting date and supervisor name are enclosed.

You are assigned to Amber Housing Zone Building 17, Apartment 404.

Due to your genetic profile indicating the presence of an Automatic Disqualifier, you are to report to the Amber Sterilization Center for mandatory sterilization tomorrow, June 1, 2075.

Jaci let the page fall to the table in front of her. "Oh my God," she whispered numbly. Her face heated, and her ears filled with high-pitched ringing. She pulled the rest of the packet from the envelope and leafed through the pages. When she got to the IQ section, she studied the scores for all of the individual testing segments. They were all good. She had an IQ score high enough to be a Sapphire. A slight sense of pride washed over her. At least she was smart enough. But, that didn't really matter now, did it?

Jaci clumsily rifled through each remaining page, trying to find the reason why she'd been designated an Amber. Then, toward the back of the stack, she found her genetic profile and zeroed in on the highlighted section.

...An Automatic Disqualifier was found in genome CD247 indicating a genetic predisposition for scleroderma and probable perpetuation of the disease through offspring...

Scleroderma. She'd never heard of it but clearly, it was one of the chronic conditions the Gov was trying to exterminate. Information regarding the disease was highlighted but she didn't read it. She put the papers down and leaned back in her chair. All of the studying or talent in the world wouldn't have made a difference. There were some genes deemed undesirable in any person, and she had one of them.

Jaci sat stunned, her gaze unfocused, unblinking.

Like an animal helplessly looking up at its demise, she experienced a frozen panic. She was road kill, unable to make sense of the unexpected ruin that just hit her. She'd been leveled by the Repopulation Laws. There was no recovering from this.

Disoriented, she followed a woman to a different cubicle to get her tattoo.

"Would you like a design or a plain band?" A young man asked as he looked at her paperwork and picked the amber-colored ink bottle from it's place in the neatly ordered row of class colors.

"Band," Jaci said vacantly.

He paused and met her eyes, opening his mouth as if he was going to say something. Then, his gaze flicked over to the surveillance camera mounted on the ceiling and abruptly closed it, busying himself again with his work.

As he tattooed the one-inch yellow-orange band around her wrist, Jaci screamed inside. She lost her bearings as the room around her caved in on itself, receded to a pinpoint far, far away. Anger and panic rose within her as she sat rooted in a state of catatonic frenzy. Only the vibrating sting of the tattoo needle marking her wrist tethered her to the reality of her surroundings.

"Can I have your left palm please?"

Jaci looked at the man. Had he been talking to her? "What?"

"I have to give you your code," he said softly. "Everyone in the Amber Zone has one." He gave Jaci a glimpse of the code on his palm, and then her eyes traveled to his wrist. He was an Amber. She hadn't even noticed.

Jaci gave the man her hand. She didn't ask what the code was for. She didn't watch as the sting of the needle pricked the sensitive skin of her palm. She didn't care.

When the tattoos were completed, she was ushered to the waiting transport bus that would take her and her duffel bag to their new home.

The border that separated the Sapphire Zone from the Amber Zone was heavily guarded. Only Ambers with the correct clearance, ones that worked outside the Amber Zone, could pass into Sapphire.

Being raised as a Sapphire, one class up from Amber, Jaci never had any contact with Ambers before. She'd been educated early that there was no color mixing. Ambers were inferior human beings, weak, stupid, and riddled with disease.

Now, she was one of them.

The transport driver had a serious case of diarrhea of the mouth and either didn't notice or didn't care that Jaci was barely there. She watched the beauty of the Sapphire Zone disappear behind her while he droned on cheerfully with need-to-know Amber Zone facts.

As they approached the ugly high-rise buildings of Circle City, the driver's annoying buzz of words continued to permeate the protective barrier she tried to erect around herself.

"...twenty story high rise that looks exactly like buildings one through twenty-eight. The buildings themselves were built specifically for housing single Ambers. They form a huge circle enclosing an entire city within the ring. You won't need transportation. Everything you're going to need is within Circle City. When you get married, you'll be transferred to a town house or condo in the Amber Zone, but outside of Circle City."

The transport pulled up to building seventeen. Jaci exited, escaping the talkative driver, and walked in. She wove her way through the crowded lobby to the elevator and then rode it up to the fourth floor. The door opened to a congested hallway. She walked through small huddles of people, like a rat in a maze, confused and not quite sure where she was going. Then she stopped short, and for a second, stared at the door of her new home. She tried the knob. It was locked. She stood for a moment longer, having trouble keeping it together while trying to remain invisible amidst the crowd of people. She fought an explosion of tears and frustration as she stared at the metal 404 directly in front of her. Then she sighted the scanner on the left side of the door. She placed her hand on it. The scanner registered the new tattooed code on her palm, and a small *click* sounded as the lock mechanism released.

Jaci exhaled the breath she'd been holding, and stepped in. She surveyed her new home, a studio apartment with a small galley kitchen and a bathroom. The entire space was about the size of the family room at her parents' house. Being a single Amber meant she would be stuffed in and vacuum packed so she took up as little space as possible.

Jaci closed the door behind her and stood frozen just inside the doorway, taking the room in. White, it was all stark white, impersonal, sterile. One large bed centered on the wall of the living space monopolized the room. There were night tables on each side. Clothes, pictures and other personal items were strewn over the area closest to the large window at the far end of the room.

A huff of air escaped her as realization dawned in Jaci's mind. She would not be in this small space alone. Another person already lived there. But there was only one bed. It didn't make sense. She glanced to the side nearest to where she stood, to what she assumed was her side of the room. She was closest to the exit and the door entering the bathroom was on the other side of her night table.

A small flat screen hung on the wall opposite the bed, and two chairs were tucked into a small round dining table near the counter that delineated the kitchen from the living space. The kitchen was small and narrow, taking up the back wall of the apartment by the entrance. It contained all the basics, a tiny fridge, a sink, and a two-burner stove.

When she got enough strength and courage together, she needed to call her mother with a list of things to send from her bedroom. She wouldn't call now. She couldn't face it. If she heard her mother's voice, she would break down. She was barely keeping it together as it was.

All her parents would be told was that she'd been designated an Amber. They would have to endure her swift, brutal removal just like she would. That's how it had always been done when someone's designation changed, a clean break away from everything and everyone they'd known in their lives.

Two visits a year. That's all she would be allowed to have to her parents' zone. Over the years, Jaci knew of some Sapphire kids who'd subsequently been designated Ambers. It wasn't unusual for them to stop visiting after a while. Maybe their families made them feel inferior, or maybe they realized they didn't belong anymore. It didn't matter that there was nothing she could have done better to change her designation. Bottom line was that she didn't make the cut, and she would merely be a satellite member of her family from now on.

A compad sat on the counter to her left. Glancing down at the large envelope she held, she lifted the flap and pulled the papers free. She searched scleroderma, bracing herself for the results, fully knowing that since it was an Automatic Disqualifier the information she found would be bad. She scanned the list of sites brought up by the search and touched the screen to get to the site she chose. Focusing on the article, she let her eyes skip quickly over the information. Scleroderma. An autoimmune disorder meaning that the body attacks itself. Genetically linked. No cure. Thirty-four percent death rate within ten years of first symptoms. Significant and intensive long-term care for those afflicted. Tissues of the body hardened and froze, essentially trapping the person inside his or her own skin.

"Shit."

She exhaled softly. It made sense. Automatic Disqualifiers weren't diseases that killed efficiently. The Gov didn't mind the quick killers. Automatic Disqualifiers were the conditions that killed ever so slowly, leaving the afflicted person in need of extensive treatment and long-term care.

The bandage over the newly tattooed amber band around her wrist caught her attention. She ran her finger over it, feeling the sensitivity of her skin beneath. She'd been planning on getting a sapphire daisy chain as her designation tattoo. Plain bands were for her parents' generation. There were options now since the Gov loosened its restrictions. Simple designs were allowed instead of only a solid band. She'd been so blindsided at the time she didn't even look at the available amber designs.

Somehow, Jaci never actually believed this could happen to her, that she'd be designated Amber. Before she received her summons to appear for her designation, she daydreamed that her testing showed her to be so genetically clean that she was designated a Diamond. Those perfect people with the ideal mixture of good genes and the absence of bad, were instantly immersed in a life of privilege and pampering. It was like winning a lottery. She supposed a lot of people had that fantasy. However, she'd totally dismissed the thought that there was even a possibility of being designated an Amber.

Jaci walked over to the window at the far end of the apartment. It offered a bird's eye view of the curious circular city. The day was gray and stormy, suiting her dire mood and doomed life.

It was quiet and still in the shadowy room as she stared out the window, brooding. Now that the influx of new information slowed, her mind started processing other things. Things she hadn't dealt with yet because everything happened so fast.

Significant things.

Devastating things.

A tear overflowed the lower lid of her eye and streamed down her face. She tried to swallow down the tight knot in her throat as she focused on her reflection in the window. But the hard-core reality of her new life suddenly inundated her, impacting with full force and striking a blow so deeply that it cut her to her very soul. Her suffering flourished, becoming palpable to her, chilling the air and seeping into her skin. The mere beginnings of it laid waste to her insides.

Goose bumps rose on her flesh. She was an Amber now, and for the rest of her life until the day she died of that god-awful disease.

Her friends and family were gone, suddenly blinked right out of her life. She was alone, utterly alone here. Her stomach swam.

She was scared.

Thunder rolled deep and ominous in her ears, vibrating the windowsill. The colorless gray of the sky was the perfect backdrop to the tiny drops of rain that landed and gathered together on the glass, forming trails that flowed down like teardrops. The window cried with her.

"I'll never have a baby," she whispered into the silence of the room. Tomorrow she'd be sterilized.

Suppressing the pandemonium of feelings trying to crash out of her was futile. Disjointed fragments of thoughts and fears flew at her, and utter grief and pain raced unbridled through her mind. She felt violent, wanting to throw something, smash anything into tiny pieces.

A primal moan rose up from the depths of her soul and burst through her mouth, filling the room as she sank to her knees. Now, all she had was the wait for her defective gene to kick in, to make her pathetic and helpless, a prisoner within her own skin, before it finally finished her off. In the course of one afternoon, she'd lost everything. Even her life had been shortened significantly with the knowledge of the deadly gene she carried. Rage and despair came from so deep within her gut that she felt like she was going to throw up between the wrenching sobs. She cried, pounded and screamed an entire pathetic performance for an audience of none until there was nothing left in her. The feel of the cold floor on her face was the only thing she registered as she collapsed the rest of the way, settling into a shivering heap on the hard tiles. She curled in on herself.

Jaci remained there sorting through all of it in her head as the hours passed. Her cheek resting on the floor was cool and wet from the tears she'd released and let fall unchecked. It felt good against the humid, New Atlanta summer heat.

Finally, trembling, she lifted herself to her knees, then to her feet, and got into bed. She lay there with her eyes open, but not noticing dusk's shadows overtake the room. Hours of monotonous, opaque blackness enveloped her as she lay awake through the night. Sleep wouldn't come.

Jaci thought seriously about committing suicide. There wasn't anything left for her. She would spend the rest of her days waiting to be diagnosed with the first symptoms of the debilitating illness that would eventually kill her. She doubted a day would ever pass in her life that she didn't feel like she was waiting to die.

If she killed herself, there would be no impact on any other person in the world. Nobody would miss her now.

She thought about others who found their lives too hard, the pathetic throng of people who slouched in the plastic chairs of the waiting room for the Gov Assisted Suicide Program, GASP. Jaci felt sick thinking of the brick smoke stacks of the cremating ovens behind the building. The acrid smoke released from the burning bodies saturated the air with a revolting smell. GASP ensured a quick, painless exit for those who sought it. But Jaci would be damned if she was going to let the Gov take that last act from her.

Lying in the dense gloom of her new home, her mind frantically groped for a foothold, something to reassure, to comfort. But, the same hopeless thoughts rolled through her mind like booms of thunder refusing to be ignored.

Near dawn, Jaci fell into a half sleep, her mind still running through her new circumstances, still seeking a way to end her life. A pleasant way. A way that she would actually have the courage to follow through with.

When she opened her eyes again, a stream of sunlight slanted through the window. She glanced at the clock on her roommate's nightstand. About a half hour remained before she was required to report to the transport.

Jaci looked around. Despite the fact that someone's belongings were in the apartment, no one had come home. She went into the bathroom, brushed her hair and teeth and washed her face.

The dark hair and brown eyes looking back at her in the mirror illustrated the lack of genetic diversity she offered the world. Weariness and misery faded her features. She expected to look different, uglier. She felt uglier, smaller somehow, but she looked the same as always.

A half laugh, half snort of despair shot out of her. Eyes closed, Jaci bowed her head in defeat. Tears welled behind her eyelids, preparing to escape. When she opened her eyes, a steady stream wet her cheeks and her nose began to run again. She grabbed a tissue for now and one for later before walking out of the apartment.

Herds of people crammed the hallways, socializing and laughing. Most of the apartment doors were open, letting sunlight filter into the corridor. Quickly, she walked down the hallway, looking at her shoes. She encountered slight brushes from the bodies of people who encroached in her space as she passed them. At times, it felt as if someone was actually trying to stop her. She didn't look up. She didn't want to meet anybody new right now. She was nauseated, physically ill. She couldn't stop. She didn't stop.

The transport was waiting for her when she got to the front entrance of the building. She climbed in and was relieved when saw she was the only passenger. She plopped down, this time out of earshot of the driver and rode the entire way with her head in her hands, still looking at her feet.

They'll escape New Atlanta or die trying.

Brave, beautiful, and not easily controlled—even within a dictatorship—Laila Lewis has finally attained the prestige of an Emerald designation. Now only one thing is keeping her from her life's goal of retrieving the Declaration of Independence and other priceless artifacts from the wild unknown of the Onyx Zone: the six weeks of training necessary to ensure her survival outside the city walls. But she won't be going it alone…

After a year as a designated Emerald, rugged, sensual ex-cop Rock Rodgers is finally prepared to leave New Atlanta for good. Six weeks of training is the only thing standing between him and his next mission: to disappear into the freedom of the Onyx Zone where the long-armed rule of the Gov can't reach him. But when the chemistry between him and Laila reaches a boiling point, with captivity just one false move away, will he have to escape on his own—or risk everything for a woman more tempting than freedom...

CONTENT WARNING: Contains explicit sexual language and content, m/f, and elements of BDSM that may be objectionable to some readers.

Visit us at www.kensingtonbooks.com

Books by Sylvia Ryan

New Atlanta Series
Being Amber, Book One
Being Sapphire, Book Two
Being Emerald, Book Three

Friday Afternoon

Published by Kensington Publishing Corporation